Trust in the Unseen

Seth Mullins

Trust in the Unseen

by Seth Mullins
Copyright 2014 by Seth Mullins

All rights reserved. No part of this book may be reproduced or transmitted in any form or by any means, electronic or mechanical, including photocopying, recording or by any information storage and retrieval system without written permission from the author, except for the inclusion of brief quotations in a review. Inquiries can be made at www.humanityswayforward.com.

This book is a work of fiction. Names, characters, places and incidents are either the product of the author's imagination or are used fictitiously, and any resemblance to places, events or persons living or dead is purely coincidental. All trademarks are the property of their owners and are acknowledged by the proper use of capitalization throughout.

ISBN-13: 978-1499668223
ISBN-10: 1499668228

First edition, June 2014

Trust in the Unseen

*For Alan,
On the occasion of
our first meeting!
Seth T. Mullins
Dec. 8, 2014*

1. The Stories We Cling To

Love was the most ruthless force in our universe. That's what I'd believed, that I'd sooner endure the ravages of hate any day. Hate wielded the honest pungency of a fist full to your face. Love eviscerated you where you stood and yet still *left* you standing.

I remember the moonlight on the little window box balcony. Janie was so nervous that she'd stolen occasional drags off of my cigarette. This had been her idea in the first place: The two of us "getting away", booking this room in the Latore Motel.

"I thought I was braver than I am," she told me.

The idea – insofar as I'd *believed* I'd understood it, had been to pretend we were on vacation, perhaps try and resuscitate the amorous mood that had characterized our rendezvous in New Mexico months before, when everything had seemed to open up and flow. I stared back into the motel living room, which bore witness to the scalds and the warm patches of love's dying embers, as if its solidity could somehow refute what was happening, what *could not be* happening.

I'd played deaf amidst all of the whispered warnings.

Janie moved to catch me in a hard embrace then. There was tenderness in her clasp; but I see it now, that it was tenderness provoked by remorse, by loyalty to *what had been,* rather than by any enduring passion. With her lips, her fingers, and all the womanly fire that her body could convey, Janie was saying goodbye. With all the unsinkable generosity of her heart, she gave me a hero's send-off.

"Rachel is the luckiest girl in the world, to have you for a big brother," she said. "Tommy and Carlos... me, too. I've never met anyone like you before. You've opened me up to so much that I was never even aware of. You do that sometimes just with your *presence*, even if you're not saying anything."

Stalling, postponing the inevitable dive into blackness, she took another drag. My tears were subsumed, inhibited by anger because anger was what I clung to to see me through this. But I never railed at her that night. I watched her retreat as if I was an impotent mute.

"But I feel as if I don't even know where you're at half the time," she explained. "The way your mind works... it, like, never sits still; it's like this madly inspired spinning gyre. And I try to keep up with it all, but it's like you go around a bend, every time, and I've lost you again."

My entire survival strategy had been contingent upon viewing my tendencies towards mental and emotional extremity as a gift rather than a curse. Of course, this had also rendered me reliant upon the presences of people in my life who could always forgive me for my excesses. Maybe Tommy's rare loyalty had spoiled me. Maybe I had let my Muse lure me into a deluded world where it seemed justifiable to sacrifice *anything* on the altar of vision.

I gazed down at the street below and felt the whole spinning and sickening free-fall that could bring me to kiss that pavement. A couple walked by, hand in hand, oblivious to the clamor of Armageddon. I gave up in that moment. I couldn't stop her. The gods had granted Janie complete executive power over my damned soul.

Her heart was turning away, shining its light elsewhere? I was never going to touch her again? Suddenly the fall from the balcony seemed the much kinder terror.

"You need someone who can really meet you in those places. And I..."

"Don't!" I managed. "Don't fucking act like you're doing this for *my* sake. *I* can decide what's good for me!"

"Fair enough." Her voice was wispy, insubstantial: An echo of the distance that had already claimed us. "*I* need to feel like I can keep up.

"It's like... you're living in this world that's being totally reinvented every day. And I'm sort of stumbling along trying to figure out what the rules are."

"There *aren't* any rules!" I protested. "Just be with me, and..."

"I can't."

Janie bit her lip. One fat tear slid down her cheek. I doubt that she'd wanted to say it so bluntly. But what gentle way *is* there?

Folding chairs, and a wooden rail rife with splinters; cigarette smoke lingering in the still spring air. Nothing there to cling to, to spare me from the plunge.

This can't be happening!

I'd once told her that if it ever came to this I would understand. I'd been a goddamn liar. The death of something so beautiful and divinely inevitable could never *be* understood; it was incomprehensible.

Janie reached over and squeezed my arm. "Hey. I *do* treasure what we've shared."

"Then don't turn your back on it and let it die!" I growled. I could feel my face curling into a snarl. I couldn't stop it. Janie withdrew. Having lost the focal point of my anger, I reverted to teetering on the edge of the precipice.

"I really tried, Brandon," she said.

It was that voice both forlorn and resolute; and every man hears his end in it. The chasm gaped even wider below me. Above me were only stars, beyond reproach or appeal.

"You'd better just leave, then, if that's what you've decided to do."

Everything within me prayed that I was calling her bluff. But the deeper, wiser part of me knew that this horrifying rift was an already-accomplished fact.

Her voice had diminished almost beyond hearing. "O.k."

For a long time, I wavered on that balcony and tried to tell myself that I'd find her when I went back inside, her heart and mind reconsidered. The roiling grief didn't fully announce itself until the receding sound of her engine merged with the rest of the street noise.

I thrust down the fierce impulse to dive down to the pavement, my salvation.

Sometime later, I fished out my cellphone and rang Carlos.

"Hullo?" His voice seemed to emerge from inside a bundle of cotton. I'd obviously woken him up.

"Hey, can we talk? I'm sorry. You know I wouldn't call at this hour if it wasn't serious."

He collected his wits pretty quick. "I thought you were spending the night at the Latore Motel."

"I'm still here."

"Then you've *got* someone to talk to, haven't you? Or what, you're *alone*? What gives, bro?"

"Look, it's over. Janie broke it off just now. She's gone." Part of me couldn't believe any of the words I was uttering, or fathom the ocean of woe that churned beneath them. "Let's go get a beer somewhere, all right?"

"Shit, bro: It's like, one o'clock or damn near!"

"Please, Carlos."

I was flailing for anything in the manifest world that might ward off the encroaching blackness. The reality of what had just happened was threatening to penetrate my brain, tear through the last thin sheets of illusion and doubt and make itself known in indisputable searing pain.

We met up at Charlie's Pub on Lincoln Ave. There were probably a dozen other people strewn throughout the place, sullen or just plain tired. There was neither a band nor any spark of life. The bartender, a middle-aged man with a mountainous beard and half-head of hair, had the look of compassion in his eyes. This carried through the timbre of his voice, too. He must've read the sheer duress on my face. When he informed us that we'd arrived just in time for last call, I asked for a shot of whiskey and a glass of lemon water to chase it down with. I had no patience for beer tonight. I needed something that was going to hit my bloodstream and brain *quick*.

Carlos, the drummer for my band back then, was full Hispanic. He'd grown up in Mexico City and, later on in his teens, moved to New Mexico in search of work. He'd subsisted for years on minimum wage or sometimes even less, resorting at times to dealing drugs. Like me, then, he was acquainted with extremity and desperation. This, alongside our passion for music and self-expression, formed the major pillars of our camaraderie.

"So why didn't you call Tommy?" he asked.

I nodded my thanks to the bartender when the drinks arrived and then gulped the stinging liquor down. I needed that moment to compose my answer, anyway.

"I just feel like he'd want to *answer* this whole twisted conundrum for me, you know? Provide some summary statement that would explain the significance of it all and the lesson that I'm s'posed to take from it. I don't wanna hear about how the pain will subside in time, or that when one door closes another opens, or that it was better to find out sooner rather than later."

"A raw wound is not to be reasoned with," Carlos concurred.

I nodded. "I hate to ever judge a friend; and I suppose maybe that's what I'm doing right now. He'd probably show more tact and sensitivity than I'm giving him credit for, really. But I just feel too vulnerable and I don't want to chance it."

Carlos seemed amenable to just accepting this and moving on. "So what did Janie tell you?"

I noticed the bartender out of the corner of my eye. We shared a wordless exchange, and he offered a conciliatory nod. When he refilled my shot glass I conveyed my sore gratitude as best I could.

Then I turned back to Carlos. "She said that I'm constantly going to places where she doesn't know how to follow me to. You know – in my mind."

My thoughts and I were still involved in the delicate game: Relaying the bare facts of the story without (for the moment, at least) believing any of it.

"But that's not the real reason at all."

This remark slipped past my guard. It surprised even me. I was now embarked upon a frightening plunge into the unknown.

"Well so what is?" Carlos prompted me.

It must be that my fresh wound had temporarily numbed me, like a clean cut or sudden burn that you don't feel yet because the surface nerves are dead. I spoke with the detachment of a sleepwalker.

"It was about two months ago; I told Janie about something that'd happened to me, something I'd done. This was right before the first gig we'd ever played, Tommy and I with Tim. I was in a fight. Some drunk – he was probably twice my age – he pushed me down. So I took *him* down.

"It ended up where I was about an inch away from opening up his jugular with the jagged end of a broken beer bottle. Who knows if I might not have done it, too, if Tommy hadn't 'a stopped me."

I'd spoken softly. Nonetheless, I was gripped by sudden panic, imagining that someone may have overheard me. I cast my eyes around the place – it was long, narrow and dimly lit – and encountered the same subdued apathy that had greeted us when we'd first come in. The dull murmur was too low to articulate the actual words that it carried. For the moment, at least, Carlos and I were left in our own little world.

"Damn, bro," he breathed. "I had no idea."

I shrugged. "That's because I never had the guts to tell you before. Tommy was there, like I said. Besides him, the only one who knew about it was Saul."

Saul was a former suicide crisis responder who was now conducting his own unique (insofar as I knew) therapeutic practice out of his home. Carlos and I had both worked with him and, in different ways, had altered the courses of our lives thanks to his philosophy and intervention. Saul insisted that we were the authors of our own destinies.

I'd always believed that if you're gonna call yourself any kind of spiritual teacher, if you place yourself in a position where others look to you for guidance and support, then you should practice what you preach. At least have the desire to, and make the effort. I'll admit that I knew a few charlatans in my day, and had even followed a couple in my youth, when I lacked experience and hadn't yet learned to discriminate between teachers who actually implemented their own philosophy and all the self-promoters who didn't.

Spirituality can be easy to talk about. There's a plethora of books abounding; and if you read a few key ones you'll learn many of the catchwords and phrases that one needs to know to get around in certain "enlightened" circles. But walking the path...ah, that is a whole 'nother ocean, my friends.

Yeah...There's genuine exploration, questioning and growth going on out there. There are also a lot of people who perceive taking on the mantle of "spiritual teacher" as being an easier way to make a buck and get laid than holding a less glamorous day job. To me, few things were more infuriating that someone espousing lofty aphorisms about love, understanding and consciousness whilst behaving selfishly in their personal lives. If you call yourself a spiritual teacher, practice what you preach! At least people who're unabashed jerks have the guts to show how they really think and feel about other people. They have that much integrity. But to con people through the rhetoric of spiritual growth and enlightenment is unconscionable. Many politicians and religious leaders know this trick, too.

It is a game that had been going on for a very long time on our planet. I hoped that as we continued to grow and awaken, more and more of us would see through it - until there just weren't enough of us left for the swindlers to swindle anymore.

Spiritual rhetoric is like any other kind of script: It can be turned to all kinds of purposes depending upon the motives of the people using it. But knowledge that one awakens to through experience and assimilation is a whole different matter. You can't really misuse that sort of understanding because it *changes you* first.

And from there it reaches out and touches others. I think that this is - in its ideal state - the nature of the teacher-student relationship. Earned knowledge isn't merely something that teachers possess: it is something they've become an intimate part of through their own inner awakening and transformation.

So now, having said all that, let me assert that I'd worked with Saul for some time and that I believed him to be the real deal.

Thinking about him brought me an insight. "When we aren't self-aware," I said, "that's the kind of place unconscious forces can sweep us away to. We can lose control like that."

"Well… maybe *you*!" Carlos retorted.

He often had *peace* on his lips. And sometimes, he reviled violence in a way that almost approached its own kind of aggression. I felt my eyes sharpen.

"Look, man, you nearly destroyed yourself with meth. Lack of reverence for life is the same across the board. It don't matter if it's killing someone else or yourself."

He was immediately repentant. "Sorry, bro. I didn't mean to get judgmental. You scared me, I guess. You just told me something pretty intense, right there."

I waved down his apology. "Yeah, it is. I don't blame you."

"So you think that's what made Janie want to run?"

"Everything changed after I told her about that. The way she'd look at me, touch me… it was all so tentative. Unsure. I think I freaked her out. I'm sure of it, actually. It had nothing to do with the explanation she gave me."

    I sipped at my lemon water and Carlos nursed his one beer until we left. I knew that I had an engagement with brutal grief, but my mind seemed to keep finding ways of postponing the moment. I didn't want to be near anyone when the psychic dam finally burst. As it turned out, though, my personal crisis never reached its culmination that night. I was still too insulated by the protective walls of disbelief.

2. Diamond Maelstrom

I awoke with deep aches so nauseating that I thought, for a moment, that the two drinks of the previous night had bequeathed upon me an absurd hangover. Every sound of life and human bustle was an affront to my raw nerves. Of course – typical of how my luck ran – I didn't have the luxury of sleeping late, even though it was Saturday and I didn't have to work.

Shortly after we'd returned from a tour down to New Mexico and then up the West Coast, our band – Edge of the Known – had signed to the Indie label Manhandle Records. The label's founder, Chas Gages of the band Herring Run, had been impressed by our ability to sell a couple hundred copies of our CD to people completely unfamiliar with us, who'd never heard of us before they'd caught our performance. The CD itself had been financed thanks to an agreement whereby we'd advertised Chas' label, and a couple of the bands on it, whilst travelling our circuit in a cumbersome van. It had been redesigned to resemble a rolling billboard for the occasion. But we hadn't been officially "on the label" back then. Our formal signing occurred only after Chas got a firsthand taste of the do-or-die attitude that characterized all of our activities with regards to the band.

He was now speculating about somehow sending us off on a tour of the *East* Coast, where we would find ourselves, once again, playing in front of completely virgin audiences. He also wanted to get us back into his studio to record a second album. In the meantime, he'd arranged for the three of us to be interviewed by Pat Stavons at the highly respected underground publication Visionary Chapbook. That was happening this very morning.

I scarcely felt capable of saying hello to anyone without snarling, much less rambling on about my music, my band and what all of it meant to me. An odd sort of tactful silence prevailed in the van during our drive over to Visionary's offices. I hadn't had a chance to explain the reasons for my nihilistic mood to Tommy; but now I suspected that Carlos had already given him the heads-up.

The low brick building resembled an old-fashioned bank or social security office, though its entryway was as plastered with flyers and announcements – the overflow of exuberant grassroots creativity – as any aged nightclub. I felt altogether too disreputable to be passing through those clean glass doors and over the immaculate green carpet. Shouldn't a paper devoted to underground music nest in a place more closely resembling a dank basement? For all of its do-it-yourself artistic ethic, the headquarters for Visionary Chapbook certainly didn't *look* very punk rock.

We met Pat. He was even slightly taller than Tommy - a few inches shy of seven feet, I guessed – and similarly gaunt. He was dressed in blue jeans and a dark corduroy shirt covered by a furry vest of gray and black. His eyebrows were bushy charcoal and scant hair remained on his head. Bristling with energy, he fetched us all coffees from the ceramic spigot and got us settled on the brown leather couch. His office space was wallpapered with old musical headlines: I saw a photo of one of my favorite bands, Foment Revolt, performing at a gig right there in Sadenport about five years before.

I liked Pat, with his buoyant, easy laugh and his obvious love for the music that his magazine was championing. And I think I can speak for the others on that count. I wished I had something else to offer him that day besides my poisoned thoughts and seared heart.

"So I've listened to your record, 'What Casts the Shadow,'" he began, "and I was immediately struck by the *conviction* of your performances. The songs are killer, and you guys play 'em like hell's pit fiends are flailing fiery whips at your backs the whole time."

His exuberance made me wince. Once – in another life, it seemed – Saul had described our band in a similar way: Performing as if our lives depended on it. Which in fact they did. And this had been before Carlos had joined, transforming us into an even more potent force.

"I may give the album a review in an upcoming issue," Pat went on. "So how 'bout you begin by sharing some of your memories of the whole process of recording it."

Tommy, our self-appointed diplomat, burst right out of the gate. "That was a good moment in time for us to capture. We'd been rehearsing like maniacs, and yet most of the songs were just a few months old and so they were still fresh and vital for us. We were also anticipating taking them out on the road, so that enthusiasm translated into what we laid down in the studio, too."

"And Brandon had a bit of a crisis of faith mid-way," Carlos good-naturedly put in.

"Oh?" Pat prompted, staring at me.

I had often fantasized myself poised in this very space and time. Grandiose as it may sound, there was a sacred dimension to the interview experience, at least for me. How the resonance of chords and melodies assumed new values, and words took on new significances, when I learned more about the people behind them! If human life is an eternal conversation – or, better yet, a sweeping symphony – then the duration of an interview is a transcendent moment, an opportunity for you to contribute a few of your own personal notes and initiate a new musical movement.

But the simmering ache within me – and my refusal to really feel it and own it – had dulled my sense of all of this. Even the most cherished gold of my soul had seemingly lost its luster. In desperation, I grasped at the one place in my life that hadn't yet fallen under the pall of encroaching thunderheads.

"My little sister brought me around," was all I could say.

Silence. I happened to glance in Tommy's direction; and I witnessed within him both the desire to speak and the firm *decision* to withhold himself and give me whatever space I needed.

"O.k.," Pat said tentatively.

"I visited her before I went to the studio, on one of our last nights of recording," I elaborated. "See, I didn't know who I was performing these songs for. They'd emerged from such a private part of me. Who else could possibly relate to them, you know? Was I really an alien in this world, or was there a place for me, somewhere?

"I guess you can get to that point where you realize that you could debate and question things forever; but if you're honest with yourself then you realize that your own truth is all that you've got. I just had to hope that it would ring true for other people too. So, I go see Rachel at recess and she's playing this game where they stole treasure from a troll's cave. This was, like, an echo of my own struggle somehow. I was trying to uncover my own voice – that was the treasure. And all the voices of self-doubt and despair inside, they were the trolls."

Realizing that this was all that I had to offer Pat, Visionary Chapbook, Tommy and Carlos - as well as whatever fans we might have out there - I relinquished the struggle for coherence. How could I even speak when I wanted nothing but to scream? I held on to the remembered moment, the one moment that resembled an oasis of peace, and continued to mine it.

"Rachel was holding this agate about the size of a chestnut. Like a quartz with a little apricot for a heart. See, some people associate stones with that inviolate part of ourselves, this kind of sanctuary where our essence lives and can never be destroyed. My relationship with Rachel has always been like that, an invulnerable place. Tommy and I were butting heads a lot back then. I was constantly challenging the therapist who I was seeing at the time. I put a lot of strain on" – I nearly choked – "my relationship with my girlfriend. But all that negativity somehow never intruded when I was with my little sis.

"So it was so fitting that she'd be the one with the stone, holding it out and telling me that it granted wishes. It's like she was really saying that she'd been holding that sacred space for me, just waiting until I was ready to carry it for myself."

That was as far as I could go. I stood up, feeling the warmth of tears streaking my cheeks. I have no idea when exactly they'd formed.

"You're a good guy, Pat. I'm sorry. I can't... I just lost my love. She's fucking gone. I hardly care about the music, what the lyrics mean; nothing matters anymore. What can you really even say about music anyway? I guess I've just always been searching for anything that could serve as a mirror for me. I can't do this today. I'm sorry."

A moment later I was out on the sidewalk. It was damp from a brief morning shower, the kind of flashing spill that our part of Oregon was known for in April. My eyes soaked up every detail as if this was the last fractured piece of earthly landscape that they would ever witness. Someone passed me on her way to the door, me with my hands braced on my knees and tears spattering the concrete. Interviews, records, songs, careers, fate... what did any of it mean to a man already dead?

I shuffled towards the van. Then an 'epiphany' visited me, deluding me for the space of several steps. Human beings were just not equipped to endure their own truth. For a moment I felt liberated. This 'insight' could serve to justify whatever I might choose to do now in response to my heart's devastation. I could fuck a whole string of loose women, get hooked on heroin, destroy myself, whatever, without qualm. The thought provoked a grim smile: My only defense against the emptiness.

I was lying in the back, left arm slung over my eyes, when the other guys finally came in. Tommy climbed into the driver's seat and began speaking at once.

"He's gonna call and see if we wanna re-schedule the interview. Carlos and I talked a bit more; but of course we didn't want to do it without you. It probably won't make it into the next issue now, one way or the other. But, maybe the one after that."

I just started jabbering out of my own bereavement.

"I don't have anything to offer you, Tommy. Just... thanks for hanging with me and not giving up. It's nothing that I ever deserved. Carlos, if we ever sign a publishing deal you're getting an equal cut of everything, even though you're not writing any songs. It's the least that you're entitled to for having to clean up my messes all the time."

My soul was so raw that Carlos' voice wafted over to me soothing as a lullaby.

"Hey, just take it easy, eh? You're in a lot of pain now, I know. It feels like a piece has been ripped right out of you, don't it? It'll take a while to move through it, bro. But you're going to."

In order to *move through*, though, I had to find some way to even *move*. As it was, I was a slug turning over and over on a bed of salt; and that dish full of salt was my entire universe. My mental hands were flailing for answers, insights, as Tommy started up the van.

Following a trek down to the Southwest and then north all the way to Washington, our vehicle had become the veritable fourth member of the band. We'd even given her a new black paint job. Had to treat her right, you know? After all, she could be serving as a home for us again, one of these days.

I stumbled upon one piece of prudent introspection. I pitched my voice over the engine's rumble, hoping it wouldn't crack. "I don't think I'll be able to handle the more vulnerable songs for a while," I admitted.

Tommy flashed me an empathetic smile via the mirror. "So we hearken back to our early days of sheer heaviness, then?"

This idea offered me a soothing breath of relief. One could always revel in negative ecstasy when that's all that remained. My love of playing – the memory of it, at least – was returning to me.

Inspired by this hope of at least temporary escape, I immediately shut myself in my room when we got back. The three of us shared an apartment – actually, one half of a duplex – on Baird Street, not too far from Siddens Elementary where Rachel went to school. My closest friends and creative partners were also my housemates, an arrangement that carried obvious comforts and conveniences as well as challenges. *Trust* was never an issue. On the other hand, minor irritations can become more serious abrasions to the mind and soul when one encounters them daily. This brought up a lot of fear for me, at times. I didn't want my relationships with the two people whom I relied upon the most to be subject to undue strain. Could it even reach a breaking point? You just have to trust that the underlying love is stronger than the accumulation of any surface conflicts, I guess. But then, my trust in love itself had been sorely tested of late…

The epicenter of my creative life lay right there on that brown carpeted floor: my miniature practice amp, which gave me a warm distorted sound even at low volume; my one guitar, which had been with me – spray-painted a charcoal ebony – since those beginning days of my first open G chord; and a notebook that still contained even my earliest lyrical ventures, often in the form of frantic scribbles. None of my contributions to Edge of the Known's first record had been created without these rudimentary but essential tools.

Lately I'd been playing around with a poignant riff, ethereal as a wisp of cloud, and had managed to draw it out further with a haunting chord progression. This, in turn, had evoked a melody line that made the whole piece ache even more keenly. Thus far I'd failed to compose even a single lyric to marry to all this music. But I felt the words coming now. For a couple hours I alternately riffed and paused to scrawl down a line or two. I addressed it all to some imagined witness to my pain and abjection – an angel of mercy, perhaps. Maybe my salvation came in the form of the song itself. It wouldn't have been the first time.

>
> Every word trusts the
>
> tongue that speaks
>
> but plays dumb to lend daring
>
> its weight
>
> The drama unfolds in
>
> every which way
>
> whether we may jump or
>
> hesitate

Thus begins "Diamond Maelstrom", which became one of my favorite pieces over time largely because I could never pin its meaning down to a logical explanation. The evocative power of poetry thrives upon certain aspects of mystery, I think.

Words oftentimes seemed to fail me at just the most crucial moments, because words can't hold the mystical experience. I think that's why so many poets become bitter and nihilistic. As sublime as their words may sound to our ears, they still pale alongside the genuine thing. But we have to keep trying, lest humanity forget that such a miracle as spiritual illumination is possible.

Reckless is the path to

faith

Fallow fields bear fruit on

the Other Side

Who seeks to lengthen his

life in Eternity?

Or cloak his wildness with

a dead bear's hide?

Transcendent experiences, moments of expanded or altered consciousness – whatever label you might want to give them, they can be really difficult to trace. Like so many events in our lives, they're often the culmination of a lot of subtle movements that went unnoticed. Altered states of consciousness can be risky subject matter, too, and I'd long kept my experiences to myself – or at least, I'd let the story go no farther than my inner sanctum, people like Tommy and Carlos - for fear of how the 'straight world', with its narrow definition of sanity, tended to view such things.

On the other hand, I did believe that if our race was to survive then it would have to embrace a wider definition of human nature. It would have to explore and develop those inner abilities that are native to us but had largely been ignored throughout our history.

Back then I didn't believe in a natural self, per se. Personality to me was just a collection of learned behaviors accrued over years of adapting to - and coping with - the world. That's what we learned in school, wasn't it? But like Saul said, if there was no inner self then none of us could hope to hold onto *any* form of sanity. Our only recourse would be to orient ourselves around the world; and the modern world believed that it had no soul or purpose.

> Word made flesh, in
>
> the Maelstrom of thought
>
> remind me of why
>
> I came
>
> Through quiet births, and
>
> bathed in trust,
>
> to be a guest in
>
> your house of flames

Through all of the dramatic changes that I weathered throughout my years of working with Saul, both internal and external, pain and fear were my constant companions. That part of my awakening was a passage through fire. There was the pain of regret: for all the limited ways in which I'd lived and felt; for all the injuries that I'd dealt myself and others. And there was a deeper pain that I'd always carried - maybe it didn't even have a 'source' in my life; maybe it was just the pain that's inherent in being here in a transitory world where everything expires sooner or later. It was a pain that I'd never wanted to acknowledge for fear that it would tear me apart. It took me a long time to realize that my feelings were meant to wake me up, not destroy me.

In the current moment, though, obscurity held out the possibility of escape from the concrete world. I was desperately in need of such a back door out of reality.

"There *is* no concrete world in the terms you're talking about," I heard Saul say. "The world that you travel through is the terrain of yourself – thought and feeling made manifest."

And then a line out of one of my own poems returned to me:

Fulfillment is a finite space where the
dreaming mind's back door is left
wide open

I told both of those voices to piss off.

After finishing the song, and playing it over again enough times so that I knew I'd never forget it, I curled up in my quilt, a tattered patchwork affair of earthy hues that was one of the last vestiges of my mother's life that I possessed. I tried to sleep through the afternoon sun and engine bustle. Life had no more demands for me until we would rehearse that night. In the meantime, *unconsciousness* was my one most feverish need. My bed was a pyre. I was burning, just like my new song said. This nest of flames was my new home.

I sought the twilight Hades realm that offers the kind of surcease that we forever vainly chase in waking. The one time I *did* slip under I immediately sprang up into full alertness again. My mind feared that plunge, and the surrender that it demanded. Janie's name rang in my ears. Had I cried out? If so, no one responded. The house was silent.

How was I going to survive this? Or – this was the more frightening admission – why was I *trying* to?

I didn't have enough skin for the world. That was it. That had *always* been my problem. My hide wasn't thick enough for reality. I was a worm turning in the salt.

3. Which Version of the Truth?

Our band rehearsed on some property on the outskirts of Sadenport that belonged to Saul and his wife June. An old bomb shelter had been tunneled out beneath the barn, the unwelcoming burrow of a former tenant who, in his near-hysterical fear of humanity and its propensity for destruction, had built this lonely refuge in anticipation of final darkness. We'd christened the place "The Catacombs". It was a location that magically befitted our quest to sound like no one but ourselves, as here we were effectively sealed off from the world's influence. We may as well have been rehearsing on one of Saturn's moons.

At one time, rehearsing in The Catacombs had elevated the quest to create music to a heroic – even mythic – dimension for me. I felt as if I was grasping the raw despair with which this bunker had been built and transmuting it into defiance, affirmation and love: The declaration of belief, cast by an unsinkable spirit against an ocean of darkness. But now all answers and purposes seemed to have fled. Artists sometimes die in such a place. Or they may linger on in such a way that the remainder of their lives amounts to a fundamental betrayal of their Muse. I was trapped in a world of contrary horrors, abhorring both fates, wanting desperately to believe and yet finding myself unable to.

Then I recalled a phrase that Tommy was fond of repeating, no doubt culled from his extensive readings in Depth Psychology and related subjects: "The only way *out* is *through*." Salvation was not to be found in any form of flight from my pain. Rather, I needed to *embrace* that pain as fully as possible, let it fuel every chord that I struck with my hands and every note that I belted from the bottom of my lungs.

I got halfway through the first verse of my new song and could already feel the medicine going to work. There's an effect that words can exercise upon your consciousness that is not dependent upon their logical meaning or even upon your understanding. There is also a magical aspect to music that has nothing to do with our conceptions of pitch, timbre and decibels.

Carlos seemed to understand the statement that was being made and where it all must inevitably lead. He captured and amplified the rhythm and attitude before I even reached the first instrumental break, punctuating my personal catharsis with his own need to transcend. Tommy was not far behind him. There is something about bereavement that marries so readily with the human voice. All of us understand the language of the wail. For all my emotional extravagance, I kept my voice under control, held its *focus*. We were all aboard the vessel now and departing from earthly shores.

When I say that music transported me to a wholly different world I'm not trying to express any sort of disdain for our physical surroundings. It just comforted me to know – to *feel* – that this dimension that we label "the real" actually exists in relation to so much else: *Infinite* something elses, really. My sore suffering in the moment was truth; but it was, at the same time, a story – *one version* of the truth. I existed on many planes aside from just that one; and the life surrounding me was not confined to the picture that my five senses painted.

I almost forgot who, and where, I was. When the song ended, as the last ripe distorted chord shimmered and faded, I had to get reacquainted with my surroundings. You might awaken from a dream of air raid sirens and frantically dart around searching for signs of Armageddon before realizing that, in the waking world, what you're hearing is the peal of your alarm clock. So it was for me, emerging from the enfolding arms of epiphany to suddenly remember that I was a mortal individual in a dusty basement space with a low ceiling and scant light.

Tommy was clutching his bass around its neck and staring at me. "Jesus!" he breathed. "That's the most shamanic thing you've done in a long time – and that takes some doing."

I tried to accept his affirmation, to honor him by letting it in. This was a challenge for the adolescent that still lived inside me, the one who faced all of life with a posture that screamed, "I can fight my way through this life alone and I don't need you!"

My eyes strayed to Carlos. Three songs into the set and he was already sweating. My own white tank top clung to my skin. Carlos nodded slowly.

"Powerful, bro."

Indeed: Powerful enough to allow me to forget, for the moment, the futility and bleakness of life, and even to question if perhaps *this* description of reality was not just, in itself, another story.

"I felt it even more, playing it just now with you guys," I said. "I can't wait to perform it live."

We'd only done a handful of gigs in the city since returning from our low-budget road tour the previous summer. We'd had a lot to attend to upon our return. I was the only one able to slide back into my previous employment, bussing tables at a steakhouse called Jaspar's. Tommy had been replaced at the pizza place and he'd eventually been hired to work weekdays at the local library. That was fitting. He was bound to spend his life surrounded by books one way or the other; and maybe the librarian who hired him had recognized this. Carlos had soldiered through various backbreaking temp jobs until the auto shop had offered him his old job back.

"Chas has been following through on all his connections," Tommy announced, "and calling in every favor, just trying to land us a steady gig somewhere. He believes that we'll make our biggest impact if we really dig our heels in and become a fixture of one certain establishment."

I frowned; and Tommy and I quickly and silently exchanged our mutual discontent. I didn't appreciate *anyone* making plans around the band aside from the three guys who were in it, and he knew that.

"He worked hard to get us that interview," Tommy pointed out. "And we botched that. I think we owe it to him to be supportive when he's trying to do things on our behalf."

"Yeah," I conceded. And I shoved aside my pride. But I had to be lenient with myself, too. Pride was sometimes the only form of self-respect that remained to me.

And there really wasn't anything else to say. I was restless; and this, in turn, made me anxious to play more. We continued on into the night, dipping into the dozen songs the comprised "What Casts the Shadow?" as well as a couple of songs that Tommy had written since that summer.

We also found some time to air our *feelings* about it all: What these songs meant to us, and where we hoped to take them. We hadn't had a conversation like that in a while, and it was needed. A vision that stirs up the embers of passion deep within your soul, that widens the skies of possibility before your inner eyes, can enable you to endure all kinds of adversity and disappointment in your daily life. And without that, even trivial sorrows and frustrations can be debilitating.

"Our pain is more easily borne when it has *meaning* for us," Saul had once told me. Music was thus a response to our collective inner *need*. It was no mere hobby or career path. It was a vocation in the sacred sense of the word. I was awakening to this truth all over again, just when I sorely needed the reminder.

"The essential pith of the lyrics, to me, is the power of the individual," Tommy opined. "It like the Nietzschean thing: 'God is dead' means that *we're* all God; divinity is ours, not Christ's or the Devil's. And by the same token, it's an illusion that the power resides with the institutions and the political structures and the military industrial complex and all that. *We the people* are the destined caretakers of the Earth, the stewards of the land."

"Society is our creation to begin with," Carlos put in; and I winced. Janie had once said that precise thing to me. I thrust her out of my head with almost suicidal force.

"Exactly," Tommy went on, oblivious to my grief and anything else that didn't fall in line with the thrust of his dissertation. "And so *claiming* our power becomes simply a matter of recognizing that we already possess it. That's the potency of our lyrics, taken as a joint statement. It's like this picture of one human being passing through the whole spectrum of joys and agonies, struggles and triumphs, as he forms his personal world."

"I think you may be right about all that," I said, slinging my guitar strap off my back as I realized that we'd tapped the well dry for this particular night. "But for myself... if I let it become too self-conscious a thing then it kills the flow right there. I have to just tune in to what's wanting to come through and not try to second-guess what it means all too much. Besides, the listener needs his or her own freedom to draw conclusions. Once we perform a song, or set it down on record, it doesn't really belong to us anymore. It belongs to the world, to anyone with the ears to hear it."

Within many other groups, such differing aesthetics might have caused a serious rift between members. Hell, I even knew bands that were notorious for fistfights in the studio or onstage. But Tommy and I had long ago learned that the tension between our disparate philosophies was actually a source of strength. Either tendency, pursued without challenge, would've landed Edge of the Known in a much less interesting place.

A band that was solely based upon Tommy's vision would've possessed the kind of ideology that was far too dense for your average music lover, of whatever genre, even if the intellectuals would've been moved to profundity. My songs wallowed in emotional extravagance; but I knew enough to realize that I oftentimes couldn't *direct* all that energy in a constructive way. So, this is overly-generalized, no doubt, but basically one could say that with Tommy alone you'd end up with a musical structure that, while brilliant, somehow couldn't come across on a street level; and with me you'd end up with a raging fire that had no container.

I was worried about encountering Saul that night and so I hurried to the van after we finished playing. I hadn't seen him since about a week before Janie had torn my fantasy of requited love to shreds. I was afraid that I'd be transparent to Saul's eyes, that he'd gather all the evidence of my internal distress with a glance. I wasn't ready to endure that level of vulnerability. Fortunately, he was rarely up at this hour. The lights in his house were all out as we made ready to drive away. And I felt closer to my band than I had in a long time. This lent me a degree of emotional equilibrium.

I could tell that the fever was going to start raging inside me again. Although I rarely drank, I picked up a six pack of strong microbrew in anticipation of my night's battle. I downed a couple of the beers quickly and then tramped off to bed. Even if sleep were to elude me I could still have darkness. Janie! Goddamn it, her shade sliced right through me like one of those fabled oriental blades. How could I banish it? The alcohol somehow only muddled my thinking; it failed to dull my emotional pain in any noticeable way.

Weariness won out over bereavement after an hour or so. It was but a flashing respite, though. I found myself upright, heart pounding,. staring dumbly at the white curtain that was outlined with the pale glow of a streetlight in an otherwise pitch-dark room.

I could still hear my father's muffled wail of anguish and despair, almost as if it was still happening in the waking world of clock time. I tried to backtrack from there, to reconstruct the harrowing dream, but could grasp nothing else. Then I had a vision of the house that he lived in, the house that I'd grown up in. Every room was dark. This was something more (or less) than mere absence of light, though. The darkness was, itself, a *presence* – a presence that had infiltrated all the spaces there that had never really known the touch of light and love. The whole place reeked of death and the void. My father was in its belly, swallowed whole.

I'd endured plenty of nightmares before, and usually their various horrors would dissipate within a few minutes of waking. Sometimes I even enjoyed the residual adrenaline, the chemical thrill of blood charging from a fast-beating heart. But I was awake now - had been for several minutes - and still the sense of dread clutched me as tangibly as it had within the dream state.

Somehow I knew that the danger was legitimate, real in the waking world of "fact".

I leaped out of bed and began dressing before I'd even reasoned through what I was doing – or what I *planned* to do. Half of my consciousness still lingered within the stark and unmerciful dream and the other half was nearly unhinged with unreasoning panic. I didn't trust myself to drive. Nonetheless, I had to go to him at once. I'd have to walk – run, rather. I'd made that trip in twenty minutes before; I could do it in ten, or less, tonight. That would have to be enough.

I retained enough presence of mind to pocket my cigarettes and lighter – my eternal antidote for rattled nerves – and my wallet. Within another minute I had my red sweatshirt on, had pulled the hood over my head and stepped out into the spring night.

The brisk air and the rigor of my exertions ushered lucidity. I realized the absurdity of what I was doing. No dream had ever before set me to roaming Sadenport's streets in the middle of the night. But I was committed now; and by the time I'd seriously begun to question the sanity behind this whole venture I was closer to my father's home than I was my own, anyway.

I stepped onto the walkway of St. Stephen's Bridge as if it was the gateway between worlds – Bifrost, perhaps. Tommy and I had often met here, in the early days of our band when the philosophy behind it had just begun to crystallize. I had weathered uncounted deaths since then. Three cars passed me along the entire length of the bridge. Matterpike River, some hundred feet below me, was slow, dark and sullen.

What had my dad ever *done* to earn my present state of panic? It seemed that with every step I recalled another stinging blow to the face, a fresh burst of humiliation, another remark full of dismissal and spite. For a few years now, I'd been strong enough to take my old man down. *He should just count himself lucky that I restrained myself all those times!* He could thank Rachel, too. If not for her, I doubt that I would have shown such forbearance.

The sounds of barking dogs drew me back into the present moment. I left the bridge and slipped onto Farrell Street which, a few blocks down, branched off into the cul-de-sac where Robert Chane lived alone. Until about two years ago, I'd called the place home also. I'd spent the better part of my teen years devising ways to stay away from it as long as possible. Only… someone had needed to be around to see that Rachel ate breakfast and caught the bus; that she did her homework and brushed her teeth; that she wasn't so scared that she couldn't sleep at night on account of being effectively left alone at the age of five, six…

God-Damn it! Why was I doing this? *Just go ahead and die, fucker! What the hell do I care?*

But I did care. My love for the man, the man who still lived (I was sure of it) beneath the inebriation and the rages and the projected disgust, was unextinguished. That love was, in fact, one of the sorest sources of grief in my entire existence.

I stopped at the opening of the cul-de-sac. My old two-storey, three bedroom home, with its dirty white walls and green trim, hovered at the very rear, perched upon a rise where the stone bared itself, like giant mangled teeth, at various points along the low hill. For a dead-end life, a road with no outlet. It was utterly fitting.

4. Death Makes for a Clean Slate?

I drew a deep breath to muster my resolve, bent and massaged my knees through my jeans. There was only one light on within the house; and at this distance I couldn't guess its source. Now that I'd come this far there was nothing for it but to enter – now, in the dead of night; even knowing that I might be doing so at the bidding of a fantastical dream that bore no relation to waking reality. This whole trek could have been naught but the irrational byproduct of fear. The odds spoke in favor of that notion. Hell, he could mistake me for a prowler and bash my head in as soon as I got through the door. He could call the cops on me, as he'd done once before. Or...

Or my dream premonition could be tangible, true, and already come to fruition. I might encounter nothing in there but his corpse.

Every time I'd ever swung my fists, I realized, it'd been as futile a gesture as smacking the tides in the hopes of turning them back. We erect thin and ultimately doomed bulwarks against life's incessant waves.

I floated towards the house as if I was still immersed in the harrowing dream that had drawn me here. Then I stalked up the stone steps, those steps that had, a thousand times before, met my booted feet in their haste to carry me *away* from this place. My sorrow, Rachel's confusion, Ma's ghost... all was encased in that cold stone. I allowed myself no time to consider what I was doing but pushed on the front door as soon as I reached it. Unlocked, it gave way.

Immediately I was confronted by the sickly sounds of coughing. They were too weak and wretched to have come from any human body that was determined to live. I now knew that my father was upstairs; in the bathroom, no doubt. There was no other logical place for him to be, unless he meant to stare into the vacant room where his daughter once had lived until his heart ruptured in his ribcage. I raced through the tiny kitchen and then up the carpeted stairs.

Time fluctuated to the rhythm of a pendulum, one moment lulled to weary somnolence and the next one thick with urgency. Perhaps this was a reflection of my alternating states of panic and disbelief. Robert Chane was in the bathtub. On the linoleum floor, an empty bottle of bourbon lay on its side beside the blue bathmat and his discarded clothes. A slash of blood, keen as a shriek, covered perhaps a two foot stretch of the tiles. Robert's head was bowed and shrouded in shadow.

"Dad!"

No answer. I reached in and pulled the drain plug. Then I grabbed him by his wet shoulders, tugged, and it was then that I discovered that both his wrists were opened. The scent of life's seepage hit me, provoking nausea. I ignored the deep discoloration of the water, the massive blood loss that it implied, and told myself that the only essential thing was to *get his arms out now*. I maneuvered my forearms under his armpits and heaved him towards the side of the tub.

That provoked the animal instinct in him, the instinct that had been perverted by its long acquaintance with my father's despair. The dream of self-preservation somehow exists even within the longing for death. Eyes still closed, he growled and resisted. I was much stronger; and it may be that some part of his inner being joined with my efforts, in defiance of his conscious intent. My second expense of strength carried him over the edge and onto the floor.

"Goddamn it, leave me!" He'd opened his eyes, now, but this protest escaped him before he'd even had time to figure out who I was. And his drunkenness delayed that moment of recognition even further. It didn't matter: His rebellion, in either case, was an empty gesture. I snatched a towel off the rack and wrapped his forearms together. My first desperate intention was to staunch the flow as much as possible, buy myself a few crucial moments in which to try and conceive of some more permanent remedy.

"Leave me, dammit!" he repeated; but his voice was muffled by general bemusement this time.

"Shut the hell up!" I grunted. My words came out in spatters – much like his blood - amidst my efforts to get cloth and pressure on those cuts in spite of his feeble struggles. Then, louder: "Maybe I'm just saving your ass so I can have the pleasure of killing you *myself* later. You ever think of that?"

Somehow that *did* shut him up; and the outburst gave me some momentary relief, enough so that I could gather my thoughts in the gap between heartbeats of terror. Robert quit struggling. I was able to ease him back onto the floor, flatten him out on his back. Feeling reassured, for the moment, that he wouldn't try to undo his wrappings, I stood and lunged for the medicine cabinet. I remembered that there'd been peroxide in there, and bandages...

He'd cut himself downwards, not crosswise; the slits were each about three inches long and they stubbornly refused to close. Luckily, drunk as he was, he'd done a sloppy job of it. The initial punctures seemed to be the only places where the razor had dug deep. The blade itself had made it to the bath drain; I could tell by the spluttering sound that the remaining water made as it pushed past it.

"There's got to be some place other than this," Robert mumbled. His emotional fever rendered him lucid for a moment. "Do you think so, son? That there's someplace we go when we die, someplace better?"

I had the supplies from the cabinet in my right hand and my left steadied me against the side of the mirror. Despite my urgency, I stopped there and closed my eyes. When had he last called me *son*? When had he *ever*? Scouring through the vast bitter fields of my memories, I couldn't isolate a single other moment when I'd ever witnessed him this bare and vulnerable.

I let out a slow breath to borrow time to compose my answer. "I think that we can make a heaven or a hell out of *this* place," I said. "And if that's true – if we have that power – then we're bound to do the same thing anywhere else we might go."

Then I turned to look at him. He'd wet his cheeks with silent tears. The sight almost stopped me.

"I know it's not the most comforting thought," I finished, "but it's all I've got."

It took me a few minutes to get him tightly bandaged. Like I said, the ineptitude of his attempt did us both a service that night. He must have done his research, though. A girl I'd known in High School, someone given to morbid fantasies like this, had once explained it to me: "If you want to slash your wrists right, do it *downwards* along the vein, not across. Make it deep, and then get it under water so that the cuts don't close."

My father tried to grasp me by the shoulders. His breath, reeking of liquor, came in ragged bouts. His eyes were wide and carried the gleam of frightened fanaticism, as if he'd just witnessed the angel of mercy transformed into something hideous. His hair was grayer, thinner than it'd been even a year ago. And although he was about the same size, he seemed lighter somehow, less substantial.

"Don't," I cautioned, easing his hands back down. "Let them sit. If you flex those muscles it'll just make the cuts open up again."

"I don't really want to die!"

The whole thrust of his fragile life lay behind that declaration. Perhaps he'd *needed* to go this far in order to finally understand. Vacillating between the poles of pity and compassion, I gazed down without speaking. Somehow his abjection enabled me to be the steady one – more focused and *capable* than I ever would have imagined myself in such a situation as this.

"Well, you're not going to," I said after a moment. "Though you probably *would* have if I'd gotten here even ten minutes later."

We were both shaking. I lit a cigarette, right there in the bathroom, and turned on the electric vent. I would've caught hell for doing such a thing back when I'd lived here. But to hell with his protests. I'd just saved his life.

The turbulence of his inner state made him pant. He stared down at his crimson bandages.

"I don't know how in the hell you came to be here just now."

That threw me back upon the very incomprehensible essence of this night.

"You'd never believe me if I told you," I muttered, half to myself. "*I hardly even know how to make sense of it.*"

He was too lost in his own inner ruminations to pay much attention to this anyway. "God, I want the peace of death." His spirit momentarily flared. "The *peace*! You hear me?" But just as quickly, his will sagged. "You should've let me die," he drawled on, in a much smaller voice. "It would've been better if you hadn't showed up. I got nothin'. Nothin'."

I gazed down at my father, this contradictory man who just a moment ago had raged "I don't want to die!" His white tank top and faded jeans, which lay on the floor a few feet from me, would've looked grubby even without the streaks of blood. In the months following his accident on a construction site – one that had virtually ruined his back – he'd amassed a layer of softer flesh thanks to a lifestyle that had largely relegated him to a recliner in front of the TV., collecting disability. But this had been largely flensed away now. He was gaunt, most likely due to malnourishment. Most of his calories these days were probably derived from the booze. But this physical change was trivial when weighed alongside the overall emaciation of his *spirit*.

"What you *have*," I iterated, "is an eight year-old daughter, almost nine now, who's not only the best reader in her third grade class but also the one who everyone wants a playdate with because she invents the most imaginative games you've ever witnessed. And although she may not live with you anymore she *does* live only about two miles away. And I happen to know for a *fact* that she loves her daddy."

I took another drag in an attempt to settle the flood of my feelings. Robert kept staring at the ceiling. I can't even fathom where his thoughts may have been.

"You have the respect of the guys who worked on your crew," I went on. "Even if you can't lift stone slabs or tall ladders anymore, still you've got all that knowhow in your brain somewhere. Hell, with a few years of schooling you could turn yourself from a *builder* of houses to a *designer* of them."

Then I couldn't contain myself anymore. That fork-tongued imp of the depths demanded his say.

"*And* you've got a son who's the most radical madman poet musician that Sadenport has ever seen – maybe the world, for that matter. And even if he'll never forget how many times you smacked him around – even if he'll never let you get away with shit like that again as long as you live – still he'll run down here in the middle of the night to save your ass when you haven't got any hope left!"

Then some of my own turmoil subsided. My ire spent, I knelt down beside him. By neither words nor look did he protest a single point that I'd made.

Presently I got back up and extinguished my cigarette in the sink. It was time to settle upon the next step: And my mind was in the dark. I remembered the full depth of my distrust of both the medical and the psychological professions. I'd had a run-in with Limn County Mental Health a couple years before, when Dad had called the cops after I'd hurled a cast iron pan through one of the kitchen windows. I'd played cagey-but-repentant with the psychiatrist, Dr. Lisbet, in order to escape with my freedom intact.

Suddenly I realized that I was willing to risk infection, other possible physical complications and even the chance that my father would suffer complete mental collapse rather than call an ambulance.

I squatted down beside him and strove to make my voice sound as reassuring as possible. "Look, we're just gonna have to deal with this ourselves. This isn't, like, an accident. If you go to the hospital, simple stitches ain't gonna be the end of it. There'll be no way to hide that it was a suicide attempt, and then you're dealing with psych evaluations and being put on crisis watch and all that. Personally, I don't think any of that is gonna do you any good. And it may even do a lotta harm. Handing yourself over to a system that's got illness built right into it ain't any way to health, in my opinion.

"So I'll stay here while you recuperate. We'll get through this together. And rest assured, if you go near any sharp objects I will be kicking your ass thoroughly."

Then I found a patch of floor that was neither wet nor stained and lowered myself to it. My dad and I both sat in silence for a while, he on the towel that I'd first used to staunch his wounds. My logical faculties had resumed their steady march. In fact, they seemed to be working double time to make up for their previous lull. A throng of hard facts paraded before me. It was actually a miracle, I admitted to myself, that my old man hadn't succeeded in doing himself in long before now. And ultimately, nothing was really resolved by the simple fact that he yet lived.

"Let's go get you dressed," I said, thrusting those larger considerations aside and focusing on the dire stains. "Then I'll get this bathroom cleaned up. It's really not good for either of our heads, to be looking at all this."

I raised my voice and strove to pierce the sickly yellow-gray aura that seemed to hover about him like a cloud. "This is now in the past, all right? Henceforth. Tomorrow is a new day."

Then I helped him to rise. Robert was silent, but I felt *intention* and *gratitude* in his effort to stand and move. Thus reassured, I was able to let him go so he could dress. He flicked some lights on as he went, dispelling some of the house's brooding menace. I went downstairs to fetch the little sponge mop that he kept leaning against the side of the fridge.

I moved mechanically, with simple and deliberate focus, trying to quiet my thoughts as much as possible. First I pulled down the showerhead and used it to rinse away the lingering traces of sickly crimson. I got the walls of the tub and the tiles above it, sending more nightmare residue plunging down the drain in the process. I ended up emptying half a can of scented sanitizer spray into the air as if I could thereby not only purge the smell of blood but also the lingering spirit of nihilism that dwelled there.

When I found my father again he was in the living room, dressed in gray striped pajamas that somewhat resembled prison garb. He looked frail to the point of insubstantiality: A sad, reduced and expended little creature that I could've perched on my shoulder. But he possessed enough courage to face me – with no subterfuge clouding his gaze.

"Thanks for everything, Brandon," he said. He sounded almost sober.

I acknowledged this with a nod and then opted to give him a dose of tough love. "Yeah, well, I can keep you from killing yourself if I happen to be around. But I can't give you one reason to *want* to live. That's gotta come from you."

His face was enveloped in still and sullen clouds; and he betrayed no further reaction to my words. After wandering slowly for a while, like an amnesiac searching for eternally-lost car keys, he finally settled into the recliner that had, over the years, molded itself to his very being. He was thrown back upon the tempest winds of self-doubt.

"Look," I offered, "why don't you get some sleep now. I'm tired too. I don't have to work until Monday, so…" I nodded towards the recliner. "Maybe I could sleep there?"

I realized, in that moment, that this was where I most longed to be in all the world: In *his chair*.

As he got up and began stumbling towards his room, I spoke to his back. "We can talk more about everything in the morning. I know someone who may be able to help you."

5. Our Self-Created Worlds

It'd been a couple of months since I'd met with Saul. Of course, we'd interact briefly here and there when Edge of the Known was rehearsing and he happened to be around. But I'd taken a hiatus from actual therapy sessions. Returning from our seven-week tour the previous summer, I'd felt *capable* for the first time in my life, really; like my existence was actually something that I could navigate alone. I trusted myself enough to skirt its edges without fear – and without blaming the world, in fitful bursts of rage, when I suffered for my own missteps.

But now everything seemed to be spinning out of control again.

Hearing my desperation over the phone – he knew that it had to be pretty severe if it *showed* through the tough exterior that I often projected – Saul penciled me in for his earliest opening. By now he had a clientele of some forty people who saw him regularly, either weekly or bi-weekly. Many of them were men and women who he'd first gotten acquainted with during his tenure as a crisis responder answering the phone for a suicide hotline. Survivors of life scenarios like that needed more than just *a reason not to die.* They needed renewed purpose, hope and a sense of direction that held personal significance. Life must be *valued,* not merely *endured.* A life devoid of meaning is unlivable. It doesn't matter how much hard-headed stamina and willpower is brought to bear.

So this is what Saul aimed to do, in the long run: Connect people with their inner sense of soul purpose, so that their problems would have *meaning* for them, first of all, and so that they could then understand how they had *created* those challenges in the first place. The power of each individual was always stressed – in a way that, insofar as I could see, it *never* was anywhere else in our cultural environment.

He'd once made an effort to summarize, for me, his particular philosophy and approach. "I think that it can and should be liberating to know that we're already carrying, inside of us, everything that we need for our life's journey," he'd said. "This is ultimately what any kind of expanded consciousness teaches us; because every reality we can perceive, in whatever state we're in, has its source within us. But as you know, the world can be such a convincing illusion! Without even noticing we're doing it, we can still slip into thinking that we're at its mercy.

"Many people look to the unconscious, to dreams and surrealism, and speak of symbols. My thinking turns that formula inside-out. To me, the objects and motions of the physical world are the symbols, symbols meant to illustrate what's going on at the inner level. If we're really the creators of our own experience then physical objects have a non-physical source; and that source lies within.

"This world is thoroughly real to us - while we're in it. But also try to remain aware that it is only a story that your senses tell you: A work of accepted fiction so dazzling that it's easy for any of us to mistake it for the whole truth. Remember that it's only one station on the radio band. And we're all tuned in to it at the moment – or else I couldn't speak these words and you couldn't hear them. But it's liberating, at the same time, to know that we can tune in to many others

"And so what happens when we embark upon this journey of self-discovery? Well, we discover that we are part of the unknown, and also part of the process through which it becomes *known*. Most importantly, we discover that the unconscious activity that upholds and replenishes the Universe is in no way separate from us. Because we are the creators of our reality, this means that the invisible forces of life await our conscious direction. That's our divine gift, to draw upon this inexhaustible source and use it to paint the picture of our lives in every detail.

"We exist at the mercy of nothing save for ourselves."

I met with him that Monday evening, after finishing up a fairly slow shift at the restaurant. I felt quiet inside, spent. I'd often carried belligerence with me into Saul's office; but not today. For one thing, I missed him. And I regretted all the times in the past when I'd sought his help and then fought with him through every step of the therapeutic process. Besides, I'd exhausted all of my own resources. I felt ready to receive *anything* that he might say. Any way forward had to be preferable to staying where I was.

Saul's office – which I had actually helped him to build and paint, a year and a half before – resembled many a psychiatrist's. A couple of plaques on the wall proclaimed his training and schooling. These were kept company by an old clock and three abstract paintings. His desk was fine mahogany, its surface neatly ordered. Saul expressed his own personal dignity in his workplace, but he was also keeping up appearances. He needed to "play the game", as he said, in order to do his real work. And that work was unlike that of any other psychologists I knew of; and I'd encountered a few throughout my troubled youth.

He looked withdrawn on this particular evening – subdued, even. His mustache and thick eyebrows could lend Saul's visage a dour puppy-dog aspect at times; but one would be a fool to assume that his sensitivity made him soft. His underlying grit and tenacity was even more formidable than what was suggested by his lean, steely physique and sleek, pantherish stride. Saul was a primal hunter beneath that therapist suit.

He greeted me with a smile, saying at once, "How 'bout we walk, do our session outside tonight?"

I was amenable, as I hoped that moving around might help my jumbled thoughts to disentangle themselves. Saul put on a sweatshirt, grabbed his pipe and lighter from a shelf and then led the way out. At six p.m., the light itself was cooler; but the air remained as warm and muggy as it'd been at midday. We began moving in an oblong circuit around Saul's land. This encompassed probably six or seven acres, and touched upon the barn (with Catacombs beneath), an outhouse and a small pond amidst various piles of rusty engine innards that had been left behind by the previous owner. I began thinking about the astonishing extent to which my whole spiritual life revolved around this yard.

Saul lit his pipe and then said: "So I want to begin by just acknowledging that I know about what happened with you and Janie. Now, I promise you that things will always be confidential between us; and the same thing applies to her. But I need to tell you that she's been in to see me a couple of times - that's how I got the story."

This revelation made me burn beneath my skin, so fiercely that I couldn't identify the underlying cause. Was I jealous of Saul, he having access to the woman I loved in a way that was lost to me? Was it the thought of her confiding in him, when *I* had so long been her most trusted confidante? Or was I just not ready to even think of her, to remember, to long for her and ache…

"How'd that happen?" I managed.

By this time we'd made it to the edge of the tepid cauldron of life that was his pond. We stopped there. Its deeper middle portion was dominated by white water lilies. Some tadpoles scampered away from the murky edge as our shadows fell upon the cattails and the sun-kissed pond floor.

"She'd heard about me from you," Saul said, "and so when she found herself in difficulty I was the one who she thought to call. You and she share similar leanings in that regard. She knows, on some level, that her life is her own creation. And she realizes that the average therapist is *not* going to work with her from that place of understanding."

I flashed him a sarcastic smile. "So much for confidentiality," I sassed.

"I got her permission to say as much as I have," Saul responded at once, and repaid the look in kind.

Then he drew a pensive puff off his pipe. Gazing over his pond towards the darkening east, he continued. "Most people look for an outside reference point against which they believe they must measure themselves. A behaviorist might try to adapt you to the social norm – whatever his or her idea of *that* is. A more, quote, spiritual person may think that the object is to surrender to God or some similar conception of an all-knowing being. It's rare that you'll find anyone who'll tell you that your life is yours, and that *you* have made it what it is.

"And so that brings us back to you and your predicament." He was facing me now. "You're suffering. You've lost the woman you love – probably the first woman you *ever* loved. How do you think that happened?"

"I told Janie about the time that I lost control with that guy outside of the Samurai warehouse, that I nearly killed him!" I snapped. "She freaked out and ran!"

"But let's bring it back to yourself," Saul insisted. "I *do* think that the incident you mentioned is a good place to start, though. What comes into your mind when you recall it?"

"I try not to – ever," I said. And this was the bare truth.

Saul was instantly animate. He snapped his fingers. "Exactly! You try to bury that part of your experience because you're listening to the voice of guilt."

My mental fingers lost their grasp on the world. I could only watch him, and wait.

Saul gave me a moment to settle. Then he said: "Our natural sense of remorse *does* carry a certain beneficial, teaching quality. Tell me: Have you ever acted out that violently, or to that extent, since you had that experience?"

I traced my way along the intervening couple of years in my mind. "Uh… no. I had that fight with my father where I ended up smashing a window. And then the Pumpkin Festival – but I *let* that guy win, basically, 'cause I just didn't want to kick his ass badly enough."

"That's what I'm talking about," Saul said soberly. "Our natural sense of regret just says, 'That felt horrible. Let's not ever do that again.' And you *haven't*, see? But I think that there's this other way in which your mind has played upon that memory. It's done some slow, poisonous work. You probably already carried an exaggerated sense of guilt to begin with. But once you nearly lost control, that guilt had a focus, some sort of apparent *justification*."

His eyes narrowed, bore into my insides. I hadn't expected us to plunge so deep so quick. I'd forgotten, during my time away, all about Saul's tendency to go for the jugular. He was as unmerciful in those moments as the fearsome killer in our dreams who really comes to free us from our mental prison.

"I'm willing to bet that, ever since that day, you've viewed your whole life in terms of 'what is wrong with me?'" he said. "Do you see that? So then it's no longer about an event, but rather seems to touch upon the essence of *who you are*. 'What kind of a monster must I be, to do that?'

"You didn't want the woman you loved to get close to that monster, did you? I'm guessing that in a thousand little ways - and probably without even realizing it – you gave her the signal to keep her distance. Sooner or later she was going to find out just how 'unstable' or 'dangerous' you were, right? And then it would all be over anyway."

It was so often this way, that Saul's pronouncements would sweep the very ground out from under me. Of course, I can look back now and see that this was because his insights undermined the very ideas and beliefs that I'd built the foundation of my life upon. Therefore, every revelation was received like a tremor – even a full-blown earthquake – that shook my inner environment to its roots. But I rarely realized this in the moment. Instead I would feel – despite all my mental commands and discipline – this rage, defiance; resentment, even. It was my old self clawing for its life - which, despite all of its myriad hells, was the only life that it knew.

Saul also had the tendency to speak as if my inner conflicts were audible to him.

"Understanding and acknowledging the self-made trap is just the first step, remember," he said. His tone was deliberately soothing. "Remind yourself, at every bend in the road, that you painted the picture of your life this way. With that same power, you can paint a *new* picture, consciously choose a different course.

"See your guilt for what it is: An emotion grown up around your misunderstanding of life and of your own human nature. Ask yourself what kind of Creator would plant us here, beginning our journey in a state of utterly-dependent infancy – 'cause that's what we believe, right? -, and expect that we'd go through our earthly experience with no missteps. And don't split hairs about how 'bad' your deed was compared to someone else's deeds. The man lived. *You* live. Life and learning continue – and *you've* learned not to go down that particular road anymore."

The abyss was howling beneath me now. "Yeah," I rasped, "but she's still gone, Saul!"

"I can't play the referee between the two of you," he said at once. "I can only tell you that if you created this painful circumstance with a false sense of guilt then *confronting* that guilt and discarding it will give you a new lease on life."

I knew that I couldn't pursue this line of discussion any further. Sometimes I could register the truth of his words and yet realize that I needed time to assimilate them. Somehow I would manage to postpone my own emotional recognition.

"O.k., I got you," I said. "But look: I need to talk about something else. I've been trying to convince my father to come and see you."

We turned away from the pond and resumed our circuit.

"I'm surprised he even heard you out," Saul remarked.

"Well, he's pretty broken. In a way, that makes me scared for him. But in another way he's more approachable now, because his belligerence is just sapped."

"He's hit rock bottom," Saul ventured.

"He tried to kill himself," I replied. "Cut his wrists. I happened to be there in time to stop it. A dream prompted me, actually."

I stopped. Suddenly I missed gazing at the still water; I realized how much I'd been relying on it to settle me. "What do you make of that, anyway?"

Saul looked thoughtful for a moment. Then he shrugged. "I've tried explaining this before, that it's our senses that weave the story, telling us that there's a world outside of ourselves that's concrete and real." He cast me a compassionate look, perhaps to acknowledge how difficult such a concept was to accept, for any of us. "Matter isn't nearly as solid as we've imagined. And so what keeps us so perfectly poised in our own time and space, amidst this maelstrom of swirling energy? Well, it's my thinking that we're able to achieve this miracle because all of life is *aware* of every other part. So, we create our world together by managing to arrive at some sort of agreement. Now, if you consider the depth of perception and intelligence that this implies... well, your ability to be aware of your father in his moment of need, miraculous as it is, is yet a small thing when weighed alongside the true capacities of the inner self."

Then his eyes forsook their clear focus and drifted off to somewhere outside of – or beyond – the immediate and tangible world. I stood and waited.

"Unless any of us have plumbed the multi-dimensional universe and every probable reality therein - so that we've got some basis of comparison - how can you really say what may be a gift and what may be a product of madness? Those are all human value judgments, see."

I nodded in eagerness. "That's why I didn't want him to go to a hospital. I figured seeing you was the safest thing."

"Right," Saul acknowledged. "Someone else would be more likely to treat what they considered his 'disease' rather than *him*. It's true." He flashed a self-deprecating smile. "So I guess I'm the best option that either of you have got!"

But he got serious – and distant – once more. "It's very ironic, what gets labelled 'self-destructive' 'insane' or 'delusional' in our society. Now, the technical definition of 'delusional' is the inability to discriminate between reality and illusion. To me, that describes our culture at large. In my opinion, popular belief puts forth some of the biggest fallacies concerning human nature that have ever been uttered.

"The science teachers I had in grade school insisted that life was an accidental by-product of atoms colliding. They said that every thought and emotion of ours was produced by chemical and electrical reactions taking place within our brains. Why weren't *they* labeled delusional?

"A slew of limiting and destructive beliefs are held by millions of people on Earth. And some of these people are responsible for putting other people, with different sets of beliefs, on psychoactive drugs, or in padded rooms... under surveillance, into enforced counseling and evaluation...

"We've come a long way since the Dark Ages, to be sure. Religious and political dogmas are not as ubiquitous and totalitarian as they once were. But when value judgments are being applied where they don't belong it can really slow down progress. Our natural mental and emotional processes are there to tell us something about who we are on the inside. We can't receive those messages if we're proclaiming that the people in group A are 'normal' and the people in group B are 'delusional' and we explore the issue no further than that.

"Am I suggesting that people who want to jump from bridges because they believe they can fly should be given the chance to try? No. But I am pointing out that beliefs are the raw material with which we create our lives, and some of the beliefs that are widely accepted in our culture are more limiting and damaging to the human spirit than other beliefs that are widely considered to be irrational. We would do well to consider how expansive and life-affirming our beliefs are, and re-train our minds to be less concerned with 'facts' - which, as the saying goes, are often just accepted fiction."

Then, as if this was just the obvious extension of everything else he'd said thus far, Saul added: "You realize that any work I do with your father will only be effective if he comes to me of his own accord, right? You can't coerce him in any way."

"No – I know that," I conceded. "I think he *will*. Something has shifted inside of him; I'm sure of it. That night changed him."

"I'm willing to bet that many people have committed suicide for no reason other than that they failed to find the kind of existential drama that their souls craved during their earthly lives," Saul mused. "And I've worked with a few people who didn't make it past their personal crisis, so I ought to know. Psychoanalysis searches for trauma, childhood wounds and destructive mental patterns in its quest to find the root of human suffering. Seldom does it ask questions like, 'Are these people able to find opportunities to use their abilities fully? Are they presented with worthy challenges that force them to call upon hidden resources of strength? Do their struggles have value and meaning for them?' Without a sense of purpose, without belief in the significance of the individual, all is for naught."

As the light cooled and dimmed, Saul and I talked more about my father's despair and my own ambiguous feelings about helping him. Without a doubt, my aggressive stance before the world owed a lot to all the beatings I'd received at home over the years. It would have been easy to blame Robert Chane for everything, even the loss of Janie.

"And so then you back yourself once again into a corner where it seems like you have no power," Saul reminded me. "I would urge you to open your mind up to the possibility that you may have *chosen* your home environment – with all its circumstances – for your own inner purposes."

It certainly had set me upon the path of learning; but that was a small consolation at the moment. I'd known the touch of love, at long last, and then had watched it slip beyond reach. And if guilt and self-doubt had wrought that cruel circumstance then they weren't going to relinquish their grip so easily. After all, perceiving the fallacy and destructiveness of a belief was not the same as *disbelief.*

"There's something that I want you to remember," Saul said. "Our inner being says 'Yes!' - Always. It says yes because it *knows*. That's what our spiritual work amounts to, basically: We're playing catch-up with that part of us that already knows. There are deeper parts of you that don't believe, for a *moment*, in any concepts of faulty, sinful humanity or guilt. When you refuse to apologize for who you are, you've got your soul and every living cell in your body right there to back you up."

"Do you think we'll learn that lesson in time, Saul?"

This question slipped past me, unbidden. And it wasn't the first time I'd asked it, either. Maybe this time it'd been spurred by my own raw need, by the pain that had rendered the whole world poignant to my eyes.

"I don't know," Saul admitted. He screwed his stoic face into a smile for my sake. "The presence of people like you in these times certainly helps. That's probably a big part of the reason why you came here" – The way that he glanced around seemed to indicate that, by 'here', he meant the whole wide world. "You think?"

I wasn't sure. Nonetheless, I derived a certain measure of warmth and comfort from what he said.

"I'll probably want to meet with you again regularly for a while," I said after a pause. "Maybe every couple of weeks. I'm in the midst of a rough patch, obviously."

The sun had dipped down below the trees; it was a red round eye in the shadows by the time we finished. My own inner conflicts had consumed my attention throughout the session. Obliquely, I had noticed changes in Saul's demeanor but never thought to ask him about it. He'd been unusually taciturn; sad… in fact, he'd carried himself with the unmistakable suggestion of defeat in his gait. Why?

6. Prometheus

I spent the next week or so job hunting in my spare time. I was in such a fragile and vulnerable state that it had become really hard to tolerate any kind of employment that involved social interaction. I searched for manual labor, warehouse positions, that sort of thing. Repetitive and mindless exertions were about all that I felt capable of. I could contain the tremors of my soul throughout the length of a graveyard shift and then pour them out in the music. It seemed a seaworthy plan. Somehow, in the space between those opposing existential extremes, I would endure.

I arrived for rehearsals one night feeling frazzled by the frenzied, distracted energies that so consume civilization. I was aching to play, to reconnect with that deeper part of myself that I so often had to smother in order to function. But Tommy and Carlos met my arrival with half-suppressed grins, as if they harbored a mutual secret.

Then Tommy waved a bundled paper. I noticed that it was Visionary Chapbook – probably the latest issue, too, because I didn't recognize the cover.

"Pat was true to his word," he said. "Obviously he forgave us for the aborted interview, judging from this review that he gave 'What Casts the Shadow?'"

He opened the paper, and Carlos eagerly peered over his shoulder. As Tommy was six-foot five, this required our buoyant drummer to stand on his tip-toes.

Tommy, having landed upon the page he sought, cleared his throat dramatically. Then he began his recitation with mock solemnity.

"As their name implies, Edge of the Known embody not just a new style of music, not just a different – and particularly relentless – approach to performing it, but also an emerging kind of new *consciousness*. We all know that the accustomed behaviors of our race have proven shortsighted and destructive. That's not news to anyone. For many of us, though, this realization has inspired little more than jaded cynicism and a sort of smug ennui.

"But it's crucial that we remember that it is the *thinking* behind our old ways that has truly failed us. And the songs on this album – every damn one of them – insist that the answers are *there*, inside of us, waiting to be unearthed. You'll find no cowardly cop-out cynicism here. Our challenges – whether they are personal or worldly – are self-chosen. And hope, belief, heroism and courage are not mere fanciful notions but rather concrete realities to the mind that has awakened to them, to the soul that has confronted its own darkness and prevailed.

In conclusion, I have recently discovered that reality is much easier to face when I play this album – preferable very loud – before I step out of my front door to do battle with the day."

The timbre of Tommy's voice eloquently relayed the underlying deep respect in Pat's words. I was the newcomer, the one who was hearing this all for the first time, so the other guys were watching for my reaction. At first I was too choked up to speak.

"That was about the middle third of it," Tommy explained. "He gives a bit of our history in the beginning and then offers a brief song-by-song analysis at the end. 'Sea Breakers' is obviously his favorite; but he seemed to love them all."

"He really *got* it," I managed at last.

Carlos nodded, as if my response resonated with his own. "It's amazing, isn't it, bro, when you set out to communicate something and then that's exactly what another person *hears*? It don't happen often, huh?"

"No, it doesn't." I replied absently. I was lost in calculations. "And Visionary Chapbook has a good-sized circulation, too, for indie press."

"About twenty-thousand, is what they say," Tommy said. "And that's where this gets even better, 'cause Chas used this review – along with our record – to convince the owner of Alchemist Brews to take a chance on us. We're gonna be the *house band* over there, three nights a week!"

This meant that, in three weeks' time, we'd deliver more performances in Sadenport than we had in the entirety of our career thus far. Most of our gigs had been abroad. This was startling news. It offered the kind of exposure that we'd thus far only dreamed of. And yet I found myself saying, "I wish I felt readier for this."

To which a voice inside me responded: *Something's still tying you to a dead world, man.*

In desperation, I grasped for something Saul had said early on in our relationship. "History is a part of a person, but it does not *make* the person. That's because it doesn't intrude upon life – is not *thrust* upon it – even though this is so often how it feels. But really, it is chosen. Our spirit is always concerned with the contribution that it can make *now*."

That was it, wasn't it? I felt powerless to escape the groping quicksand of my past – and that past seemed characterized by failure. My broken relationship, my father's suicide attempt, Rachel's displacement, my own struggles with self-destructive tendencies... somehow these seemed to all be kindred phenomena. Distinct, yes – and yet still manifestations of the same underlying nightmare.

"What is it?" Tommy prompted me, drawing closer and trying to catch a glimpse of my eyes, the secrets they harbored.

Anticipating an argument and wanting to forestall it, because my own feelings were too ambiguous to clearly side with either end of a protest, I waved my hands.

"I'm not saying I can't do it. But I'm gonna just come clean about this. A part of me – a *big* part – doesn't want to come out of my shell right now. I don't want to *express* and I don't want to *connect*."

"So, fuck everything," Tommy said. But he actually wasn't antagonizing me at all. His voice was as clinical as the intern at Limn

County Mental Health who'd once set all my interview responses down on a clipboard. Tommy was just making sure he had the facts straight.

"Heartbreak is not a laughing matter – I know," Carlos put in. "It will take some time."

Thinking, *just to fucking hell with vulnerability and feelings*! I decided to abort the whole discussion. "Well, let's jam," I said. "I'll start us off with the new one."

"Diamond Maelstrom" was the easiest song for me to play because I'd written it in the same state of escalation that I existed in most of my waking hours these days. I therefore didn't need to make any kind of effort to get 'into character' for it. And if I ever forgot what was great about our band, this song could remind me within six minutes.

Over the course of playing it, I became more aware of the root of my inner paralysis and the intense frustration that it engendered. Nihilism basically amounted to giving myself an ultimatum: "If my life can't look like *this* then it's not worth continuing." Existence could only have meaning and value if certain conditions were met; therefore, I was always judging what *was* – and thereby failing to love and appreciate it.

Hidden in there was the myth of perfection, which is a really perilous idea. Saul had often warned me about it. "You insist on seeing around the bend," he'd once said, "even though you have no idea how a shift in belief may alter the picture of your whole world."

I was judging my anger. That was it. Having confronted my penchant for violence, I'd begun to swing the other way, where I was wary of any emotion that *resembled* the way that I felt when I lost control. But *feelings* are neither right nor wrong, neither good nor evil. They're the very motion of our aliveness. The voice of guilt was trying to shut me down, cut me off from the wellspring.

Of course I was pissed at Janie for abandoning me! Of course I had rage around being put in a position where I was trying to save my father whilst all the while knowing full well he'd done little to ever nurture or encourage *my* spirit.

With each increment of new awareness, I gave myself over more fully to our music's aggression. Tommy and Carlos, joined with me by the telepathic bond that we all understood, though we could never explain it, responded in kind. I'm surprised the very salt-gray walls of The Catacombs didn't begin to heat and steam.

Afterwards, Tommy said "I got it!" Then he stopped right there, swaying before his mic and milking the dramatic pause.

"Well?" I prodded, feeling half amused and half irritated.

"We'll perform at Alchemist Brews with a light show," he said. "Like those liquid light, slide projector affairs that the psychedelic bands used in the late Sixties, particularly in London and San Francisco. We'll have to find someone to run it for us during the gigs, but it'll be perfect. You'll just be this shadowy figure, Brandon, blended right in to the psychedelic display. We'll make it darkened. Then you won't feel exposed at all. You can be in your own imaginary world up there."

Well, we had a somewhat psychedelic sounding name anyway – and sonic template to match – so the notion of some accompanying visual phantasmagoria wasn't too far-fetched.

"It's a pretty played-out concept, though, isn't it?" I asked.

"Well, so is video," Tommy argued, "and that doesn't stop all these new bands from *making* 'em. It's not the medium but the way that we use it that decides whether it comes across as cliché or not."

That's all that it took to convince me. I strongly ached for anonymity, for the opportunity to merge with - and lose myself in - the shadows. Once we wrapped up rehearsals the three of us returned home and hung out in the living room, munching on cold pizza and sipping lemonade while we bounced around ideas.

Oftentimes, the challenge inherent in creating something is due not to the *limits* imposed upon one's freedom but rather the *overabundance* of possible avenues to explore. We were brimming with too many thoughts; and not one of them seemed to possess any inherently greater merit than the others. At least the excitement of brainstorming allowed me to forget my own pain for a while, though.

Even as I participated, another part of me passively watched as each notion hatched, evolved and then ultimately fell by the wayside as it was replaced by a fresher concept.

At last, we settled upon the idea of using a succession of images that would illustrate the progression of human life from infancy to old age. The entire cycle, we figured, should last about as long as our average song – about five or six minutes. We also wanted to somehow convey the sense that this whole cycle represented, on another level, a mere day in the life of the soul.

Chas ended up hiring his dour, humorless cousin Ken – the same tall and lanky guy who'd spray-painted our van with Manhandle designs – to create the actual slides, based upon our sketches. The liquid slides would run over the static images to add a hallucinatory dimension. The majority of the drawings were done by me, as I was actually the most competent of the three of us. I was grateful for the escape that this activity offered me. Perhaps plugging up all of my life's spaces was the only possible salvation, at least temporarily. Imagination could slip into realms of frightful darkness if it wasn't actively herded in other directions.

I produced about thirty sketches; and Tommy and Carlos made roughly another twenty between them. Then we experimented with different running orders for the images. For a couple days we existed in a sort of microcosm of the film industry, playing at pre-production, production and direction. We found a cheap projector at a thrift store and put Ken's show to the test one night, shining the images on the living room wall and taking turns either engaging in shadow play or dancing in front of it.

I sorely missed Janie that night. She had always been a part of creative ventures such as these, ever since conducting our first photo session. She'd been there for the gestation of such ideas and also for the celebrations that would inevitably follow those bouts of hard work. She loved photography, and would have relished this particular project. Every time I saw our three silhouettes on the cover of our first album – the same image that graced our flyers – I was reminded.

I excused myself early and laid down in the dark, counting my uneven breaths. I told myself that somehow the flow of life continues:

sweeping up new joys in its wake. I could scarcely keep from putting my fists through the wall.

No drug or therapy could possibly douse the fire that raged in me. Sometimes the pain was monstrous enough to forbid sleep, thereby denying me even the escape of unconsciousness.

From the outside, Alchemist Brews looked like a giant circus tent made of wood instead of tarp. Its coat of ochre paint was old, and varied with a greener hue around the upper storey, which the owners – a middle-aged hippie couple who'd lived in their van for several years before opening this establishment - had taken for their apartment. It had its back to the Matterpike River – one of Sadenport's widest bridges was a block away – and faced the runner's track that belonged to the technical college across the way. I suppose this kept the neighboring apartments at sufficient distance so that no one complained about the noise.

I couldn't look at the building without imagining rowdy barn stomps on a hay-strewn wooden floor, abetted by a fiddle band and frenetic clapping from the hayUpstairs above. Inside, however, it smelled more like a whole foods grocery store – the scent of Chai most predominant – and there were tapestries all over the place, depicting the full sweep of religious iconography. You'd see Buddha, Krishna or Christ any which way you turned your head.

Our friend Todd Jacobs joined us that first night. He'd agreed to run our slide show. Todd was two years my junior and one of the few congenial souls I'd encountered back in High School. He was that rarity amongst rabid music fans: A free-spirited punk who carried himself with easy-going humility. He had no underlying chip on his shoulder. I don't think he'd cut his hair since sophomore year. It was the color of corn husks, and now braided down the full length of his back. He also sported a goatee and thick sideburns. Todd just had an *intent* way of looking at everyone and everything. He was so absorbed in his own trip, at all times, that people tended to instinctively give him room to pursue whatever it was. I think it elevated our aura of professionalism, just having such a person in our orbit.

Tracy, one of the owners, was bartending that night. She'd been amenable to keeping the back row of lights off for our benefit.

We got our gear set up and plugged in. Tommy solemnly intoned, "America must learn to dream new dreams!" in a half-dozen different inflections, into both mics, as Todd adjusted the levels. Then, as soon as he got the projector started, we began.

Some are given to relating it to sex, or to certain kinds of drug-induced euphoria, but you really can't compare the indefinable sensation of *reaching* people with your music to anything else. When it's good, it's the fruition of that pollinating push of spring wonder that already lived, somewhere in the depths of your soul, when first you wrote the song. Maybe it had already been alive, waiting, like the fetus of a future savior, as I'd struggled to learn my first few chords. You already have this idea that, somehow, some way, others are going to participate in this phenomenon with you. What you're really creating is the incipient part of a communal experience, an electric bath of rousing, soothing, affirming and ultimately healing intent. Both you and the audience know when such an exchange happens, and there's no need to try and speak of it.

God, I'd *missed* performing.

I felt the chords rattling the tables and the wood of the walls and knew that, for these few hours at least, no one would miss the voice from the mountain. And all the while I felt almost amphibious, bathed as I was in the oceanic flow of light and surreal imagery curling over my body and over all of our instruments. I was safe and secure somewhere in nameless dark depths.

At least, I was until I heard someone shout, "Man, you're *God* on the guitar!"

I'd been trying so hard to *elude* my self-consciousness. Maybe that's why I reacted so vehemently.

"Look, if that's all you're getting out of this then we've failed!" I shouted back.

It'd been a male voice, but I could scarcely see the person, what with the dim light and the way the slideshow refracted reality all around me. He was probably thirty feet away.

"The thing you're seeing in me... it's in *you*, man. That's what these songs are all about. Just fucking kill me if I ever look like I'm in danger of becoming a rock star, o.k.? Seriously!"

"Jesus – can't take a compliment, huh?" someone else muttered.

I ignored that, as best I could, and we dove into another song.

At some point during the gig I noticed that members of the local band Ashur were seated a couple of tables away from us, off to our left. They were an intimidating bunch, even for someone with the "live by the sword, die by the sword" philosophy that I'd long adhered to. This was partially due to their appearance: Rigor-mortis pallor; tall, jagged beanpole frames; acres of leather embellished with pointed steel. Then there was the aura that surrounded them. Underground musical folklore of this city abounded with whispered rumors of what intended members had to do in order to be initiated into the circle of Ashur. I'd never seen them perform; I only recognized them from a photo that I'd seen in Chapbook. But those in the know all agreed that the extremity of their lyrics, and their overarching creed, was *in no way an act*. I wasn't sure exactly what that meant; and the mystery somehow made the concept more chilling.

As we finished up for the night and began gathering up our equipment, I watched the members file out. Their singer and bandleader, a gaunt albino as tall as Tommy who went by the name of Saveel, met my gaze. He bowed low, with an air of complete and solemn reverence, and then strode out.

Feeling unnerved by this silent exchange, for reasons that I couldn't identify, I packed hurriedly. Before leaving, though, I tracked down the guy who I'd snapped at from the stage and apologized. I just muttered something about being overwrought.

"It's all good, bro." He was anxious to make peace, and shook my hand.

When we returned to Alchemist Brews a couple nights later, Saveel and another member of his band were again present in the audience. They were sitting hunched over one of the tables closest to the stage, talking low and staring at us intently. Their scrutiny made me uncomfortable, and I masked it with irritation verging on anger. Was Saveel looking to recruit one of us into his own band? If so, he was going about it in an obnoxiously blatant way.

But it was my job to create, alongside the two musicians with me, the atmosphere in the club this night – *not* to let it be dictated by anyone who might walk through the door. I closed my mind off from Saveel – and whatever other lingering earthly concerns I possessed – with the fury of Edge of the Known's music.

There were probably a dozen other people there who had returned to see us following our debut performance. This was tremendous affirmation of the path that we were on. The average Sadenport band gigged once a week or less, simply because they didn't have the drawing power to support more frequent appearances. We were becoming local heroes.

I *lived* very close to this music and so perhaps couldn't view it with the objectivity of an outsider. But it was obvious even to me that this melodic mayhem was as powerful as anything currently pulsing in the Underground and *superior* to just about anything one could hear on corporate-owned radio. If every age must have its Prometheus, lest the flame of humanity's collective spirit be snuffed out forever, then our band fulfilled the dictates of that myth more fully than anyone else currently performing.

So maybe Saveel's here 'cause he's pissed. My lips curled into a smile of relish, mid-way into a song, as this thought streaked through my transcendent flight.

The floor was covered with whirling, cavorting bodies, each lost in personal transport and yet still connected to the ubiquitous Gyre of Pan that spun us all on the ecstatic wheel. Sometimes when I was onstage I'd feel as though I was presiding over a very ancient ceremony, a rite that's recognized by the breath and the blood, the Earth below and the sky overhead, though the mind may never grasp its source.

7. The Gift

Saveel's companion approached us as soon as we finished our last number and the back lights were turned back on. He looked young – no older than seventeen, I would have guessed – and *scarred*. That word leapt into my mind at once. I swallowed hard when he smiled at me, as that expression completely belied what I *felt*. He was wearing a jean jacket (plain, devoid of patches), ripped jeans and some kind of thick woven, tan sandals.

"I am Abass," he said; and of course I immediately thought that this could not be his birth name. His tone was eerily formal, and partially a whisper. "Of Ashur. We've brought a gift with which to honor your great band."

At once my eyes fell upon the long gray knapsack that had lain between them on the table.

"We cannot offer it here," he went on, as he followed my gaze. "Will you meet with us?"

By this time Carlos and Tommy had both joined me. But though they watched Abass intently, his attention remained fixed upon me.

"You choose the place," he pronounced.

"Saint Stephen's Bridge," I responded at once.

My mind had been racing through frantic calculations. It seemed potentially dangerous to refuse an offer made by these people. At the same time, I didn't trust the entire scenario; and I knew that it would be futile, trying to pry more information out of Saveel's acolyte. The bridge was close to home – and it was familiar. It was also out in the open, more exposed than most of the streets.

"We will follow you," he said, with the same walk-of-the-dead inflection. Then he bowed low to the three of us, just as Saveel had done the previous night.

As soon as Carlos, Tommy and I were in the van, I aired my underlying unease. "The thing I don't get is why they're so interested in us in the first place. This is bizarre. I mean, they were right there at the first gig we played, as if they were waiting for us."

Tommy was driving. He shrugged. "It could be the record – 'What Casts the Shadow?' It seems to have been making its way around the city – taped copies, anyway. Actually, it's not just tape trading anymore. The Internet makes it easier than ever for people to share music nowadays. Chas has been pulling his hair out trying to figure out how to capitalize on that – or, really, he's trying to find ways to keep making money off records that kids are finding so many ways to get their hands on for free."

I chewed on all of that for a moment. It was odd to think about how the fine edge of modern technology was being utilized to disseminate something that felt (at least to me) so primal – primitive, even.

"None of which is helping to feed *us*!" I muttered.

"I hear that!" Carlos concurred from the back.

"Well," Tommy offered, "it does seem to be spreading the word about our band, anyway."

By now it was well past midnight. The streets saw few vehicles; and the homes were predominantly dark. Tommy took a winding shortcut to the bridge.

"And these guys are, like... I don't know if they're a *satanic* band, necessarily, but they're definitely occult through and through," I said. "What the hell's their interest in us?"

"When you write songs that are deliberately oblique, metaphorical..." Tommy let that thought dissipate. "You and I are both guilty of that," he told me. "Not that it's something negative. I personally think that the best songs are the ones that you can never plumb the depths of. But it *does* leave it open for people to interpret it however they want and to draw their own conclusions – even twisted ones."

There was a grassy pull-off not far from the south side of the bridge where people often parked so that they could take the little footpath down to the water. Tommy stopped there; and the three of us moved at once.

"I said meet at the bridge, so that's where we'll be," I grated. "If they choose to be insulted because we didn't greet them at the parking space then they can explain why they're in such a goddamn hurry, riding our ass like that all the way over here."

The two members of Ashur had pulled up in a bus that could've been twenty years old. But it sported a much more recent paint job – as much as I could descry it in the dark – composed of spidery and serpentine etchings in black that covered the entire metal surface in sinuous darkness. It seemed intended to ensnare the eyes, though, so I didn't stare for long.

We moved swiftly and kept our faces fixed forward. No one spoke. On a practical level, I wasn't frightened for our safety. There were three of us and two of them; and we were all well worth our salt in a tussle. Before leaving the van, I'd also retrieved my hunting knife, with its four-inch sharpened blade, from the glove compartment and tucked it into my boot. Hey, we'd spent weeks sleeping in that vehicle; you can't begrudge me a few precautionary measures. So, unless those guys were packing hand guns...

I didn't stop until we'd reached what I judged to be roughly the halfway point of the bridge. A subtle power-play was being enacted here, and I didn't want to begin the proceedings with any show of compromise. I deliberately turned at that point to watch the two of them approach.

Sure enough, Abass was hauling the knapsack. Saveel strode a few paces in front of him. He stopped about ten feet away from us. Once more, he bowed. Somehow his solemnity conveyed more incipient menace than any overt show of aggression would have.

"Ashur greet you, great minstrels!" His lilt was surprisingly high-pitched. I'd been expecting a harsh growl.

He waited until Abass caught up with him before continuing. "Have you all heard the legend of Damien Pratt, who was a resident of these parts until his death some fifty years ago?"

I shook my head; and I sensed, rather than saw, Carlos doing the same. Tommy muttered, noncommittally, "The name sounds familiar..."

Saveel looked pleased to have the opportunity to enlighten us. "He was a great sorcerer of his time. His long – some would say, *unnaturally long* – lifespan attests to it. His forays into deeper mysteries of the Craft were as exhaustive as Crowley's, Levi's."

Then he nodded in Abass' direction. Saveel's acolyte dutifully unzipped the pack he was holding and began rummaging through it.

"It is believed," Saveel went on, "that he even mastered the transubstantiation of the flesh, allowing him to assume other forms – wolf, crow, bat."

Abass withdrew a head of sullied ivory, a bit larger than a softball, and proffered it in our direction. Tommy stiffened and retreated a step.

"Looks like a human enough skull to me!"

I absorbed the stark fact of it as soon as he uttered the words. This was no carving. All the signs of organic nature, of something that had once served as a vessel for life, were writ upon it in a script that my deeper senses could somehow decipher at a glance.

"You dug that up?"

In a matter of heartbeats, I stooped and snatched my hunting knife. I bared the blade to their sight. "Stay. The fuck. Away from us." I held it with both hands – its wooden pommel was long – about a foot in front of my chest. If Saveel wanted to be ceremonial... well, I could play.

I was swept on by outrage, by the dim sense that somehow I had conjured up this cruel misapprehension of all of our intentions. "Don't come to our performances! Don't tell other people that we're affiliated with you, or that somehow we've been an influence. Nothing! This is your travesty. We've got no part in it!"

Saveel's eyes smoldered. I'd caught a glimpse of them in the club, earlier, beneath much stronger light. Glacial blue, man; iciest eyes you'd ever see. He let out a slow breath of disappointment but didn't move.

"I had hoped to honor the potency and dark majesty of your music," he pronounced. "And to recognize our brotherhood. Alas!"

He nodded towards Abass and the skull that he held. Abass, intuiting the gesture, shuddered.

"Are you certain?" he asked.

Saveel frowned. "The gift was offered and spurned. It has no value to anyone, now."

Abass deliberated a moment longer. Then he madly hurled the grim ivory relic so that it arced over the twelve-foot high railing and sped down to the deep, tranquil waters of the Matterpike below.

"That was really Damien Pratt's skull, huh?" Tommy mused. "I have to admit, I'm impressed."

"It seems I misjudged you all!" Saveel spat. Then he turned on his heels and strode away, Abass following after like a dependent cur.

The silence that followed, nearly devoid of breeze or thought, was finally broken when Carlos quipped: "Damn, bro... I'd just been thinking 'bout how we had a perfect space for that up on the mantel!"

We all burst into laughter, abetted no doubt by our need to relieve tension. I didn't lower my knife, though, until Abass and Saveel were a good fifty yards from us. Those two never looked back.

I sobered quickly. "We've gotta do something to ensure that shit like this doesn't happen again, that people don't take our words and just go off the deep end with them."

Tommy had been peering over the side of the bridge at the spot where the skull had finally made its splash, as if he was debating whether some means might be contrived to fish it out again.

"What's that?" he muttered, distractedly, as he turned around. "We *can't*, Brandon. That's the thing. Once we create it and put it out into the world then the world can react towards it however it will. That part is forever out of our hands."

And I had to content myself with that, because – despite the molten heat of my frustration – I knew that it was nothing but the bare truth of it.

And although we kept talking about the experience over the short drive home, digesting the whole bizarre arc of this late night adventure, I just couldn't drive the creepiness out of the marrow of my bones.

***

I was so unnerved, in fact, that I ended up calling Saul and requesting an "emergency" session. I met with him the following day, in the early evening. The air was misty and the ground damp from the rainy first half of the day, but the parting rays of the sun reached over and dispersed the clouds as I made my way over to his house. It seemed like the only thought that sustained me through my days was that of landing on my session with Saul. I judged myself for this, and considered it a sign of weakness, but it was the truth.

When we greeted each other, I again received the impression that he was making an effort to smile at me through a haze of pain. And once more, I assumed that it wasn't my place to intrude and inquire about it. Instead I offered him an abridged version of our encounter with the members of Ashur.

"Wow. Those guys are pretty fanatical, huh?" Saul mused. "You could go to jail for a long time for digging up a body."

"I guess we'll have to come up with a new descriptive angle for our band," I joked. "It seems that 'extreme' is already spoken for."

Saul chuckled, but also took advantage of the opening. "If you could just steer clear of labels altogether – at least, as much as possible – then it could really limit this sort of thing. Once you *symbolize* something specific in people's minds then the things they project upon you become a lot harder to shake."

I lit a cigarette, craving not only the tobacco but also the added moment to gather my thoughts and courage. "Yeah," I said, exhaling my first drag, "that's what I was wanting to talk to you about. Why are we attracting these sorts of reactions? It's *not* the kind of attention I was looking for. And it goes against the grain of everything that we're saying in our songs, too."

Saul was quiet for a long time. And this is part of the reason why I'm given to describing him like a shaman or medicine man: He gets this faraway look, as if he's engaged in silent conversation with forces or entities that the rest of us can't see. Then his eyes return to the familiar world, and there's a light of *recognition* that seems to emanate from him.

"What it boils down to is a basic misunderstanding of the very nature of creativity itself," he said finally. "So many people carry the belief that the deeper forces of life are locked away somewhere; that they're inaccessible. So then it seems necessary, following from that belief, to have all these elaborate rituals and procedures to help us access the psychic places that we think we're so separate from. And it doesn't matter if we're talking on the small scale – this band that you encountered being one example – or on the larger scale of major religions and whatnot. All of it is acting out of the deep conviction that we're just these little disconnected egos that have to go to drastic measures to feel like a part of Creation. And of course, religions will explain to us *why* we're supposedly so separate to begin with – original sin and all that."

Then he smiled at me. "I'm willing to bet that if you were to scratch the surface with the guys in that band then you'd find some scared young men who really worry about their own significance in the scheme of things."

I shivered, recalling how Abass' aura had screamed to me like a raw wound. Saveel, on the other hand, certainly hadn't *seemed* like a man who possessed any fear whatsoever.

"But of course," Saul said with a gleam in his eye," we don't want to get too caught up in the general state of the world, because you and I know that the real work is done inside. And so this leaves us with two possible avenues to explore, insofar as your personal work goes. First, we can talk about how this sort of 'I am a tainted stepchild of the universe' idea may be working within *you*. And then from there we might better understand why you attract these kinds of shady characters into your life. In other words, how do they mirror *you*?"

I didn't particularly relish the thought of pursuing *either* of these avenues. "Fuck, Saul," I burst out, "I'm in enough goddamn pain as it is! Do we really have to dive into more 'brutal truths' today? How 'bout we get one place bandaged up before we start worrying about other injuries?"

Saul waited for me to simmer down before he spoke.

"So you know why the idea of self-exploration feels threatening? Because you don't see the *value* of it. Because you still don't believe that your life is mirroring your own inner condition. So examining your own thoughts and feelings seems beside the point. But it is, in fact, the *essence* of the point.

"All right – so maybe you don't want to look at your possible connection with these cult members because you still don't understand why your girlfriend left you. But what if I could show you that there's a clear relationship between those two circumstances?"

I sat up straighter on the couch, almost despite myself. But I didn't say anything.

"The woman you love turns away from you," Saul iterated, "and then some strangers give you the kind of attention that you don't want, based on some perception of you that isn't true. Do you see? Neither side *affirms* you, which leads me to believe that there's some way in which you don't affirm yourself."

I shook my head, feeling my morale – what little had been left to me – plummet.

"So I don't feel worthy. And I guess that's where it fucking ends, Saul."

"Where it *ends* is where you uncover the reasons why you're so convinced of your basic unworthiness," Saul retorted. "And then, when you see through those beliefs, when you see that they're erroneous, you discard them and find yourself living in a different world. But right now, for you, it's all coming back to guilt again."

Having no clue where he was heading with this, I just stared back. Saul seemed to be waiting for comprehension to crystallize within me. Then he sighed.

"This was a band that's heavily influenced by black magic – the aura and imagery surrounding it, at least," he said. "Now, you've done your own experimenting with the occult arts, right?"

"That was a while back," I protested. "And for a very brief period of time. I don't see…"

"People only ever pursue those kinds of avenues when they're convinced that they have no real power to begin with," Saul interjected. "So here's my pitch: I would suggest that you disown your power because the voice of guilt has convinced you that if you *had* power you'd misuse it. And that same denial of self is what makes you hold love at bay. *There's* the connection."

"Well, I didn't hold love at bay this time," I muttered, a bit petulantly. "Janie ran."

Saul stared at me somberly. "Do we really need to rehash this argument?"

I waved a hand. "No. I hear you. Somehow I initiated the whole thing, even if I wasn't conscious of doing so."

"Somehow? I've told you *exactly* how. The voice of guilt, Brandon. Examine it. Learn to recognize the distorted picture that it paints. 'Don't give me power over my own life 'cause I'll abuse it.' 'Don't bring a lover into my life 'cause I'll endanger her. I can't be trusted.'"

I sank into the couch, tore my gaze away from Saul. I felt myself immersed in a battle that I had no chance of winning.

"If we dispensed with guilt, Saul," I argued, "then what would be left to keep us in line?"

"You see? You see how willing you are to accept the idea that human nature can't be trusted?"

I glared at him. "Maybe it was guilt that restrained me that night at the Samurai. Maybe that's what held me back, kept me from assaulting Saveel."

"Maybe it was your *heart*."

This was no easier to hear.

"My heart is chock full of pain," I pronounced. "I'd almost rather have the guilt."

"Sure," Saul responded, "until you actually step back and take a look at what it's done to your life. Natural regret just says, 'don't ever do this again', It's a *preventative* measure. Guilt says we should be punished again and again for the rest of our lives for *ever* having done it."

I was on the verge of weeping by this point. "Maybe I should just see a psychiatrist who'll prescribe me some fucking drugs!"

Saul nipped my imminent rant in the bud. "I want you to do something for me," he said. "Take a moment, here and there throughout your days, to tell the voice of guilt to go to hell. Then remind yourself that you trust yourself and can navigate your life just fine without it."

8. Sister/Satyr

The following day was a Saturday, and I'd made plans with the Friedman's to take Rachel out for the afternoon. This in itself was typically an unpleasant process. My aunt Gail was my father's sister. She and her husband Ernie had won custody of Rachel about a year and a half earlier. They treated me like a peripheral part of the family, at best. Apparently the fact that I had essentially raised my little sister since Mom died, and that the two of us had developed a powerful bond during that time, had completely escaped their notice. Instead of acknowledging it with any word or gesture, they instead spun their own variations of my father's favorite derogatory question: "What are you ever gonna *do* with your life?"

But whereas it was easy to deflect my father's challenge back at him – because what was *he* accomplishing? – The Friedman's had a cozy, solvent and insular reality to feed their sense of smug superiority. They drove new cars, inhabited a lavish home, were deeply entrenched in high-paying careers and all in all exhibited the trappings of success. The fact that I had no desire to succeed in their particular world, or even *participate* in it, was not something that their minds could ever compute.

But they never made it difficult for me to see Rachel, so long as I asked in all humility and never put on an air of *expectation* like I had every right. And Ernie, at least, was able to hide whatever judgments he harbored about me beneath a veneer of surface friendliness.

It was hard for me not to feel like a derelict whenever I drove up their sleek-paved circular driveway. It was edged with white gravel and patches of spring flowers that seemed to mock my grayish-blue little two-door; faded, and twelve years beyond her prime. My car seemed worth about as much as their front door knocker. Ernie was a jeweler and Gail an accountant... but I don't know when – if *ever* –

they found the time to actually enjoy all the wealth that they were so busy amassing.

I'd never had the chance to see how Rachel existed in her new home, what her room looked like, where she ate, because I always waited at the door for her. The suggestion to do so was never overt but rather subliminal, and yet it screamed to the senses of one as sensitive to the jarring flail of rejection as I was.

Because I didn't see her as often nowadays as in years past, the changes manifesting in her were more obvious each time. Her countenance was a bit more somber, unsure. She often paused a moment and reflected before speaking, whereas her younger self had oftentimes been spinning too fast for introspection. Now there was the hint of underlying *questions* behind much of what she said, behind even the most innocent-seeming expression. I wished that I had even one answer to offer for the riddle of her life.

"Can we go to Iris Park?" she said at once.

Well, *some* things apparently hadn't changed at all. She nearly always made this request; and I laughed, now, as I questioned why we even went through this ritual of asking each time.

"Can crows carry French fry trays?" I responded.

We'd once seen a crow do this very thing. He'd been eating out of a paper dish of tater fingers that had fallen in the middle of the road. I'd watched him devour as much as he could before the oncoming traffic arrived. Finally, at the last possible moment, he'd gotten one edge of the tray in his maw, lifted it evenly and flown off without dropping a single one of the remaining fries. References to this incident had become a running joke for us ever since.

"Well we know *one* that can!" Rachel gushed as she opened the passenger door.

It was now a longer drive than it once had been from the old house. I had time to ask her about school. She was nearly wrapping up the third grade.

"The only subject I like a lot is history," Rachel said. "But it makes me sad, too. Everything disappears after a while so that something else can come along. You learn about dinosaurs but then don't get to go see them. You learn about Indians and then find out that a lot of *them* are gone, too."

"Maybe they all still exist somewhere," I suggested. "Someplace we just can't see or go to right now. You think?"

Rachel flashed me a sly smile. "My teachers do *not* think like you do. They'd tell you to get your head out of the clouds, Brandon Chane!"

She giggled. *That* sound had not changed, either. It was still high and contagious as ever.

"Well, Rachel Amber Chane," I responded, "I have heard it said that only those of us who believe in magic have any hope of finding it, so I guess maybe I feel sorry for your teachers 'cause they're missin' out!"

She just giggled some more. "You're funny!"

Me lecturing *her* about magic. Ah, the irony...

We were favored with a fair day: A bit balmy; and the grass still wet from the previous night's brief rains. Rachel may have visibly matured before my eyes – she was going to turn nine come midsummer – but she still wanted to play all the same games that we'd indulged in for years. This involved monkey bars, chase, the merry-go-round followed by more chase. Our routine typically involved running, in one form or another, until we were too exhausted to continue.

Then we lay on the grass, talking about animals, boys, girls, school, God, whatever. Rachel was dressed for the occasion in an old pair of overalls, well-worn sneakers and a sturdy gray woolen shirt. Ernie and Gail weren't about to risk any of her "good" clothes on an outing with me.

A few minutes later I glanced to my right and caught glimpse of the cruelest sight my eyes had been afflicted with in an age of the world. There was a sidewalk across the way, beyond the swing set and slide and the tall maples that bordered the park. Janie was walking there... with a man. She was listening, head slightly lowered: receptive. He was talking. His cheeks were colored in a way that bespoke nervousness or excitement, probably both. The intimacy of the scene was palatable. In one hand they each held paper cups of coffee, most likely. Their other hands were entwined.

Mind and body at once were aflame. I could scarcely breathe.

Rachel followed the line of my sight.

There was this distinct air of a first or second date. Their body language was tentative, exploratory. He was probably asking a lot of gentlemanly questions.

They were apparently taking things slower than Janie and *I* had.

And I can hardly recall what he looked like because in that moment I was completely consumed by the fantasy of grabbing him by the hair and yanking so hard that it divorced his head from his neck.

I do remember – one of the keenest torments of this vision – that Janie was wearing the same light-tan fringed blouse that she'd had on when I'd met her in the Albuquerque airport, in another lifetime; when I'd swept her up in my arms and felt appeased to the depths of my soul.

That quaint detail was nearly potent enough to unhinge me.

"Is that Janie?" Rachel asked. She sounded confused.

"Rachel... just don't."

The only thing that could have made my abjection any more complete would have been for Janie to see me, to witness my state of horrified paralysis. And that's precisely what happened. She chanced to meet my eyes – and *hers* widened. She turned away, then, and quickened her pace. Once more, the only answer she was able to latch on to was that of flight.

"Why is she holding that guy's hand?"

The two of them were disappearing. Reality was unravelling.

"Doesn't she love you still? Is she not your girlfriend anymore?"

"Look, *shut the fuck up!*"

I yelled that loud enough to startle a woman nearby who was pushing a stroller. Rachel recoiled... and before she drew her next breath, the full horror of what'd just happened rebounded on me like a storm wave hitting a ship's prow.

Bastard! After all she's gone through, all the ways she's been hurt... now, to get screamed at by the one person left who she thought she could depend on without question...

I held my hands out; but an agonized moment passed before I could muster any words.

"Honey, come here! Please. Oh, God, I'm sorry!"

Rachel approached slowly. Once she made up her mind, though, her caution morphed into eagerness. Love is always ready to rebound. It is far wiser, and more far-seeing, than doubt, forgetfulness and fear.

I leaned against a bench and cradled her on my lap.

"That will *never* happen again," I whispered. "I'm sorry."

"That's o.k." She was quivering like a rabbit; but her voice, though it was low as mine, was steady. "I'm sorry you're upset." She risked a glance up at my face. My cheeks were already wet. "I wish she still loved you," Rachel offered.

I made a clumsy swipe at my tears. "I'm sure she does. It's more complicated than that... but I just can't talk about it right now."

Something odd happened to me then, at this critical threshold of my anguish. The world receded; or perhaps my mind relinquished its attachment to its surroundings. Nothing existed except for Rachel and I, for the love that passed between us as simply and undeniably as the breath of skies. The sensation was divorced from all notions of time. This was a single moment that always had been and always would be.

My feelings bubbled up from their molten core, lightening and quickening as they rose. They mustered up vibrations in my throat.

Sounds demanded expression, so I opened my mouth wide. The notes slowly joined hands and formed a melody. Words sprang out of it like foam from the denser flesh of a wave. I sang without even stopping to consider what I was actually saying.

And thus, I serenaded Rachel with what would grow to become the song "Sister/Satyr". Fortunately, I repeated it enough times to commit it to memory.

You're the wild imp, the Fountain Sprite

Giggling as you're kicking your tin can

Chasing me down those long, lost alleys

All those days we blindly ran

But now my joints, they need some oiling

They could use some of your Elfish grease

Your laughter moves me past the train wreck

Your smile brings me dreams of peace

Satyr of my soul

Resuscitate my heart and ripen my mind

I'll trade this entire world of "facts"

For whatever precious trinkets you find

Take this vagabond by his hand

Fill his pockets with your magic sand

Teach him the words when the moment's ripe

Build your pagoda out of his spare parts

Remind him of your ancient arts

To pull his head out of the world's stove pipe

Satyr of my soul

The universe, it melts inside my brain

But I'll let it go without pang of doubt

For love of you, little Rachel Chane

9. Outsiders

It ended up being the closest I'd felt to her in a long time, so I guess this was the hidden gift of that horrible moment of my reaction, the reciprocal swing of the pendulum. After I dropped her off I drove around aimlessly for a few hours. I'd stare down each paved lane, before turning onto it, like it'd betrayed me. The brutal world was waiting to ambush the tattered remnants of my heart and soul. The sun went down and no answers emerged.

When I stepped inside the house Carlos came out at once to meet me in the kitchen. He raised his hands in a slow shrug as if to say "I'm just the messenger, bro," and then told me that Janie had called a couple of times. I didn't understand this at first, until I fished for my cellphone and realized that it wasn't in my pocket. I must've left it in my room. I felt a surge of wild, unreasoning hope – and then chastised myself for it. What the hell was I thinking? That, fresh from her date, she was gonna say, "Oh, Brandon, I've reconsidered. I love you. I've never stopped"?

"How long ago was that?" I asked.

Carlos gave me a wry smile. "She said she'd wait up 'til you got in, however long it takes. 'I know he's not gonna sleep otherwise,' were her words."

I nodded, trying to somehow *will* my gratitude to show through my turmoil.

I'd finally broken down and purchased a cellphone because it'd been getting on Carlos' nerves, my borrowing his all the time. Now he was obliged to answer *mine* at home.

I shut myself in my room. I didn't even bother to turn on the lamp. I put on some ambient music to muffle the sound – and to help steady my psyche. Janie's number wasn't saved anymore – I hadn't been able to bear seeing her name on my device – but I still knew it by twisted, limping heart.

I could practically hear a deep bell tolling with each key I punched.

She answered at once. The sound of her voice, its earnest *presence*, stirred up the voice of betraying hope inside me again.

My efforts to strangle it almost made me snarl. "I heard you called."

"Well, yeah, of course. I didn't want to just *leave* things like that." Her tone was a strange admixture of compassion and rectitude.

This resurrection of my pain served no purpose. What was this, a funeral revival? I couldn't respond.

"Look," she said, "just because I can't be your lover doesn't mean that I don't still really care about you and want to continue being your friend. And I definitely don't want to hurt you, like I'm sure it *did* hurt, seeing what you did today."

My mental environment swayed as if, somewhere in its depths, tectonic shifts were deciding the fate of continents. I clung to the darkness. Nothing sapped the fight in me so quickly as someone refusing to react. And Janie had adopted that strategy a long time ago.

"I don't even really know what to say about it," she acknowledged. "It's not a serious relationship. We've gone out a few times... I guess what I'm feeling is that I just don't want you to go away with the idea like you're so easily replaced in my life. What we had was *not* something that I took lightly. And I don't in any way want to trivialize it, like 'Whee! I'm back on the horse again! Life is great!'" She paused for a tension-laden huff. "I've been testing the waters, taking little steps."

I sat on the edge of my bed and wondered whether a quick skewer might not be preferable to this sort of slow flagellation. For all of her compassion and honesty, Janie was essentially just prolonging my agony.

I was so tired of futility, of the sense that all existence would ever allow me to do was roll back and forth within the wound.

"Am I supposed to congratulate you?" I burst out. "Christ, Janie! I don't care *what* it is, *how* serious you say it is or isn't. I'm still fucking in love with you, all right?"

She sighed, as if conceding that all her explanations had accomplished nothing. "I love you too, you know. May be hard for you to believe right now, but…"

"But now you've found a safe guy to give your heart to, someone who'll never scare you!" I snapped.

"That's not it at all!" Janie shot back. She was moving at my speed now, her temper rising to the same pitch. "You're like this spinning gyroscope. I can't keep up with it. Sometimes I just feel *dim* next to you, lackluster… I don't know what-all."

"Sorry, Janie, but I'm not buying it. You were frightened, plain and simple. I'm not saying you're cowardly, all right? But just don't throw me all these red herrings."

"There was probably some fear in there, too, yeah," Janie admitted, so low it was almost a whisper.

While I shook my head, realizing that winning this concession had gained me nothing at all, she plunged on. "Maybe I did the wrong thing in calling you. I feel like it's just made things worse for you."

I bit off a mirthless laugh. "Worse? If you really knew where I've been at you wouldn't worry. It can get to a point, you know, where it just isn't possible to fall any farther."

Her voice was now hollow and broken. "I'm sorry."

I was free-floating. Because I could grasp nothing tangible, I was scared to trust any of the words I might speak. One way or another, they were bound to reach out and claw her. As if I could assuage my own pain by making Janie a participant in it. I grit my teeth, clenched my free fist and let the last whisps of that foolish hope burn away.

"I'd still very much like to be friends," Janie said. "I don't want to disappear completely from your life."

It took every bit of strength I possessed to respond without bitterness. "Yeah – I want to keep in touch too."

"O.k. then."

"O.k."

So the conversation ended there. And how was it that the walls around me refused to crumble, that the world withheld its last dying convulsions?

***

On Monday evening we were scheduled to do a makeup interview with Visionary Chapbook's Pat Stavons. I was looking forward to it for a couple of reasons. For one thing, I was grateful for his review of our record. Not only had it been sympathetic, but it had also indicated to me that at least one person out there could actually *hear* what we were trying to convey through our songs. Because of this, the interview was a means of moving forward. Movement was what I most sorely needed. And there was no point in trying to distinguish between the band's momentum and my own. The band *was* my life.

Of course, the very act of being interviewed touched upon a core place of tension within my contrary nature. The part of me that felt fundamentally ostracized by the world wanted seclusion. My creative soul, on the other hand, ached to *join in the conversation*, to dip into the vast collective stream that encompassed, within its sweeping myth, both the life of ideas and the evolution of humanity. Within that context, words preserved within a magazine were, much like words spoken from the stage, as much a part of a band's art as its music and lyrics were.

And aside from everything else, I wanted to make things up to Pat, Tommy and Carlos for my having squandered our previous opportunity.

Pat certainly didn't seem to bear any grievances. He held the door and waved us in, got us some refreshments (coffee for Tommy, tea for Carlos and ginger ale for me) and made us feel right at home in his little office.

Once his tape was rolling, he began: "How 'bout we start by talking about the genesis of the band. We already know that you went on tour before you'd even played out a whole lot in your home town. That in itself gives you a bit of an air of mystery."

"As far as the real origins go," Tommy said at once, "you'd have to trace it back to two misfits in High School – Brandon and I – who bonded over our mutual love of underground music. This was after some initial animosity fueled by philosophical differences, which were ultimately inconsequential."

And we were off, Carlos and I already biting our tongues as we watched Tommy do his thing.

"And that was a lot an expression of the desperation and isolation we were feeling at the time," I put in. "People – young people, particularly – can get so marginalized by society that lots of times they'll gravitate to music that gives voice to the frustration, and even the hopelessness, that they may be feeling. It's a mistake to try and suppress those feelings – *any* feelings, really. Like, if you're in pain then this in itself indicates that you have the capacity to care. If you *didn't* care then you wouldn't hurt. So, pain is really an aspect of love. Any feeling is as essential to love as shadow is to light. That was our main motivation, in the beginning: To give voice to *everything* within us. No repression, no rules, just let it all out. With vehemence."

"It comes across as threatening to a lot of people at first, that sort of thing," Carlos said. "But if you give it a chance, don't listen to that voice of fear, then you can *recognize* yourself in it. It's like the music is giving you permission to just fully be yourself. That's how I felt when I started playing with these guys. It's a real gift."

Pat was already grinning, clearly enjoying this. "So there's a way in which it's all therapeutic, is that it?"

At this, we cast our glances around at each other, wondering who should go. We did this because we intuited that we *all* had personal responses at the ready. Receiving encouraging nods from the guys, I stepped up.

"Carlos was talking about people feeling threatened... well, when something is perceived as threatening then we resist it. Pain, for instance - like I was saying before. So then it never gets a chance to cycle through. How does it find an outlet, then? Well, it gets distorted into nihilism, depression, these other debilitating emotions..." I thought of Saul, and it spurred my next insight. "It also gets projected onto the world outside. Then, because we haven't given our pain or anger its due, we might overreact to really trivial things. Any situation can serve as a trigger for it. Hell, this is what's behind wars and other mass conflicts, even. Any brush with the outside world becomes, like, stubbing a toe that's already sore."

Carlos was nodding the whole time. He could scarcely wait to have his say. "Deep inside, people really want that honest expression, even if they usually don't want to admit it, you know? It reminds me of back when I was drinking heavily and using drugs, all those tiresome party scenes. They seem to promise fulfillment – to the point where you just about catch a glimpse of it, around the corner. One more drink, one more smoke, and maybe finally, the door will open. Feelings will gel with that guy you're trying to connect with, that girl you're hoping to make it with. Magic words will be spoken. You keep tellin' yourself that 'til the room's spinning, bro; and tomorrow you're paying for oblivion.

"But what is everyone hoping that next drink, or snort, or smoke, is gonna do? Well, you hope it will open you up, get you to show your real self. If anyone was just brave in that moment and said, like, 'I really want to connect with you and I just don't know how, I can't find the words,' then it'd cut through all that. Everyone else could lower their defenses and be genuine and human too. They wouldn't have to wait in the hopes that getting fucked up would lend them the courage to expose themselves. And that's what good music does. When it's real, it gives *you* that permission to be real – with yourself, with others. It exposes so many things that we're all thinking and feeling, on the inside, even if people so rarely come out and *say* those things."

"And yet the artists who express themselves so openly, who let everything out, are so often the misfits, the outsiders," Pat observed.

"Exactly," Tommy concurred. "In order for society to evolve it must always have its misfits. And they'll create their own artistic productions, which society typically frowns upon – and feels threatened by, as we've mentioned – until it finds some way to assimilate it."

"Is being outside of society something that's *integral* to the identity of your band?" Pat asked.

"It's essential for any kind of *real* art," I said.

"Truly," Tommy agreed. "If you're completely bought in to the status quo then you're not going to have any contribution to make, no new vision."

"You're just repeating the ideas that the culture at large already lives by," Pat suggested.

"Exactly," Tommy said. "Whereas if you exist on the margins of society then this obliges you to search for your own kind of personally resonant truth. And that truth, in turn, can become a gift to the society. That's where you find the irony of our cultural response to rock stars: They're outcasts, and yet they're idolized.

"When the social order somehow manages to assimilate a new form of expression then there's a movement forward: Expansion. A lot of people will claim that it's naïve to think that art can really change the world. But art changes the world all the time.

"For us, the journey began about five years ago when the Internet was still in its nascent stages. Half our music collection was cassettes. We were involved in the tape trading scene, all that. We were influenced by bands that never even went out on tour, some that never played a single gig. Real underground stuff."

"And now, Carlos, you weren't the drummer for the band back then, right?" Pat asked.

"I've been playing with these guys a little over a year – maybe a year and a half, now," Carlos said. "I'd only rehearsed with them for a few months before we hit the road for about seven weeks."

"Before that," I added, "we had a member – Tim Peralta was his name – He was a real good guy, you know? And he had the technical ability – great drummer – but the chemistry was weird. Maybe he was just a bit too happy-go-lucky for Tommy and me!" I laughed. "I mean, Carlos is hilarious. But then he gets behind the drums and he's got the same maniacal do-or-die mentality that we do."

"We didn't *fire* Tim, though," Tommy pointed out. "He left of his own free will, realizing that he just didn't want to make this band his life."

"And so now that you three have joined forces," Pat said, "and you've made one record and honed your chops out on the road, what's next? What are your plans?"

"We have too many," Tommy deadpanned at once.

"Yeah, I guess we do have some prioritizing to go," I elaborated. "I'm to blame for some of that, too, man. I can be temperamental. I either feel passionate about something or else I just can't even approach it at all."

"It's the Dionysian thing," Tommy explained. "He's Dionysus and I'm Apollo. If you ever saw one of our rehearsals or listened in on some of our band discussions then you'd see how this plays out. You should definitely put that in your write-up. Journalists just love to run with that kind of stuff.

"But getting back to your question... there are ideas being bounced around for getting back in the studio. We've got five or six new songs written at this point. And we may be doing a tour of the East Coast sometime – New England, particularly. Chas is a transplanted New Yorker, so he's still got contacts back east. How we'll get ourselves and our equipment over there is another matter..."

At this point, all three of us simultaneously eased back in our seats and sipped at our drinks. The interview was complete: You could palpably feel this in the room. What more could we say? Upon the occasion of our very first appearance in print, we'd already distilled our essential philosophy and delivered our mission statement.

"O.k.," Pat said, with a brisk and satisfied air. He clicked off his recorder. Then he looked right at me. "Now, I'd still like to use some parts of our first interview, but I'll only do so if you feel comfortable with it. I just think that there are some real human moments there that readers, your fans and potential fans, might appreciate."

I thought this over for a moment and then shrugged. "Sure. Why not? It wasn't the most coherent interview, for sure; but then again, it was *real*."

"That it was," Pat said with a smile. "And therefore very much befitting for your band. It's been a real honor, guys!"

In the face of all his magnanimous support, we expressed our gratitude to Pat as best we could as we shook hands and said our good-byes.

10. Everything Born to Perish

I finally learned the reason for the underlying sorrow and conflict that I'd sensed in Saul since I started seeing him again in the last month or so. This occurred about a week after we did the interview. I showed up for my scheduled session at his house in the early evening. This had been the hottest day of the year thus far. We were on the cusp of summer; but it began cooling as soon as the sun started to dip. For the second time since we'd resumed our unique kind of student-teacher relationship, Saul suggested that the two of us take a walk.

This time we left his property and followed the bike trail that snaked alongside Townes Street for a while before it cut through several acres of heather that were strewn with litter. Traffic was sporadic. The entire city of Sadenport – half of which was visible, off to the left, from our high vantage – felt subdued. Maybe Saul's somber mood was affecting my senses.

He was quiet for a long time; and I didn't feel like it was my place to initiate conversation. Finally Saul said, "I won't be charging you for today." He was distracted, his eyes cast vaguely over the yellow grassland towards no point in particular. "So let's just get that out of the way and not worry about it." Then he glanced my way and allowed me to see his pain. "I'm sorry that it's taking me a while to get myself together tonight."

In a rush to help, or to at least *feel* helpful, I replied in earnest. "Look, it's no problem. And I got the session. Hell, there's been times when I've gotten everything I needed from you inside of ten minutes. I'm not gonna split hairs now."

"Yeah, well, I'm not counting it," Saul insisted.

We began making our way across the field. The sounds of human bustle receded even farther. "I'm probably going to have to pull back on my practice for a while anyway," he continued. "June needs me. That's where I feel like I have to devote my energies now. She's not well."

For a moment I was stunned, fixed in place as if I was buffeted by chill winds hitting my soul on both sides with equal force. I was frightened for Saul's sake, and by the thought of how such a strong man could be brought to this place where he appeared so frail, almost defeated. Also, I realized how attached I'd grown to him. In my wounded and thwarted human need, I'd turned him into something *other* than human, a being absolved of ordinary hang-ups and sufferings. I felt it sorely, as this illusion was rent from me. In some deep recess of my haunted psyche, I could hear my lost mother wailing.

"What's wrong with her?" I managed.

Saul slowly shook his head. "I'm not sure what anyone would call her condition, in conventional Western medical terms. I don't really care."

"Yeah, but... what's *happening*?"

He scowled. This was the angriest I'd ever seen him. He spat the litany of June's woes as if each sentence was a curse hurled at the Creator.

"She shivers and aches. Her whole body... it's wracked with pain and fever. I sleep next to her at night sometimes and, goddamn it, it's like her living flesh is a furnace. She sweats through clothes, bedding, changes everything three or four times a day. Not that she's hardly got the strength left even for *that* task."

He looked at me and hugged his shoulders, mastered his outburst. The rage receded and the raw pain returned.

"God, and she looks so frail. Like a reed – like a stiff wind could just break her."

But something in his attitude, in the implied defiance in his eyes, had riled me. "But what do you mean, you don't know what anyone would *call* it? She hasn't been *diagnosed*?"

Saul glared at me. "Diagnosed by *who*, Brandon? Some doctor who'll turn her into a guinea pig for the drug companies? Or put her through chemotherapy that could kill her quicker than cancer? Just what do you think it actually means, to live outside of convention?"

This was yet another revelation that I was unprepared for. I'd never been on the receiving end of Saul's ire before. I could only make my best effort to swallow what he said and nod.

Then I processed the import of his words aloud. "So you've decided to work through this on your own, you and her."

Saul looked distant – and not the communing-with-spirits kind of distant that I was used to.

"Yeah," he said, as if the word was a latch intended to lock in impending tears. "And there really isn't much that I can *do* except be there, be her support. It's all up to June.

"We actually did seek some medical help in the beginning. I didn't mean to snap at you about that. I was reacting to my own sense of helplessness there. But her condition has been stubbornly unresponsive to treatments and antibiotics. And then we tried the natural methods. A complete overhaul of her living habits. A transition into a largely raw food diet. No good. June has tried acupuncture and Chinese herbs, Ayurveda and yoga. Nothing makes a difference; at least, not for long.

"Nowadays she has to force herself to eat at all, because the very thought of it makes her nauseous. She hardly has the stamina left to enjoy, appreciate, the little joys of life. All she really wants is the oblivion of sleep."

His face flushed with color, and I wondered whether he was torn between consideration for his wife's privacy and his own need to share his pain and sense of futility. I wished that I'd known June better, had shared more with her during those times in which our paths had crossed, as if this could have enabled me to be of help somehow.

"But let's talk about what you're working through now," Saul said, clapping his hands together and thus summoning his self-control. "And let me just say it, and get it out of the way: I know that you had a painful experience involving Janie lately, and that you and her talked since. I know that it's unprofessional of me, blah blah blah; it's not my place to say; but I'm glad you two have communicated on that level finally. That feels a lot more real to me than the place where things were left at before."

I didn't know how to tell Saul that the mere mention of Janie's name stirred up in me a kind of senseless, betraying hope. I grimaced at the turn of my own thoughts.

Before long, though, our talk drifted away from my personal life and back to June and her difficulties. And I didn't mind this, because I realized that there were lessons for me in all of it. Saul's love for his wife was evident in the way he spoke of her. There was also a note – the merest suggestion – of fatality. The idea of death had a way of reminding me of what was really important in life. It was the sheerest form of catharsis, really.

"It's been a learning experience for her," Saul said, "in the sense that her crisis training and work never prepared her to be needy and dependent herself." He grinned – it was the first time I'd seen him do it that day. "Her pride is taking a blow."

But the shadows pounced over his visage quickly once again. "This is not about her physical body! I know that. It's about the need for some sort of life change, a whole change of orientation for her." He shrugged in a way that expressed more eloquently than words the underlying question: *But would she discover what it was, in time to save herself?*

"We just spend a lot of time sipping tea together and waxing nostalgic," Saul said. "We talk about the year that we lived in a bus while we saved up the money to buy this house." He looked distant once again; his voice turned as much to himself as to me. "We were different people back then. We were poor and uncertain; but somehow the moments of our days had been *full*..."

I didn't know how to respond to any of it. I did make one plea to Saul about halfway through the session, though.

"Please, can you just find some time to keep working with my dad?" Then I was bit by the old bitterness. I shook my head. "I don't even know why I give a shit, really. But I do. Somehow I still do. Besides, he's Rachel's father, too; and I know that she'd love to see her daddy get better."

Robert had already come to see Saul a couple of times. I knew that much, although Saul had stuck to his personal resolution to keep things confidential. It would be up to my father to discuss what he was working through – or not. And I didn't *expect* him to share much at this point in time, anyway. No doubt it was all very new and raw.

Saul nodded. "There's several people who I'm keeping on during this period," he said. "He can be one of them, if he chooses to come."

"He needs it," I said. "I mean, I don't know if he'll ever be able to face his life, but... I'd say you're the best chance he's got."

"Making that first appointment was a good step for him – a strong symbolic gesture," Saul said. "He took the initiative at least. But of course you know that I'm only the messenger. The real healing's gonna have to come from him."

Then he took a moment to delve into my eyes. I bore his scrutiny as best I could. "What about you?" he asked.

"I'll be fine," I assured him, although I didn't know how much I meant what I was saying. "You know how it sometimes takes me months before I really start to understand and live by the things that you tell me, anyway."

Saul suddenly smiled; and in the expression I saw glimmerings of his old impish self.

"You know, I had therapist once," he said.

"Oh yeah?" I was genuinely intrigued by this.

"I was about your age, actually," Saul explained. "Maybe a little older. I saw this man... he was an analyst of the Jungian persuasion."

"So what happened with that?"

Saul shrugged. "Ah, it just wasn't a good fit, for a lot of reasons. The main problem I had, I think, was that I got to feeling that the inner self – soul, whatever you want to call it – was far away, almost inaccessible. Like it lived someplace you could only reach after a lot of conflict, pain and arduous work." He chuckled. "I've tried real hard to spare *you* from that trap!"

I smiled in return. It was such a relief for me to see him in this more relaxed moment. Saul's voice was wistful.

"When you feel that you're separate from the environment that surrounds you, when you *believe* that you are, it engenders a lot of fear. And that's exactly the kind of belief that our culture instills in us. Then a lot of other destructive ideas sort of gather around that one, support it.

"I mention this because I'm realizing now, looking back, that what I'd really wanted my therapist to do was *contradict* that belief. It had made my reality look so bleak, hopeless and gray. I wanted him to say or do something that would totally refute it, that would give me a new kind of conviction. But of course that's not something that he or any other person could ever have *given* me."

He met my eyes and offered me another glimpse into the turmoil and doubt within him. "It wasn't easy for me to believe that I existed within a world of my own making. I battled that one for a long time."

"And now this crisis with June has brought it all up again," I blurted, almost without thinking.

Caught in a state of surprised delight, his eyes wide and aflame, Saul burst out laughing. "Did I not tell you that we're here to learn from each other?" he said, once he'd recovered himself.

But I could only partially participate in his momentary good humor. My most recent insight had led me on to another.

"That's why you don't want to take clients," I said, even as it occurred to me. "It's not that you don't have the energy, but that you feel like..."

"A hypocrite," Saul finished. He was somber once again. "Yes. How can I teach people something that I'm reluctant to place my own full faith in?"

I responded much like a child would, one who was in need of a strong father. "Well you need to *find* that belief again, Saul! Seriously!"

Unguarded and vulnerable, he regarded me for maybe half a minute. Then he said: "In all the time we've worked together – coming up on two years now – we've never hugged. And I know you can feel uneasy about that sort of thing. But I could sure use one now."

I entered his embrace as soon as he opened his arms. My own feelings were pretty raw and insistent too; and my mind's objections didn't stand much of a chance. I held him while his muscular physique shook with quiet sobs, refusing to let go until Saul withdrew of his own accord.

11. Short of an Album

When I got home that evening I learned that Carlos had gone out. Tommy, though, was hanging out in the living room practicing finger exercises on his four-string. Occasionally he would stop and scribble a line or two in a notebook that was laid open on the coffee table. I watched him work for a while. He seemed to be in the midst of yet another killer song. Damn, did this guy *ever* get writer's block?

Then he looked over and asked me a question that he never had before, in all the time that I'd been seeing Saul.

"How'd your session go?"

I stopped – I'd been halfway en route to the bathroom – and groped for an answer.

"Well, I found out that Saul is just as human as the rest of us, which was probably good for me."

Then the deeper reservoir of sadness rose up and engulfed me. "His wife's not doing so well. June. She's real sick."

In a stumbling manner, I described what I knew of her symptoms. And I explained that Saul and June had decided, after a few half-hearted forays into conventional medicine, to move through this crisis on their own.

"Jesus!" Tommy muttered under his breath. He leaned his bass against the table. "It sounds like *cancer*, man. And they're not seeking help? I don't know... odds are she ain't gonna make it."

"I basically told Saul the same thing, at first..." I trailed off, feeling unsure of *what* I believed anymore.

Suddenly I was crying. The reservoir rose over the dam. I felt like my face bore trails of blood from twin wounds. When Tommy slung his arm over my shoulders I began blabbing, spluttering.

"Do you ever wonder, man... the music, the inspiration – is it even *enough*? I mean, I love it. It's the reason I live: You know that's how I feel about it. But it isn't the sum of life."

A minute or two later I calmed down enough to catch my breath and try and proceed more coherently. "I guess it's like I was saying that night at Toad's in Albuquerque, when I talked the crowd's ears off. I just realized that it wasn't the answer to everything. I don't *just* want to be this mad, inspired poet and musician. I want to have a happy and healthy *life*. too. God, I don't think I really realized that until Janie left."

Tommy repositioned himself so that he could grip my shoulders and face me. I could tell that an *unaccustomed* display of emotion was coming from the way that he deliberately composed himself.

"I gotta tell you," he said, "I haven't been there for you to the extent that I really could have, lately. I've seen what you've been going through. I see how heavy it all is. And yet I've had this attitude, like, 'Well, all right, but we still have things we've got to accomplish.'"

He let his hands drop, perhaps realizing that I wasn't going to turn away. "I guess what I'm saying is, if you need to take a break from all this, put the band on the back burner..."

"No!" I protested at once. "It really isn't that."

There's something that you'd need to understand here. I had the tendency to *wallow* in certain feelings. It's like they were deep, dark pools of water; and I was curious to see how far down one could go. When Tommy felt intensity he immediately looked for the *solution* to it. Maybe that's part of what he was getting at with that "Dionysus and Apollo" remark he made during our interview. Apollo is an expert swimmer. Dionysus knows how to drown in style.

"All right," Tommy said, with a half laugh. Then he considered for a moment, reached for a new strategy. "How 'bout we ease up on the whole quest to enlighten the world, then, and give ourselves that much breathing room? Let's dig our heels in over at Alchemist Brews, make another great record and the go from there. All right?"

A few days later, Edge of the Known met with Chas to discuss the band and our future. At thirty-one, Chas was still lean and driven: As high-rev a personality as you're ever bound to encounter without uppers figuring into the equation. It was hard, at times, for me to work with him in any state of vulnerability because he was such a believer in *action* over introspection. But on this particular afternoon I felt focused. Even though we only had enough new material written to fill about half a record, I suggested that we spend some time laying down tracks in the studio.

"I think it would just give us a sense of *momentum* at this point," I reasoned. "We don't want to get too comfortable, you know, just playing at being local heroes over at Alchemist Brews."

"How big do you hope for your band to become?" Chas asked suddenly – and rather *pointedly*.

This left me thoroughly nonplussed. I'd never really thought about it in those terms before. In the naiveté of our original vision – mine and Tommy's, some five years before in High School – 'success', in the abstract sense, had meant salvation. I suppose we'd hoped to find ourselves surrounded by congenial minds, kindred souls; that we'd never again have to exist within the system that alienated us, if only we "made it".

For a moment, I gaped at the shortsightedness of this vision. I couldn't respond.

"Big enough to eat," Carlos offered. "And to pay the rent and not have to hold day jobs."

"Unfortunately, it's such a feast-or-famine industry," Tommy added. "Either you've got some big company at your back, throwing money at your band until you're living large, or else you're struggling as unknowns."

Chas looked thoughtful. He ran a hand through his short-cut, thick black hair. "It's interesting to me, though, how well you guys went over with people when you did that last tour. There seems to be something about you that average people can really grasp on to. I mean, you seem to appeal even to those who aren't metal-heads, punks or even music lovers in general."

"The honesty of it?" Carlos suggested.

"There really isn't a hell of a lot of competition out there," Tommy opined.

"Well," I said, "whatever the secret to our magic may be, I have a feeling that we'll spoil it if it becomes too self-conscious a thing. We gotta just keep trusting our instincts and not try to analyze the whole thing."

"Yes," Chas muttered, distractedly. He was still following his own mental loop to its culmination. I could see it, when the resolution came, 'cause the focus of his whole being returned, in a swoop, to the immediate.

"I think I may be able to get you guys into a showcase gig in a couple of months," he announced. "You know, there'll be a couple of big-draw bands on the bill alongside you; and hopefully some A and R guys – who've been specially invited to the thing – in the audience. There's this event being planned in New York. I know the promoters. Between the power of your record and the rave review in Chapbook... well, I'll call in every favor I can think of, on top of that, and hopefully get you guys in there."

There followed a half-minute of silence as we all absorbed this. Then we tumbled over one another in our eagerness to express our interest in the idea and our gratitude to Chas.

Then my thoughts hit a disconcerting snag, as another dimension of this idea revealed itself to me.

"But wait a minute, Chas," I said. "A'n'R people. That means possible major label interest. Why are you doing this? I mean, if we sign to a big label then you'll lose us."

Chas met me squarely. "That's why I was asking you guys how big you want to become. My resources are limited, obviously. Manhandle is like for bands that otherwise wouldn't be heard *at all*. I think your music deserves to reach as many people as humanly possible. If someone can give you that wider exposure, better than I can…"

His generosity caught me off guard. I was bereft of speech. Tommy came through for all of us. "In the event that that happens, I'm telling you this: Manhandle's getting a mention somehow on every record that ships out!"

Chas acknowledged this with the merest humble nod. Then he clapped his hands together, his mind already embarked upon the next venture. "So now let's talk about the new record. If you guys are anywhere near as inspired as you were last time…"

Then, suddenly, the bottom fell out of my fleeting sense of happiness. Despite my prideful efforts to keep the dam erect, sorrow welled up and pushed at the backs of my eyes. In that moment I was alone, distanced from my band as well as from Chas, who was articulating a kind of faith in us that I couldn't partake in.

"Not a record, man," I sputtered. "An EP. I can handle an EP."

When Tommy and Carlos turned towards me their eyes and body language conveyed a kind of quiet sympathy. It told me that they weren't actually so surprised, that they guessed at the underlying reasons. But I kept my awareness fixed on the compass point of Chas' face.

"I've been through too much upheaval in my personal life lately," I explained. "It's hard for me to concentrate on anything for very long. The couple of new songs that I *have* written both just leapt out without any conscious intention on my part."

Then I couldn't look at him anymore. My visual field panned down to the hard little curled knots of the gray-white carpet. "Last time I *did* get blocked, at one point, but I had Saul to help me work through it. And he's just not available now. He's got his hands full with his own nightmare. Then I had another dry spell for a few months after we got back from the tour. It seems to all come in fits and starts for me. I'm sorry, Chas. I really don't think that I've got any other songs in me right now."

Tommy stepped up to support my flank. "And in that case, it wouldn't be right for me to pick up the slack and fill the record with my own material, even if I was able to. We've always had this kind of unspoken pact, that we'd divide everything up more or less evenly. Edge of the Known is a lot about the balance that we've found, the middle ground between our voices and visions. We've got some differing tendencies, both lyrically and musically, and it's oftentimes the tension within that field that really makes the band strong."

We were both much more earnest than our producer was. Chas just nodded in acknowledgement. No skin off his back. "An EP it is, then," he said simply. "So what length are we talking? How many songs?"

"Five songs, one of them being an instrumental," Tommy said. "We've got about a half-hour's worth of music ready to record."

"When do you feel like starting?" Chas asked.

"As soon as possible!" I blurted. I suddenly envisioned those hours in the studio as refuge, escape, forward motion. I needed to feel useful and effective again. I'd witnessed too many things that I cherished withering and dying, right there in my hands.

'Soon as possible' turned out to be the very next night. And I have to admit that by this time I'd grown superstitious around the recording process. I needed to visit Rachel and soak up some of her faerie magic for the venture. Making time for this was a tricky endeavor. She had school and I had work, which left a window of just a few hours in the late afternoon and early evening. In addition, I hadn't *planned* this in advance, which meant that I showed up at the Friedman's door and knocked, unexpectedly. I'd never done that before.

Their reaction surprised me. Ernie stood in the doorway and – quite humbly – told me that it was fine with him. When Gail saddled alongside him, in her utilitarian khaki pants and plain button blouse, he passed the question on to her. She deliberated a bit longer than he had, frowning in concentration, but was just as amenable in the end.

"Rachel!" she called. "Your brother's here! He wants to take you out, if you want to go."

I actually heard her squeal with delight from her bedroom upstairs. It was the most delightful sound imaginable. And I wondered, in that moment, if it was her love for me that was slowly softening the manner in which the Friedmans responded to me, in spite of their inability to relate to either my physical circumstances or my mental world. They had apparently decided to perceive me as a human being, regardless.

Rachel appeared in pink overalls, brown sandals and a white long-sleeved shirt. Her long auburn hair (most of the red having faded with maturity) was tied in two tight braids. She was visibly excited, but didn't say anything: Just watched, and waited.

"I know this is so last minute," I told the Friedmans, "but maybe if I could take her out to dinner, just to give us a little more time?"

Gail presumed to speak for the both of them. "All right: That's fine." Her tone seemed to say, *permission is granted this time, but don't think to turn it into an expectation.*

Rachel was quiet and demure as we walked to my car – reflective. I felt suddenly unsure of how to initiate conversation. Then inspiration hit me.

Ah... but did I dare to act upon it? For this was precisely the kind of thing that could erode, if not completely obliterate, the goodwill that I'd so painstakingly accrued with the Friedmans. I vacillated a moment longer and then thought, to hell with it.

"Hey," I said, pausing at the door on my side, "do you want to go visit Dad?"

Rachel lit up at once – not with joy and excitement, necessarily, but with a definite alertness. Her imagination was engaged. She nodded.

I'd always sensed, with her, that there was more going on in the inner world than the surface revealed. But now the subtle signs that had previously shed light on that internal activity had become harder to isolate.

I got inside and started the engine. While Rachel buckled up, I said: "So, I haven't talked to him about this beforehand. I actually got the idea just now. So we'll be dropping in and surprising him. Hopefully he'll be o.k. with it.

"And," I added, "if Ernie and Gail get upset about this then they're going to take it out on *me*, not you, all right? So just don't even worry about it."

"I don't want to get you in trouble, though," Rachel said.

"Hey, it's not like they're *my* parents," I responded – and then immediately regretted having done so.

"They're not *mine*, either," Rachel shot back, with an intensity of emotion that I didn't know how to interpret. Was it bitterness? Sorrow?

I let out a long breath as I began backing the car around. "If they make it difficult for me to come and visit you then that'll be unfortunate," I said. "But I don't think it'll come to that. And kiddo… you *do* have a loving home, at least. Not everyone does."

You didn't before, I wanted to add.

"I know," she said, sounding much more at ease. "But it's different from how it was when I didn't live there, and they were still just Aunt Gail and Uncle Ernie."

"How so?"

"Well, they want everything to be *perfect* all the time, for one thing! Nice clothes. Perfect grades. They even sometimes say things, like I should be friends with this person but not that person. It's so stupid! I can make up my own mind! And what do I need good grades for, anyway? They're not gonna help me be a good rock singer, like you. And that's what I want."

I nearly steered us into a rut off on the right shoulder of the road.

"Since *when*?"

Little sis giggled. "Marla told me that Rachel Chane sounds like a rock star's name. I think so too."

I recovered from my shock and glanced over to smile at her. "Well... yeah... I suppose it does."

After that I drove in silence for a while, marveling at this new perspective that she'd given me. I was so accustomed to thinking of my own life path as something that I pursued for lack of *any other recourse*. That it should have romantic implications in someone else's mind was startling.

"Hey, you've never heard me play – I mean, like, with a full band," I said as it occurred to me. "You should come to one of our rehearsals sometime, if you want to."

"That'd be cool."

Oh, how many changes were I going to have to race to catch up with? "And since when do you say things are 'cool', rock star Rachel Chane?"

She laughed again – and that was her only reply.

It was unfortunate, at least in terms of my own emotional preparedness, that our banter made time speed by, because before I knew it I was pulling into the cul-de-sac where our father's house sat and pondering the possible imprudence of what I was doing.

"Here we are," I breathed.

The walk from the curb to the door transpired inside a dream. I pulled open the screen door and then rapped on the wooden one.

A minute later, Robert opened it and then met our gazes with the expression of a man who'd lost the capacity for any kind of expectation. He blinked like he suspected we were phantoms.

I was spared the burden of having to break the ice. Rachel beat me to it. With humility and innocence the likes of which I'd scarcely witnessed in the entirety of my life, she stepped forward and said, "Hi Daddy."

That such soft, quiet words could wield such power. They literally brought him to his knees. Robert knelt; and his moist eyes burned towards her. Then, with obvious effort, he offered his open arms. Rachel entered his clasp with a kind of eagerness that I'd often been on the receiving end of myself – and indescribably grateful for, every time.

"Oh, I love you," he panted, nearly hoarse.

"I love you Daddy," she returned, much more clearly.

It was a fairly stiff display, on his part. But it was also, to my knowledge, the first time those words had passed between the two of them in both their lives. They bridged chasms, sealed rifts, opened views onto wide skies never before glimpsed.

As they disengaged, I looked at each of them in turn. "I think I'll just let you two hang out for a bit, o.k.? I'll go take a walk, maybe to the bridge and back. See you in a few."

12. Fool's Gold

Of course, following this outing with Rachel, the song that I most wanted to record was the one that I'd written for her. Tommy, Carlos and I had been wood-shedding it over the last couple weeks and had solidified an arrangement that was somehow edgy and dynamic without ever overwhelming the delicate, aching melody – which was, all in all, the quality of the song most dear to me. Some experiences just can't be conveyed with words alone, and love's primal force is one such phenomenon.

I used a distortion pedal while recording my guitar part so that it could ring clear and twangy during the verses - just like how you hear it on a lot of vintage '60s garage band records - and crunchy through the chorus. Classic grunge trick, I know; and I typically disliked processing my sound with anything other than the distortion that my amp on high volume could produce. But it was difficult, in this case, to convey the alternately escalating and subsiding states of emotion without resorting to a bit of technical aid.

Feeling reluctant to commit my sister's full name to a recording, as it existed in the original lyrics, I ended to last line with the innocuous "Sparkle Lane" instead, just so I could preserve the rhyme.

Then, following an obscure impulse (as I was wont to do when the tapes were rolling - or when I was onstage, for that matter) I began intoning a piece of surrealistic poetry over the spacious, psychedelic outro that we'd composed to finish the song. The poem had been an offshoot of the original lyrics anyway, written a couple of days later, so it seemed to just be finally settling into its intended spiritual home.

I'll trade this whole

world of facts for
your comic collection and
trusty sea pets

If you could just help me to
wade
beyond the jellyfish
Then – no doubt –
once my head's below water it'll be like
that time in winter when
my reasoned construct of the
universe melted and
I found myself thinking
clearly for the first time in
my life

I was so excited by the result of this experiment that I suggested, a couple of nights later when we entered the studio again, that we try to wed another poem of mine to the instrumental piece. The other guys, Chas included, were enthusiastic and supportive. I had in mind the poem that I had drawn upon for source material for a song on our first album: "Stage Props". This song had, in fact, been the first composition that the present incarnation of Edge of the Known had ever played together. That run-through had earned Carlos a place in the band forevermore.

Again we were blessed with a miraculous marriage of words and sonic landscape; and so, "Instrumental No. 1" was transformed into "Stage Props II", utilizing the last two verses of the original poem.

Logic, standing anxious on its
patch of ever-shifting ground, seeks
the comfort of finality

May it be eased into
recognizing its own source in
the grinding mill of mortality, which
disguises Eternal Nature behind
the stage props of

all who have loved and
lost

This was a new depth of vulnerability and exposure for me to sink into, speaking words like this without adopting a vocal mask beforehand. I tried to be as natural as possible and avoid any posturing. But I was in the throes of an intense inner maelstrom of feeling, so there would have been no need to try and abet this with an overdose of contrived angst anyway. For better or worse, the words ended up sounding like they came from someone who *lived* them.

Though our intended disk was still unnamed, we finished recording the songs within three sessions. Then we treated our next performance at Alchemist Brews as our celebration.

We'd begun to notice *regulars*: people who went there to see us nearly every time we played. By now they'd become familiar with the tunes that would soon surface on our new record, too. We were all bursting with too much enthusiasm, and the keen rapture that the act of creation alone can bring, to keep our compositions a secret for long. The spoken sections, however, were new to everyone on this night. We'd also decided, beforehand, to abandon the slideshow. Much as I'd enjoyed that exotic departure for a while, it just didn't fit in with our overall ethic of being *transparent* within the music. Exposed as I was, the words seemed to emerge with just the right ring of candor. And the near-complete *silence* within the bar during those interludes was the ultimate homage.

"We've got the best fucking fans in the world!" I shouted, as we finished "Sister/Satyr". And this sounded neither gratuitous nor scripted. I meant it; and the audience, some fifty or sixty strong, responded with cries of tribal blood-deep assent that rolled like pristine waves onto the stage.

We typically played about two hours on any given night, taking a brief breather mid-way. Obviously, bands with a slew of cover songs in their repertoire can comfortably stretch out even farther than this. But none of us had ever seen much point in promoting songs that people were already familiar with. *Challenging* the audience, stretching both their minds and the bounds of their emotional territory, was our inimitable art.

My spirit felt akin to wind or fire, transcending the limitations of fleshy sinew and pushing through to a sphere where nothing could touch me – nothing *harmful*, anyway. Or maybe I was already completely immersed in the fire and therefore no longer had to fear being burned. My voice sounded particularly raw and forceful. It strained a bit at times, trying to encompass all of this mad rapture, but held in there.

Then we finished the last song, and all the energy that we'd poured out rebounded upon us from the audience in pelts of adoration. I'd scarcely unslung my guitar when the cocktail server, Kayla, came right up and grasped me in an urgent hug. She was there on most of the nights we played, so I'd chatted with her on and off on previous occasions. She had honey colored hair that ran to her shoulders in mild ringlets and usually (as was the case tonight) wore high heels and a single piece dress of deep blue that showcased her shapely thighs and hips. Hoop earrings dangled from both her ears. She also displayed a tasteful arc of golden eye-shadow over each eye; and this last detail threw my otherwise sweet indulgence in the spectacle of her into pained disarray, as it reminded me so much of Janie.

"God, Brandon!" she gushed. "That was incredible!"

I could tell at once that this went beyond a simple compliment about the music. Undeniable sexual warmth oozed through both the words and her smile. And I was filled with such a sense of plentitude, following that cathartic apotheosis onstage, that I was able to smile back.

"Thanks, Kayla," I said, as humbly as I could manage.

"Can I buy you a drink?" she asked.

"Hey, I'm not broke! I can cover myself."

"No, seriously, let me. I get 'em discounted." Her eager pursuit was making me hot all over. "So what'll you have?"

I shrugged. "Just a beer. Any kind… something stout!" I amended.

"Be right back," she replied with a merry twinkle – and an implied promise.

Tommy had just returned from packing his bass amp in the van. His cool nod somehow acknowledged that he was privy to what was in the air.

"Looks like maybe it'd be worth your while to hang out here for a bit," he observed.

This made me more self-conscious about what I was, by slow degrees, surrendering to. I was suddenly apprehensive. "Oh, I dunno... I'll probably just stay for one drink."

Tommy's gaze followed the trail of Kayla's departure. "It's a nice night," he argued. "I don't mind a walk home; and I'm sure Carlos doesn't either. You could drive the van back later."

Kayla returned then with a pint of dark ale for me, and Tommy retreated to give us space. After a moment he left, probably to find Carlos.

"It's such a trip to actually know someone who can write and perform like that!" Kayla said. "It's one thing to hear a record – you know? – and just sort of admire this musician who you know you're never gonna meet."

I waved a hand. "There's nothing too special about it, really. Everyone has their own different gifts. Hey, you can navigate this place in half darkness, weaving around all the people who're jerking back and forth, a tray of drink balanced on your shoulder and not spilling a drop. That's something I could never manage."

She sparkled again. "Oh, it is an art form, isn't it? And speaking of which, I'd better get back to it." She cast me a look that was part gauging and part insinuating. "You wanna hang out until I get off, or...? It'll just be, like, another hour."

"Sure," I said; and by this I was acknowledging that I was now swept up in the inevitability of it all.

One part of me was already sampling her wares, sating the places that were so starved for touch, closeness, release. When Kayla left I sat on the edge of the stage and nursed my beer. Now and then someone would come by and say "hey", compliment me on the performance. It *had* been a righteous outburst of Pan's madness. Tommy had managed to announce the imminent release of our mini-album in the midst of it, too. None of this touched me like I longed for it to, though. Kayla, and my own want of her, posed an essential dilemma that I had no answer for.

She returned a while later with her purse slung over her shoulder and her server's apron all folded up and clutched in one hand.

"I know it's late," she said, "and they're doing last call now, but... you wanna do something tonight?"

The underlying suggestion could hardly have been more blatant. And I realized that I had either already lost this fight or else I just didn't understand the battleground to begin with – nor which side represented what.

"The other guys walked back, and I've got the van," I said. With a subtle lilt, I made the word 'van' sound like 'conveniently close love nest'.

Kayla stepped right up then, took me securely by the belt loops beside both my hips, pulled herself closer and then tilted her head up (she was half a foot shorter than me) to kiss me.

"Just thought I'd get it out of the way," she explained, as we parted from this sharing of flesh and breath.

I soaked up the scent of her, and the loosening of my own feelings and inhibitions, and leaned in for more.

We flowed and swayed together, through the bar, out the door and to the van. Kayla's whole body was taut with eagerness; and it drove a fire straight to my brain.

A stash of condoms was always kept in the van, in the event that situations like this ever occurred. Not that they very often *did*. After all, we three guys typically occupied the van at the same time; and at this point in time, none of us had steady girlfriends. Kayla slid back into a space between the equipment, hugging her knees and quietly acquiescing to my intent, as I rummaged for my protection.

She had her dress pulled down by the time I returned. Her arms stretched out, she alternately curled and extended her fingers to give me a 'come hither' command. I tore off my shirt. Then, kneeling on all fours, I suddenly froze.

"Jesus, Kayla!" I breathed. "I gotta tell you. You gotta know. I'm still real attached to someone. I mean, there's someone who I still love, even though it's over."

This hardly even slowed her down. "Well, it sounds like you're not *with* her now, so... there's nothing stopping us." She started wrestling with my jeans.

"No, I mean..." I had to pull a deep breath in order to settle enough to continue. "I don't know that I can give myself to you, like, *fully*. My feelings are still over there, with someone else. Well, a *part* of me is still there, anyway."

My discomfort just seemed to create a challenge that she was delighted to be confronted with.

"Will you relax? I'm not asking you to marry me, you know."

She leaned forward and kissed me, real soft, on the neck. That loosened me enough so that I stopped forestalling her hands, which had paused right at my zipper. My nipples were the next to receive her lips. Her fingers were deft. Somehow, by the end of this brief foreplay I was entirely naked.

By now my lower brain was doing the lion's share of the decision making. Well, I could dispense with guilt, anyway. Kayla had been warned. Besides, she seemed the far less vulnerable one, between the two of us.

"You get hornier after a night of playing like that?" Half tease, half challenge.

And then the time for talk was past. Her lips smothered me. I cupped the back of her head and the small of her back simultaneously, went in like a dog straining at the uttermost limits of its leash.

Neither of us apparently had any interest in pacing ourselves. I felt like I was panting my lungs' last hoarse reserves, every time. When I came I almost couldn't comprehend what was happening. A train gone off the rails had finally collided with an unmovable obstacle. My spate of wild flight was over; and no one – nothing – had been saved.

A few minutes later we were both lying on our backs, facing the shadowed roof and indulging in the honored movie cliché of sharing a cigarette.

"Please tell me," I pronounced, "that you didn't just fuck me because I'm in a band."

She elbowed my ribs. "If you weren't in a band, a band that happens to play in the bar that I work at, then I probably wouldn't have even *met* you." She seemed immune to all intimate insecurities. "But I *slept* with you because I like you and I'm attracted. The passion you have up onstage is part of that, yeah. I won't lie."

Her candor eased me slightly. I reached over and massaged her head with my fingertips.

"I don't know if there can be another time, Kayla."

The force of my voice was nearly neutered by the trepidation I felt.

She turned on her side. "You sure? It was really nice, wasn't it?"

"It was beautiful. Don't know if that's even the right word for it, really. I was pretty *animal*!" I barked a laugh. Might as well acknowledge it – my body was still quivering. But my mind was morose. "I'm just fucked up around intimacy in general. I tried to tell you…"

"You *did* tell me," she said. She searched my face for clues in the darkness. Then: "She must be pretty special to have you all hung up like this."

"We're *all* special," I responded at once.

Thank you, Saul, for teaching me that. *God I need you!*

"Well, I won't act like I'm not disappointed," Kayla said. "If you change your mind, you know where to find me."

"Yeah." I leaned forward and gave her lips all the tenderness that I was capable of, leaving it up to her whether or not to consider it a kiss good-bye – though I knew the truth.

"Come on. I'll walk you to your car."

The streets of Sadenport were dead that night. Well, there was plenty of traffic; but it was dead in the sense that none of it possessed the power or life to touch my entombed heart. My body, at least, was sated. My mind was as gutted as a Jack-o-Lantern.

My only consolation was Kayla's state of being – which, judging by the casual ease with which she made small talk all along the sidewalk and down the alley behind the bar, was wholly intact. When we reached her car, she didn't move in for a kiss before saying goodnight. I guess that told me how she chose to interpret the *last* one.

When I got home, I pulled my phone out and dialed as soon as I'd closed the bedroom door behind me. And I lit into my father the moment I heard his voice on the other end of the line.

"Look, I'm glad that your near brush with death has apparently made you see things with new eyes, made you maybe see the worth of living in a way that you never could before. I really am. But don't think that any of this makes me forget one single time that you ever smacked me around just because you couldn't find any other answer to the goddamn helplessness that you felt inside.

"And let me tell you this, too: It will *not* ever be happening in the future. You put a hand on me again and I will lay you out on the motherfucking *floor*! You got that?"

He was quiet so long that I wondered if he was just going to hang up. Had my vehemence provoked a heart attack? Then his voice, possessing a kind of dignity in its honest resignation, reached me.

"Fair enough."

Then *I* hung up.

13. Gail

No doubt you've heard some psychologist or another – teachers, even – talk about how we humans supposedly lean towards one of three possible responses to trauma, pain and fear: Fight, flight or freeze. And I'm sure by now you can guess, easily enough, what *my* default position had long been. But my heart was sickened by all the fighting; had been for a while. Saul was no longer available to help me find another option. In lieu of his guidance, I naturally began to fantasize about *movement*.

The road, as it had during another period of time not so far in the past, held out my only hope of salvation. In my mind, it was getting time to *go*.

"If you can just spot us a couple grand for the gas," I told Chas, "we'll take the van. We'll just bomb right out there and be on the East Coast within a week."

I'd dropped by to "hang out" (i.e., peer over his shoulder and perk my ears at every note that moved through the soundboard) while he was mixing our new EP.

"We've saved up enough money to ensure that we can eat and survive during the time away," I went on. "Just help us to *get there*, is all."

He finally looked up from the mixing board. If he felt any irritation, he hid it well.

"Getting you there doesn't do you much good if I don't line up a bunch of gigs to begin with," he pointed out.

"Send them the record," I urged. "Look, 'Shadow' convinced twenty-three club owners to give us a chance up on their stage, even though they'd never met or even heard of us before that. And now we've got Patrick's review – and pretty soon, the interview in Chapbook - to give us even more clout."

Chas acknowledged this quietly. He was that rarest of creatures: Artist and businessman in equal measure.

"That's a fair bit of change you're asking for, though," he said. "How can you expect to recoup that?"

When all the chips were down, when the avenues of the manifest world had been pursued and exhausted, I forsook reason and restraint. That was just my way.

"Look, Chas, if I'd *ever* stopped to worry about what I could recoup, about what possible assurances I had, then I never would've picked up a goddamn guitar in the first place. You can't separate that out of the music that we make, man. The desperation and the power are wedded together. We write songs like we do, and perform like we do, mainly because this band is *all we've got!*"

He turned back to the console, perhaps so that he could think without me marking the reactions as they played upon his face. He tweaked a few knobs and let the current song run its course before responding.

"O.k.: So obviously I can't protest *too* much since I'm the one who planted this idea in your head in the first place. I just was never clear about how we'd actually accomplish it, what with the travel and whatnot. Maybe your idea is really the way to go. Maybe it's the *only* way. I'm gonna draw upon the profits from future record sales to make back what I invest in this trip, you understand..."

"Oh, definitely," I assured him.

"And I think it's time you guys got some proper management, too," Chas said.

An unfamiliar sensation stirred within me when I heard that word: *manager.* Now, you might suppose, given my turbulent history with authority figures – which began within my own home – that I'd rebel against the notion of someone else coming in and trying to chart my band's course. *I* would've expected such a reaction, from myself. But instead I seemed to settle inside – it was a strange premonition of peace, of protection. As Chas continued to speak I just stood in silence, nodding occasionally and marveling at this foreign feeling, using my mind's fingers to sort of delicately probe its edges.

"I've got someone in mind. A lady who's actually *very* interested, having heard your record. But of course, it's up to you guys."

Hearing that the person was female seemed to articulate my hope more clearly, clarify it. Yes, I know – how convenient, a mother substitute for a guy who hadn't had one since his early teens. But you know, this world can be pretty austere; and I'd spent time in some of its most parched deserts. I relished what oases I could find and tried my best not to judge myself *or* them.

But I was also momentarily brought up short by the speed at which everything seemed suddenly to be developing. *Management* suggested that we were – or were fast *becoming* – professionals.

"Uh...who is she?"

For the first time since this conversation had begun, Chas looked pleased. His smile put me at ease.

"Maureen Connelly. She lives in Boston, so what I would do is arrange for you guys to meet once you arrived out there. She's in this game because she's a music lover, Brandon. That's rarer in the industry than you might realize."

"Actually," I said, "I distrust most of the people who are in the music business and feel pretty damn sure that they're involved for all the wrong reasons."

Chas nodded in acknowledgement. "I think you might like her," he went on. "This is her trick of the trade, because I've seen it in action before: When she believes in something then she has a way of making *everyone around her* fully aware of her enthusiasm. After a while they're just like, 'All right – I'll give it a listen!' almost with an attitude of capitulation! And" – his smile widened – "she happens to think that

Edge of the Known exhibit signs of – I quote – 'true and rare greatness'."

***

For the second time in the course of our career thus far, we were about to forsake our fragile links to our livelihood – our homes and jobs – and let our fates be determined by the waiting audiences of the world. There may have been an element of courage in this; but then, risks are more eagerly undertaken by those of us who have little to lose.

"Chas could have the record pressed in a few weeks, and shows lined up not too long after that," I told Tommy and Carlos during rehearsals that night.

At this point Tommy turned off his amp, unslung his bass and leaned it against the wall. The surface of The Catacombs was so gritty with old cement that it created a rain of gray dust whenever anything rubbed it.

"This is what I make of all this," he said, with a ceremonial air. "Now, we've been out there once already; and the whole time, we were of the mentality that if we *survived*, if we earned enough to eat and keep moving and complete the tour, then we could count it a success. This time around I really think we ought to broaden our consciousness around the whole thing, elevate our vision."

Carlos intuited the thrust of Tommy's imaginative flow at once. "This could be our opportunity to risk what we *have* for the dream of something larger," he said.

"Exactly!" said Tommy. "To hell with 'hopefully we'll still have our jobs or find new ones when we get back'! Let's make this leap with the intention that *we land someplace else*!"

"There *is* the big gig in New York," I said. "Chas seems pretty confident that he can get us on the bill. And there's supposed to be industry people there…"

"That's all we need," Tommy said. "Our music speaks for itself. Everyone who hears it knows how far it can go. It's at least as good as anything else out there, and a hell of a lot *better* than most of it. It just needs to *reach* people!"

Then it was quiet for a while. Personal revolutions often follow this arc: A burst of bravado, to get things properly initiated – and the energy moving in the direction of desire – followed by more sober reflections. Finally, into the uncertain dim light, I ventured: "So we're all in this, then? It's unanimous?"

There really wasn't much to consider. We were three young men utterly sidelined by the American Dream. It'd scarcely had a flicker of light left in it by the time any of us had reached the age where we were even aware of it. *Change* was our one holy and unassailable god. *The way things stood* was the enemy. Following from this line of logic - and filled out by our quite potent imaginations - upheaval, disruption and recklessness were all welcome prospects so long as they had any hope of breaking through the dead pale China casings of *where we were.*

Edge of the Known where ready to unleash their mayhem upon the world once more.

Of course, I couldn't embark upon another road trip without seeing Rachel again. And I hadn't spoken to the Friedmans since making the executive decision to bring her to Robert's house for a visit. I wondered if perhaps I'd burned that bridge permanently.

In my doubt and trepidation, I deliberated over making that phone call for a full week. Then, one Saturday morning, I awoke with the distinct feeling that I was tired of guilt, tired of berating myself for all of my perceived 'mistakes' - which had all, in fact, constituted necessary learnings. And I was tired of feeling like a second-class citizen every time I talked to my sister's foster parents. The very vulnerability that had seemed to sap my essential courage mere days before now cut through, like a bright sword aflame, the din of negative self-talk that had so long cluttered my mental environment.

I rolled out of bed and scrambled around for my phone. I dialed while the impulse was still fresh in my veins, gave myself no pause within which to reconsider what I was doing. *Trust yourself, dammit!*

There's no Janie, no Saul, no God in Heaven. You're all you've got. Sink or swim, right now!

Gail's voice sounded tentative, probing. Maybe she was unused to receiving calls at that time of morning.

I launched right in.

"Hi. It's Brandon. Look... yeah, I took Rachel to see Robert. And I didn't ask you guys beforehand because I'd made up my mind that it was a good idea, that it needed doing, and I didn't want to risk your saying no. So, if you're pissed at me I understand.

"But I want to point this out, too, that I'm not about to take sides in this thing. Look, I've had my issues with Dad – more than you or anyone else have, truth be told. I didn't create any conflicts when the custody battle was happening and I'm not going to now. I just want to see my sister without having to jump through hoops all the time."

Then I had to settle down onto the edge of my bed, alternately pushed and pulled as I was by the internal winds of emotional inertia. Part of me waited for judgment to be spoken like a guillotine blade descending on my neck.

But Gail sounded measured and calm. In fact, her voice evinced a quality of softness that I'd never heard before.

"I never intended that Rachel should not *see* her father," she said. "I questioned his ability to raise her; and I think I was right in that. But what you did was fine. Yes, I was a little upset that you didn't ask beforehand. But I also recognize your right to make your own decisions with her. And believe it or not, Brandon, I completely trust you with her."

This was such a novel concept to me that I was rendered speechless for the moment.

"I don't disapprove of *who you are*," Gail clarified. "I just don't always understand your *choices*. And I'm a woman who speaks her mind, typically."

There was a hint of humor and self-conscious irony there that made me chuckle. It loosened me up enough to voice the revelation that hit me.

"You've changed towards me. I can't put my finger on what it is, but..."

"I've come to a different understanding," Gail conceded at once.

"Well *I* don't understand."

I heard reluctance in her sigh. And I guessed its source: Persisting in her present course would require Gail to admit that she'd been *mistaken,* something that she loathed doing.

"Rachel has been telling us things: little bits here and there, but enough so Ernie and I can piece together a story," she said. "We hear about how you'd come home late and yet still be up in the morning before her, have a plate of eggs and toast ready for her when she came downstairs. You'd have her school lunch all packed. Stuff like that. And apparently this had been going on for years, from what I can gather."

Gail laughed then. It was a sound that I do not believe my ears had ever before received.

"She explained to us" – this was broken up by even more laughter - "that the reason why she has so many pajamas is because you give her a new pair for Christmas every year. And the stuffed animals – they're in the garage now; she's outgrown them – a lot of them came from you, too. And all the books you read to her. Oh, I could go on and on. She's told us so much. And she adores you."

My personal and private universe began to tilt around the hub of my stunned mind as I realized that Gail – stoic, unsmiling, all-business Gail – had worked herself up nearly to the point of tears.

"Oh, you have to understand, Brandon...when I see someone wearing a skull necklace, and a t-shirt covered with fire and demons and blood, someone wearing a belt and bracelets that look more like weapons than functional clothing... well, I just don't think of that kind of nurturing instinct. It all just looks like violence and hate to me. I

118

think" – she nearly stumbled – "I think I've been a little afraid of you, for quite a few years now."

I felt that her confession deserved a little reverential silence. I allowed the space for it. Then for the second time during the course of this conversation, spirit moved me to speak before I'd mentally rehearsed the words.

"I might be to blame for some of that, too. Maybe part of the reason why I've dressed like that is 'cause I *wanted* to scare people a bit."

This prompted another revelation from Gail. "We've heard other things from Rachel, too. I know that Robert has been abusive with you, especially when he was drinking."

At this point I brushed her off. I didn't want to be brusque, especially during this moment when she was showing me her vulnerable side for the first time ever. But I didn't want the shadows of my past home life to become anyone else's affair to either explain or mitigate. It was *my* reality; and I would define its pitfalls and consequences for myself.

"Yeah, well, that's in the past now," I said. Then I moved on: "Anyway, I'm going to be heading out on the road with my band again, soon. I don't know how long it will be this time. Maybe a couple of months. I'd really like to take Rachel out again, for some kind of day-long outing, maybe, if I could."

"Yes, of course."

"And Gail... it's been real nice to talk to you like this."

She was reserved once more; I could almost hear the sluice gates rise up within her, closing off the free-flow of emotion that had so recently frothed over her high stone walls: The walls that (presumably) had protected her for so long. But I didn't begrudge her that. Maybe we'd gone as far as *I'd* dared to, too. And anyway, the truth once heard cannot be unspoken.

14. Crab Shell and Crystal

Rachel and I ended up taking a drive out to the coast the following Saturday. Spring's soft air had heated up in the onset of June, but many of her blooms endured; and Rachel drew my attention to every flourishing lilac that she could espy off to the side of the road. She loved all things of a violet hue.

I was still feeling spring's renewal, too; but it was a remote spark; tiny and undaunted; resolute. It was that diminutive voice that wields such inexplicable might. It will not give up at the last, no matter how the world might rear its shadows, because it knows the underlying truth of life, the truth that refutes those shadows.

This led to deeper ponderings than I wanted to indulge in at the moment, though. I tried to latch onto something more earthy and concrete, and took something from our last conversation as my cue.

"So you know, if you really want to be a singer then you'll have to do this a lot – travel around, play in different places, sleep in hotels. You think you can manage that?"

"I guess so," she said – simply, and noncommittally. There obviously wasn't any imminent decision that needed to be made about the matter, so... Then her brow furrowed with contemplation. "I thought you said you already had a place to play, a lot of nights. Why do you have to go off to other places, then?"

I grinned, while at the same time acknowledging the underlying love in her that was essentially asking *why can't you just stay here where you're close to* me?

"If you just stay in one place then the best you can hope for is to become what they call a 'local hero'. That means that you may have a lot of fans near you, people who love your music, but then what you're doing can't grow any bigger because you keep playing to those who already know about it. The rest of the world never gets to hear it.

"You know, it's not just rock stars who live like this, either. This sort of thing has been going on for a *long* time. Centuries. Like, troubadours used to travel constantly. They'd even perform for kings. Towns would celebrate when a minstrel came along."

Rachel's eyes widened. "Really?"

"Well, yeah, because that was the only way they got to hear music. Unless there was someone in town who really knew how to play — a local hero." I winked. "They didn't have stereos and digital players. The only way you could hear a song is if someone right in front of you performed it. It was the same with books, too. They were a lot rarer back then. It's more likely that you'd hear tales of the outside world from a storyteller than that you'd read about them for yourself."

"Sounds like it was hard to live in those times," Rachel opined. "I'm glad I'm not there."

I considered this for a moment. "Yeah, but imagine how magical a song or story would sound to you if you'd waited all winter for the warm weather to come so that the minstrel could visit your village."

Rachel stared out the window for a while and then mused, with keen curiosity, "I wonder what they sang about?"

My mind was stumbling through associations, fragmented connections, so I answered distractedly at first. "Probably places and happenings that most people didn't know anything about. The world was a lot less known back then."

But the insight that I'd stumbled upon was this: The world was no more truly *known* in our own time. Its surface had been explored, sure. We knew its *skin,* for the most part. But all that we were really familiar with was our own perceptions, our own stories about it — and oftentimes we were only half-conscious of *those.*

"That's the same thing that musicians should be doing nowadays," I finished, at the same time thinking: *That's why we're Edge of the Known.*

We arrived at our destination in the late afternoon. The high waves of the full tide, churning up a white froth, were visibly cold even from a distance. The breeze blew right off the water, carrying the tang of salt, sea life and sailors' longings. Couples skirted along the beach's edges here and there; but it was still early in the season, and few dared swim or surf.

"I have something for you!" Rachel announced suddenly. "It's a going away present."

Today she was dressed in overalls, of a sort of light periwinkle color, and brown sandals. She'd pulled her hands behind her back. And the smile she gave me made my heart melt and run like heated wax in my chest.

"You do?"

She nodded fervently. "Yup! But you've got to find something for me, to give in trade."

"Well yeah, of course."

It was, in a way, an odd time for us to be exchanging gifts. My twenty-second birthday had occurred almost a week earlier. And Rachel's ninth, which landed near the middle of July, was more than a month away. But then, I figured it was *always* a good time for the two of us to give and receive.

Shaking my head in wonderment, I began scouting around for washed-up treasures. Eventually I found the prize: A perfectly preserved shell of a blue crab, just a tiny hole at the top of its head where a gull had probably poked in order to suck its insides like a salty, gooey cocktail.

Yes. Rachel was a Cancer. I cupped it in my hand and proffered it. "Will this do?"

I wasn't too worried about disappointing her. Tomboy that she was, she would no doubt be more interested in this particular find than she would have been with a more elegant conch shell, for instance.

"Sure!"

Then her hands reemerged; and she opened the left one to reveal a sight that tugged at old memories: A translucent, milky-white stone with orange in its heart, much like a tiny apricot sealed within a sanctuary of quartz.

"I brought this home from the playground one day after I saw you, and been keeping it," she explained. "When I told the other kids that you'd made a wish on it they let me keep it and didn't argue."

I shook my head, trying to dispel my sudden stunned bewilderment. "I know. I remember," I stammered. Was it possible that she actually *understood* its significance to me? "Do you have any idea how amazing you are?"

She just laughed, briefly, and blushed.

So we traded presents then, Rachel cupping her crab in both hands like it was a precious relic. I don't think it'd been dead long, as the shell and limbs were still somewhat moist and supple. I put my new agate in the pocket of my jeans and promised myself that I'd keep it forever.

We stole it from the trolls... It grants wishes.

Saul had taught me that the trolls were all in my mind. I was beginning to believe him.

So this was the night when Rachel would finally get to sit in at one of our rehearsals. I was still struggling to comprehend how Gail Friedman had actually been amenable to this, as it meant that I'd be bringing her adopted daughter home at ten at night, or possibly even later.

Rachel was quiet as I walked her down into The Catacombs, soaking up the sight and the damp, musty scents as if it was a dungeon from antiquity. "The guy who built this," I whispered, "had the idea that he could come down here and survive in the aftermath of a nuclear war or some such catastrophe like that."

Carlos and Tommy were already set up and laying down some grooves together. A joyous meeting ensued. Carlos, in particular, was always especially animate on the few occasions when he'd hung out with Rachel. So there they were, many of the people whom I loved most, gathered into a shadowed and claustrophobic space that we routinely transformed into our vessel of exploration, a submarine of the astral, with our music. My heart swelled with plentitude and the urge to play.

But before we began, I needed to address the other guys. I was nearly grinning from ear to ear as I showed them the stone Rachel had given me. It wasn't as awe-inspiring a sight as it could've been, in the pale light of the couple of lamps that we had turned on down there, but my own enthusiasm compensated for this. Carlos leaned over his drum kit, alight at both the spectacle and his recollection of the story behind it.

Tommy deliberated for a moment and then suddenly proclaimed: "That's gotta go on our album cover somewhere!"

Although she couldn't possibly have grasped the implications of all that was taking place around her, Rachel was, nonetheless, obviously enjoying her place in the spotlight. She smiled and twisted from side to side with delight.

"Well then, the title ought to relate to it somehow – eh, brothers?" Carlos said.

From there we launched into a debate about possible symbolism, metaphor and allusion. Rachel got to witness Edge of the Known's mental gears in motion firsthand.

The agate had originally evoked, for me, such phrases as The Light That Can't Be Extinguished and The Light That Never Left You. But we all felt that these were somehow overly lofty phrases to bestow upon an album containing a mere five songs. So we simplified things and settled, at first, upon "The Essence". Same essential (pardon the inevitable pun) significance in fewer words.

Carlos, meanwhile, had been intermittently glancing over at Rachel, who was still cupping the crab mummy that I'd salvaged for her. With the look of inspiration grown to fruition, he suddenly rose and approached her. "Hey, can I see that for just a moment?"

Rachel gladly obliged; and the two made the slow, gentle exchange.

"Come here, guys," Carlos bid us. "Brandon, bring that stone. Let's have a look at this!"

So we all crowded around Carlos as he first took the crab and positioned it in the center of one of his floor toms. Then he requested my agate. This he situated between the crab's claws, nudging them closer so that they seemed to clutch – or guard – it.

"What do you think?" he asked, with a smile of satisfaction.

The montage was rife with implications. I again thought of Rachel's astrological sign, Cancer, and its associated domesticity. Home. Within the context that we were exploring, 'home' and 'essence' and 'the undying light' all conveyed similar references to our spiritual origins. Then, of course, there was the symbolism of the shell itself – what is visible to the eyes of the world – 'guarding' the precious treasure that lies within it. And the agate had a 'coat' surrounding its colorful core. Layers within layers...

As Tommy and I nodded in joint eagerness - and Rachel gushed, "Oh! Cool!" – Carlos dug his phone out of his pocket. "Let me see if I can get a good picture of this!"

Tommy pulled one of the lamps closer and kept experimenting with different positions until Carlos got what he felt was his ideal light. He snapped four times.

Turns out one of the crab's legs had gotten separated from its body during all of this creative abandon. But we were nonetheless all ecstatic when we saw the resulting images.

"That's it!" Tommy said. "Edge of the Known – The Essence – with *that* for a visual."

"Cover image inspired by Rachel Chane!" Carlos added, winking at her.

We were all so exuberant, so enraptured by the free-flowing of new ideas, that we had to take some time to make small talk and ground ourselves before we were even able to play. Then Rachel took a seat on my amp (only to leap up again about twenty minutes later when it started getting hot) and we began.

My little sister was, of course, thrilled to learn that a song about *her* was going to be on our new EP. I couldn't look in her direction when we performed it, though. I was flushed with the kind of nervous adrenaline that you only get around people who really know and *see* you. Onstage, one can achieve a sort of detachment, sublimating one's ego within the music as it sweeps self-consciousness away. On the few occasions when I *did* glance over, her face was unreadable. I would have given a great deal to know what her thoughts were.

Then, throughout the drive home, the winds of mourning wailed in some deep caverns of my mind. I tried reasoning with them. Surely I'd be seeing Rachel again before too long, squeezing another couple of visits in before my departure. But the tour that Chas was putting together felt essentially different from our self-made excursion of the previous year. I couldn't shake the odd certainty that we would not, in any way, be returning to the life that we'd hitherto known. The notion carried notes of hope – glimmers of wild ecstasy, even – alongside loss. But I was beginning to realize that my oft-repeated assertion that I had "nothing to lose" was just an artifice intended to hold fear at bay, engender courage through illusion.

I played it cool, albeit not aloof, when I said good-bye to Rachel. I worried that anything approaching a raw display of the real emotions that were roiling inside me might frighten her.

15. The Road East

Well, all the shared enthusiasm that'd been stirred up at the rehearsal spilled over into new conversations, which eventually resulted in a final title change for our mini-album. Tommy initiated the process, speculating about all the coincidences in our lives that are really too uncanny to even be *called* coincidences. Then I voiced an idea that Saul had put forth to me, one that I'd now struggled for a couple of years to try and accept: Our experiences don't actually *come to us* from the world at all but are really woven from within us. Consciousness comes first, in all things. The world as it is perceived is essentially a mirror for the inner state of the perceiver.

There was actually much more that I wanted to share about this, thoughts that had been provoked by recent experiences, but it all seemed too delicate a matter – perhaps unfit for the rapid-fire style of our band discussions.

Anyhow, we phoned Chas at the end of all this and informed him that we had finally settled upon a name: Trust in the Unseen.

The clearest digital image that'd been captured on Carlos' phone still seemed to us an utterly appropriate one. When you think about it, *any* picture would be suitable for a title like that because the image that you see is, at the same time, dependent upon all that is *not* seen. Everything exists in relation: There are no isolated worlds or realities. A camera simply freezes one moment of the kaleidoscopic display in flux and then leaves you to speculate about past and future shadows that may be cast by that moment. Every picture not only *tells* a story but also evokes countless others – if you let it.

You might just be standing there in the photo with your blue graduation gown on, but that captured instant is, at the same time, poised in a reality within which it affects everything else. We tend to see ourselves as sitting, standing or lying at the very hub of the universe. And if what Saul says is correct, that we *are* the authors of this dream, then this sensation speaks truly. We are always at the hub of perception, the choice point from which our world is determined.

During this same conversation, Chas informed us that he'd booked thirteen solid dates for us on the East Coast, including a spot at the coveted showcase at Broomstick Belladonna's in New York. This was a scant number of gigs compared to our foray of the year before, but they were (for the most part) more prestigious. We were actually being advertised as a band that was generating a bit of a buzz in the West. There was a sense of curiosity, and anticipation, whereas before we'd simply shown up to play as near-complete unknowns.

"It begins mid-July, in Boston," Chas said, "and it's gonna take you several days to get out there. So basically you've got less than a month to settle your affairs."

He said that, and I felt the instinctive lash of mortal fright clawing at my insides. I just breathed and let it wash over and through me. It's called a leap of faith precisely because you can offer reason and logic nothing in the way of assurances beforehand. And "faith" was a word that religion had soured inside my psyche; but Saul had helped me arrive at a more expansive, and truer, definition. Belief in ourselves is the prerequisite for belief in anything else. We were, after all, Edge of the Known. It was time that we returned to our proper place on that potentially perilous frontier, peering forth into the unmapped Beyond.

"These gigs *are* our affairs, Chas," Tommy told him. "The rest of reality can attend to itself, as it always has."

Chas laughed in appreciation of our collective bravado. He was the veteran and visionary behind a punk band that had defied all the conventions of a movement that was supposed to be *devoid* of conventions. He knew that we were not making idle boasts. Hell, this was a major reason why he'd signed us in the first place.

"If you manage anything like what I've seen you do at Alchemist Brews," he said, "then you'll conquer them down to the last man, woman and child."

We all gave our employers our notice the following day, and told our landlady Megan that we'd pay through July but be vacating the premises even earlier. This was our token gesture, our demonstration of belief in the new paradigm that we were struggling to create. We were convinced that security of any sort would only entice us to grasp at what we were trying to transcend, to wax nostalgic about what rightfully belonged in the past.

We carried the gesture further by holding a weekend lawn sale, during which time we shifted obsolete equipment, records, books, furniture, clothing, posters and memorabilia to a throng of Sadenport bargain seekers. The entire time, we felt as avid to *shed weight* as we did to amass cash.

In the aftermath, we were left with about a week's worth of clothing apiece, our gear, maybe enough books between us to fill one shelf of a case, and a milk crate's worth of personal mementos. By the time July rolled around, my existence was austere even by *my* standards.

Adolescence is a time, for many of us, when something cracks open inside and our senses suddenly awaken to the perception of new worlds. My sense of the spiritual life – and I mean this as something distinctly separate from any religious concepts that I grew up with – really began there. Maybe that's why it was such a hard era to truly let go of. I missed the intensity of those times, and the prevailing sense that everything was in motion and nothing was certain. I guess the unpredictability of the road was the closest I could come to recapturing that sensation in my adult life.

And so at long last, we three were staring at a packed van and pondering our course. The house was bare and cleaned. I realized now that, comfortable as it'd been, I'd always thought of it as a transitional space – never a *home*. Once again, I was going to have to train myself to consider every environment that I found myself surrounded by as "home". Perhaps, like Saul insisted, it was a place that I carried *with* me and not an eventual destination at all.

Carlos, with his newly-reinstated license, took the wheel and got us onto I-80 E. We hoped to stay on this route for most of our journey east. The weather within my psyche shifted and swirled, painting the world in front of me, the world I was rushing to embrace, in alternately ominous and alluring hues. Evening brought rain; and I watched, from my shotgun position, as the sweep of the windshield wipers constantly enacted the erection and demolition of all my dreams.

By about nine o'clock we'd crossed over into Idaho. The skies had cleared, and we stopped at the nearest gas station to fuel the van and stock up on road rations.

The parking lot, in the lambency of the streetlights, looked recently paved. I'd no sooner stepped out than my phone began vibrating in my pocket. What the hell? Nobody ever called me…

Janie's name on the I.D. smote me to the very pit of my gut, from which the storms had already been issuing all night. Now they reached a crescendo. I wasn't ready; I couldn't *get* ready. There was nothing for it but to answer without allowing myself time to consider what I was doing.

Sapped by the old wound, my voice came out hollow and unsure. "Hello?"

"Hey. It's me. I just… I ran into Tommy the other day at the library…"

"Oh. He didn't tell me."

The conversation, such as it was so far, was so jagged and disjointed (no doubt due to our shared trepidation) that it couldn't get off the ground. But Janie pressed on like a trooper.

"Well, yeah, he just told me that you guys were going out on the road, playing some shows around Boston and New York, and I wanted to wish you luck."

The high point of our first tour, for me, had been reuniting with her for a brief time in New Mexico. Her presence had inspired me to expose myself to the audience in Albuquerque in a way that I'd never managed before. I paced around the van for a moment – the other guys were already inside the store. I felt immersed in the warmth that her voice often awoke inside my body. Then I decided to drown this sensation by having a smoke. I fished a cigarette out of my jean jacket pocket. Although I'd cut down quite a bit over the last year, I'd never managed to quit entirely. *Maybe if life ever give me a goddamn break!* I thought. Weak, I know.

A hard lump had formed in my throat, one that I couldn't speak past.

"So good luck," Janie said, in a voice brimming – almost to the point of spilling over – with all that lay unsaid between us. "When do you get back?"

"Uh, in like five or six weeks," I managed. "But I'm not sure where 'back' will be, exactly. We let go of the house we were living in. We're really just throwing our fates to the wind with this."

"You always were *brave*."

She gave that word peculiar emphasis, as if it was one that she'd been spending a lot of time thinking about of late. It seemed to have layers of significance: One meaning for her and an entirely different one for me.

"Or desperate!" I returned; and I almost chuckled despite the deep tremors of anguish.

"I think it's *courage*," she said, even more intently now. Then, after a pause: "Well, if you don't end up back in Sadenport then I do hope you call and let me know. I don't want to lose touch with you completely, all right?"

"Deal," I said. I was now anticipating the end of this conversation, and torn between the impulse to grasp for her and the longing for some reprieve from the unbearable tension.

"All right, then. Go bring your gospel to those thirsty souls."

"Thank you Janie." Even my own ears heard the echo of my heart's former warmth for her.

"You're welcome. Bye for now."

I was grateful that Carlos came out almost immediately and joined me. I craved *any* distraction. He was clutching a tall bottle of lemon iced tea. He nodded towards the quick stop.

"Tommy's got the rest of the stuff. They've actually got a great selection of metal magazines in there. Rare thing to find these days, bro. He's checkin' 'em out right now."

I latched on to his presence to help me detach my mind from the conversation that I'd just had. I took another drag. Then inspiration hit me, the memory of something that I'd wanted to bring up at our last rehearsal. I broached it now.

"I had this pretty uncanny phone conversation with Aunt Gail – Rachel's guardian – the other day," I said. I groped for the essence of my puzzlement. "She sounded *sympathetic*, in a way that she never had before with me."

"Were you being nicer than usual with *her*?" Carlos suggested.

I smiled. "Actually, yeah. But I feel like there was more to it than that. See, I've just been feeling so tired of having this animosity between myself and others. Saul told me over and over again that I perceive the world as my enemy. I really want to let that go. And I guess my way of doing that lately has been to insist on seeing everyone as a human being rather than as an obstacle in my path."

Carlos pursed his lips in thought. He was always fully *present* in a conversation; involved. He really heard you out, whereas so many others are just itching for their chance to speak. This quality made him one of my favorite people to talk to. It suddenly occurred to me that he and Tommy were *both* unusually good listeners. How lucky was I?

"Well, people can feel your attitude towards them, bro. And react to it. They'll hear it in your voice…"

I nodded in acknowledgment but cut in nonetheless. "I'm thinking something even deeper than that."

Carlos cast me a look that seemed to say that he half guessed what I was getting at but wanted to give me the space to articulate it for myself.

"Saul says that we're the authors of our lives," I elaborated. "You and I have both heard that a thousand times from him. And I've always found it hard to accept. Also, I've played this sort of mental game where I think that the rule applies to certain circumstances but not to others.

"But is it possible, Carlos, that if I hold to a different image of Gail in my mind, to a different feeling of her, that she becomes, like, a different person? That who she is actually changes, in my experience? Does it happen so literally like that? Because I swear I felt like that's what was going on."

He took a drink and then screwed his face into an exaggerated 'who the hell knows?' expression. "Like you say, it's hard to accept. But I do think that Saul means it literally. People have a lot of faces, you know? The one that they show *you* will depend upon your attitudes and beliefs. I think that's what he would say."

"Right," I acknowledged. "And then, no one is in our lives by accident in the first place. We've attracted everyone to us, for our own inner reasons."

Tommy came out then, holding a tall, stuffed paper bag in both hands. On the occasion of our first night out on the road he was dressed in gray leather pants, tall, pointy black boots and a long white shirt with fat buttons that reminded me of Celtic nobility. And of course, even in this heat, he still had on the trench coat (albeit unbuttoned) and leather cap.

"Reality is our own creation," I remarked when he reached us. "We've just decided."

Tommy accepted this with characteristic nonchalance. "Can I create a reality, then, wherein I ride shotgun now?"

I was amenable. "I'll drive for a bit – get us into Wyoming, at least."

We'd never actually *been* through Wyoming before. We'd done a gig in Salt Lake City, on our last tour, and followed it up with a performance in Denver a few days later. But we'd taken a 'scenic' route back then, driving south to the town of Salina and then cutting across on I-70 E.

We traveled mostly at night, we three nocturnal right-brained madmen. But from what I could descry through the general darkness, this was a rugged land, with its mountains of high chiseled grooves filled, in places, with snows that endured even the summers. We rolled down our windows and inhaled the kind of air that one associates with lofty and lonely heights. Then there were low hills, dreaming of peace beneath their blankets of heather, and flats that allowed for miles-long views of the moonlit straight road ahead of us. I quite forgot that we were embarked upon a tour, after a while, and let my reveries carry me to a mythical land somewhere out there beyond the final boundary of stark rock, where nature reigned in her own inviolate harmony.

We passed well over a hundred miles south of Yellowstone, a place I'd often fantasized about as a child; and as it turned out, our road skirted clear of all the major national forests in the state. There is always that war within the heart of the traveler, between the allure of the longed-for destination and the beauty of the myriad places in between – all of which, when you think about it, serve as the object of someone else's most cherished dream in this vast world.

My solution to this particular paradox, as with so many others, was always the same: Keep *moving*.

Many leagues now lay between me and my troubled father; and the lost, desperate young people who projected upon me their need for clarity and solace in this confused world; and the woman who I had lost, but who somehow still held my heart clenched in her fist.

Some part of me felt strongly pulled back towards Oregon, where so much was unresolved. Perhaps that was my problem – the belief that there had to *be* resolution.

"Is that part of the Dionysian thing that you talk about?" I asked Tommy. By this time he was across from me at the wheel. "You allow that there will always be the element of chaos within life? You don't try to control it?"

He formed a wry smile. If my question had caught him off guard, he didn't show it.

"Yeah – don't waste energy, either mental or physical, in trying to put the universe in order. It already is. Just give yourself over to the inherent madness of the moment." He glanced over at me. "But you don't need *me* to tell you. You take that even more in stride than I do."

Carlos leaned forward, looking intent. "Saul says that our souls, in this universe, are eternally safe. But in order that we can have our adventures in the world, we use our minds to convince ourselves that we are *never* safe. So we strive, and learn, and grow."

I nodded, soaking this in. His words just made me miss Saul all the more.

"And yet Dionysus doesn't care for that one way or the other!" Tommy shouted back. "Safety or non-safety. This life that we know, that we identify with now, could be obliterated at any moment. So let's live in the ecstasy of this time, however we find it. That's the principle. 'Be drunken ceaselessly', as Baudelaire put it."

And with that, I slowly began to give myself over to the intoxication of the road, as the sore patches upon this Earth retreated behind. There would always be the music within which to dissolve myself and my troubles.

We eventually pulled into the parking lot of a 24-hour grocery store, where we shared the space with some half-dozen other vehicles. This was about an hour after the sun began to rise over the small Great Plains town. We'd turned off a road that was bordered on its far side by a high green mound, featureless save for a single radio tower at its peak. The day was inching towards cheery yellow calm; and I regretted having to miss the majority of it.

Normal life began to stir and quicken all around us as I stuffed earplugs into my ears and found a space where I could lay with nothing between my face and the van's steel wall. I was too sensitive to sound and vibration to ever sleep in the middle, a fact that the other guys forgave me for. Carlos could probably curl up and snooze on an airport runway if he made up his mind to do it, so it all worked out. In fact, the zeal with which he abandoned himself to sleep was my major reason for bringing the earplugs.

We just hoped that within an hour or two the spaces around us would fill in and our presence wouldn't elicit any comment.

The world let me go slowly. I was ambivalent about both realities, unready to fully relinquish one or embrace the other. I ached for the stage, for the catharsis of distorted chords and volume and the release of screams. But finally I forgot to worry, to count my sorrows and my fears, long enough for dreams to reach up and pull me under.

16. A World with No Adversary

Another couple of hours saw us crossing over into Iowa, with a fair bit of sunlight still holding overhead. Traffic was languid, the road smooth, and the other guys' spirits running high. For a moment I got lost in selfish introspection and envied them for their 'simplicity'. Then I quietly chastised myself. What did I really know of their personal battles, or of the inner fortitude that might have enabled them to laugh in the face of it? *Carlos is a recovering hard drug addict, for Christ's sake!* Seriously – I was going to begrudge them any of the good cheer that they were able to wrest from this world?

So I relinquished my judgments; and yet I still felt almost anxious for night to roll over. I craved the anonymity of darkness, the hypnotic pulse of passing car lights and median reflectors, the monotony of American twilight. I ate and read poetry while the sun endured, letting Tommy and Carlos, who occupied the front seats, carry the conversation.

Tommy drove this stint. At about four in the morning he announced: "There's a sign here for a rest stop ahead. Twelve miles. Might be our best chance."

We decided to take it, figuring that the couple extra hours of travel that we might otherwise squeeze out wouldn't be worth the uncertainty of finding sleep at the end of it.

If you travel often enough, particularly in the dead of night, these truck stops end up looking all the same. Same dead white glow from the high street lights, glaring at a little oval green and a building with some restrooms and (during its open hours), maybe historical plaques and brochures and water fountains. At the same time, these areas form the hub of the spiritual life of the road. Here travelers can meet and tell of their adventures, thereby adding to the myth of the great wide expanse. And here your thoughts of the journey thus far finally have a chance to catch up with you.

But most importantly, they allow you to get out, stretch and move. Carlos and I made two laps around the green while Tommy smoked. I noticed that there was another vehicle in the dim space, a high, bulky truck as dark as the tree shadows that it was set back within. I tried to jog quietly, lest I disturb possible sleepers in there.

After the other guys returned from their business I took my turn in the bathroom. I only had to piss, so I walked up to one of the two standing urinals that were set a couple of feet apart. I'd hardly unbuttoned my jeans and gotten started before another figure stepped up, with a heavy tromp of boots, to the stall to my right.

Yeah, I was well aware of the public restroom etiquette that says you must stare straight ahead and pretend that you're all alone in the universe until you empty your bladder. I always hated conventions, though, particularly those that had grown out of social anxiety and knee-jerk fear. I almost instinctively pushed their boundaries whenever I encountered them. Also I was irrepressibly curious, nearly as much as a child. So, while the last bit of tinkle was still working its way out, I couldn't help but glance over and see who I might be sharing this ritual of ablutions with.

Every part of his wide face was either pale or deep red, particularly beneath the fluorescent lights. He had a bunched, muscular jaw that probably didn't allow his lips to part into smiles all too often. I reckoned he was in his mid-forties. And just my luck… I don't know if he was moved by the same curiosity, or if he sensed my attention, but he glanced over simultaneously – and our eyes met.

Apparently this occurrence was - from his point of view, at least, - cause for horror. He bit down so hard that he seemed to redden even more from constricted blood flow. Embarrassment and outrage carried out a fierce turf war behind his eyes.

"Thought you were one of my buddies – sorry!" I said quickly. Then I buttoned up and dashed out of there – making some effort not to look *too* obvious – without even washing up.

A few minutes later I was standing by the van and smoking a cigarette to calm my nerves. Tommy was pacing, occasionally lifting his knees chest-high to stretch, and Carlos was doing push-ups on the sidewalk.

I saw the man who I'd encountered in the restroom: He was marching towards the truck on the other side of the lot with the air of a man in uniform with orders to *keep the peace.* Premonitions curled around themselves within the pit of my stomach. An unseemly vibration wove through this conjunction of time and space; my very hairs seemed to be picking it up, like antennae; they twitched at the reception. Any fighter knows when violence is in the air. I was hardly even surprised when four men emerged from the pickup truck and stomped straight towards us.

Tommy looked merely curious; but Carlos seemed to pick up the same perilous vibe as me. Being the eternal peacemaking diplomat, he stepped out in front of us, ready to toss water on this fire. Somehow I knew that this was my battle, though, and I couldn't let him stand on the front lines of it. I laid a placating hand on his shoulder and then stepped past him.

All four guys stopped a few paces from me; and I noticed that the one I already knew held himself back a bit from the others. He pointed a bony finger in my direction.

"That there's the fucker! He tried to take a peek at my dick while I was pissin'!"

They were all dressed conservatively: Overalls or suspenders, jeans or khakis, flannel shirts one and all. As I looked these men over, I didn't sense any deep acquaintance with the ruthless side of life. I imagine they were some good 'ole boys who might've met one another on bowling league nights.

But fear can do strange things to a man, particularly fear that fails to recognize its own underlying source. And so it was with the one who had his arm extended in my direction. He seemed, somehow, almost unhinged by a phantom of his imagination.

"I thought you were one of these guys," I lied once more, continuing my line from the bathroom. "It was an accident."

"Accident my ass! You were peeking over and then you were makin' eyes at me, goddamn *faggot*!"

One of his buddies started rolling up his sleeves.

"You don't want this," I informed them all.

Tommy, who himself constituted a veritable wall with his arms folded across his chest, stood now on my left flank. He kept his peace, though, perhaps intuiting that his *silence* would be more ominous than anything he actually said. I harbored no doubts that we were a match for these guys. All three of us were capable of doling out some serious physical consequences, outnumbered by a man or no. But I didn't want to land a single blow. I understood, in that moment, something that Saul had tried to impress upon me for a long time: I dealt *myself* every ounce of hurt that I ever inflicted upon another.

I blinked, shaking myself out of my personal epiphany, and realized that my antagonist had brandished an aluminum baseball bat that he'd thus far kept concealed under his coat.

"What the *fuck*, man?"

"It'll just be one less lecherous faggot!" he babbled. I saw hysteria in those eyes. "No one'll know, and no one will miss you!"

"Well, except that there's two witnesses right here," I hissed through my shock, "and I happen to know for a fact that you don't actually want to kill *me*, much less all three of us."

He wavered then; and while he did so, I bent down and pulled my hunting knife out of my boot. I was in the habit of keeping it there during my travels since our encounter with the guys from Ashur. It was in its leather sheath. A couple of the guys started as I tossed it, perhaps thinking it a grenade. It landed close to the homophobic bat-wielder's feet.

"No matter what you decide to do," I stated, "I'll die when and how I choose to. But if you really think that you're the man to do the deed then use that. Easier for you and quicker for me."

I'll never know what prompted these words, or what enabled me to utter them with such unshakeable inner equilibrium. I recall that I meant everything that I said, though, utterly. I knew that I was done with giving myself over to violence towards anyone. I'd renounced it before my brain even verbalized the pact; and so I recognized, almost in hindsight, a transformation that had already occurred in me.

It must have happened by slow degrees, steps too insignificant to be marked day by day. I don't know how to retrace them, to recount the myriad inner 'eurekas' and subtle movements of remorse, forgiveness and love that finally added up to this crucial renunciation. But it was over. That answer would no longer serve. If there were other solutions available then I would find them. If not, I would suffer. Either way, I wasn't going to fight fire with fire ever again. My life had been twisted away from its natural courses by the lie that says, "One must fight for self-preservation." The biggest victim of my own violence had always been myself.

My 'adversary' was so bewildered by this point that he forgot to even hold his bat upright.

"Well?" I said, still sounding furious despite my conviction. Emotion is oftentimes the last to listen to resolutions. "There's no art in this. It's the most cliché fucking thing in the world. There's millions of people on this goddamn trip, and all just because none of them have ever been able to come up with a better idea. Well, I'm done with it. If you want this fight you've got it. But I tell you, it's gonna be one-way. It's all on *you*."

By now it was quiet enough for one to hear every bend of knee and shift of posture. My friends and I were scarcely breathing.

"He's fucking psycho!" the guy barked at last.

Perhaps that was the only frame of reference within which he could put all the illogical movements of this night. He said nothing more, but just turned sideways and indicated, to his buddies, the direction of their truck with a swift snap of his head. They all filed out; and only on a couple of occasions did anyone spare a backwards glance our way. My knife still lay where it'd landed. I walked over and retrieved it.

My senses were tuned to a pristine pitch, nearly pushing against the edges of the world, where all must give way to the dream dimension that birthed it. I could almost feel the river of time's passage, hear the birth of moments.

When I got back the other guys were still holding their same positions, digesting this tumultuous and strangely beautiful crisis. Finally, Tommy said: "Well, I suppose that's *one* way of handling it."

Carlos whistled in disbelief as he watched their truck disappear down the shadowed road.

The very human reactions of my two closest friends made me realize how shook up I really was. Emotional responses that had been temporarily swept aside in my leap of transcendence began to announce themselves. I clutched my torso to still the sudden tremors.

Saul had once warned me that a time could come when I'd find myself thinking and behaving completely at odds with my own sense of who I was. "Your definition of spiritual transformation - how you envision it unfolding, what you think it means - is bound to change as you grow," he'd said. "That's the irony. You start out with a certain goal in mind and then the path alters your very desires and values. You may no longer want what you wanted at the onset.

"It can be a very bewildering experience when your values, beliefs and sense of identity all shift in mid-stream. Life becomes a moment-to-moment matter of 'Who am I?' and 'What is real?'"

"I think," I pronounced, "that I'm gonna need to be alone for a little while."

Well, we ended up having to fly out of there in the pre-dawn. I'll tell you how this was precipitated. I went back into the restroom – probably the last place I should have revisited at the moment – for privacy. And there my underlying outrage, fear, anger and confusion caught up with me. I grabbed the top of the green toilet stall with both hands and tried to give this upheaval an outlet. Then I turned to the sink and attempted the same thing there. Unfortunately, I managed to tear it from the wall with a dozen spasms of fury. Panting, and on the edge of weeping, I watched the ceramic fixture tip and droop like a downcast face. Though it didn't completely fall, it was nonetheless rendered useless.

I tried to soothe myself. This was an inanimate object. Sure, the act that'd caused this destruction had been aggressive. And someone was going to bear the cost of what I'd done. I wasn't entirely without guilt and misgivings. But by the personal standards that I'd so long lived by, this was progress. I hadn't vented my rage with my fists on a living, feeling man's body. The guy who'd confronted me was unharmed. He was free to go and face the consequences of his own hate – or not. I was free to work through my own sense of powerlessness and the anger that it spawned. What lay in the balance was a little bit of property damage. So long, Nebraska. I'm real sorry. Maybe we'll make reparations by coming back someday to play a benefit gig...

Tommy was continuing his stint at the wheel. "Pulled the sink right out of the wall, huh?" he mused. "Still... I'm surprised stuff like that doesn't happen on a weekly basis in places like that."

We'd decided, to hell with rest stops of any kind, from here on. We had three capable drivers among us. There was no reason to park the van for anything other than bathroom breaks and purchases of food, cigarettes and coffee. We could sleep in shifts until we got to Boston. And personally, I was too shook up by my recent brush with mortality to even *consider* sleeping.

"I don't wanna talk about it anymore," I murmured. "Goddamn it! I don't want to leave this life feeling like I did more damage and harm than I did good during the time that I was here."

Carlos, from the back, leaned forward and gripped my shoulder.

"That's certainly not the case with *me*, bro," he said. "And I'm sure Tommy here would say the same thing. You just take all those times that you lost control or acted out and give them a bigger place in your memory. You forget those thousand other little positive things."

"If you were actually a prick," Tommy surmised, "then I wouldn't be in a band with you. Simple as that."

Remorse just says, 'don't do that again'. Saul's words emerged in that moment to soothe me. Yes: It neither demanded nor even implied punishment. I managed to smile for my friends, just for their being there.

In time, as the miles raced beneath and behind our wheels, my angst began to subside, to be more fully replaced by a sense of victory – or satisfaction, at least. I'd proved to myself that I was able to act from someplace other than my familiar 'default' position. And I began to question how many other assumptions, equally erroneous beliefs, I might be carrying around with me like dusty dead debris in my mind. Saul's artistry was to lift the stones and expose such skulking creatures. Might I not be capable of the same sort of excavation on my own?

After we stopped at a salad buffet for our first healthy meal thus far on this road trip, and returned (highly caffeinated) to change positions on the van once more, I settled in the back seat with my notebook. While Carlos got us back onto I-80 E and pushed us into Illinois, I began writing down bits of my own internal dialogue whenever I could catch it. If I noticed my imagination tugging me towards feelings of gloom and despair, I tried to identify what I'd been thinking beforehand. I isolated the unspoken assumptions, let them roll around in my head for a while, questioned them. I could feel how my thoughts and emotions were linked. Black moods and rage-filled episodes didn't just "come over me". They had always been generated somehow by my own internal monologue.

I felt the kind of excitement that often accompanies the discovery of an unforeseen new way forward. Was this the trail back to the sources of all my misery, frustration and overall dearth of hope? In a way it was. At the same time, though, I was daunted by the *immensity* of the mind and all that its vast corridors held. How could I possibly ever sift through the near-endless strands of thought that I'd used to weave my life?

Once more, I felt the keen pang of Saul's absence. But it was from him that I had first heard of the unseen source. If *it* really held the answers to all of my questions then all I had to worry about was how to be clear with my own intentions, right?

I nodded out, with pen in hand and notebook in my lap, an hour or two later. Nearly three pages had been filled with the fruits of my self-analysis. When I awoke, my first sight was of Tommy at the wheel and what looked to be late-afternoon sun filtering through the windows.

Via the overhead mirror, he acknowledged my waking. "We've put Chicago east of us," he announced. "You slept through a view of Lake Michigan, but it wasn't much on account of the hanging clouds anyway. I'm bound and determined to get us to Akron, Ohio in one run. We'll need to gas up by then, though. And stock up on some more food."

I gazed out over the alternating brown and green flats, broken up in places by fingers of deciduous forest, the trees filled out now in their summer prime. For a moment I felt lazy and content; and I marveled at the sensation. Then I voiced my insight as it occurred to me.

"When I was writing earlier... it hit me that I don't have to feel like I'm at the mercy of my own ideas. I mean, what in the world is there to fear if I trust and don't fear *myself*?"

"You proved that at the truck stop in Nebraska," Tommy responded at once. "If the Brandon I once knew had made an appearance there, *somebody* could've ended up dead."

Carlos looked over at him and smirked. "That's a hell of a way to make a point!"

Tommy just curled his lips. "Sometimes the best way to encourage yourself to keep moving forwards is to remind yourself of where you started from."

I didn't want to follow that line of thought at the moment, though. Even fleeting glimpses of *where I'd come from*, that nest of webbed darkness, gave me icy soul shudders. And yet... my efforts to steer away from self-reflection only landed me in territory just as troubling.

"But see, the guy who taught me how to move through all this is struggling with his own crisis of belief. What does *that* mean? Is the faith that I think I'm finding just another comforting illusion?"

"Look," Tommy shot back, "you don't know what Saul's challenges *are*. You don't know what kind of learning he came into this world to do – he *or* his wife. There's no end to it, once any of us start making comparisons. It's best to just not start down that road."

"If you *feel* faith inside, then it's real," Carlos added. He maneuvered around to face me. "It's funny, isn't it – those habits that we have? Most of us are so willing to accept any kind of negative expectation as truth. But when a positive sort of belief starts stirring in us we're quick to question it, doubt it."

On one level, what he said made absolute sense. But Saul's hardships had really undermined my morale. I realized in that moment how monstrous was my need for a hero, for someone in my life to be more-than-human – transcendent.

"That's the real irony of this whole thing," I murmured. "Our band, our whole quest to bring our music out into the world… So many people look to musicians to serve as their guiding voices in the wilderness. Look at those guys from Ashur, treating us like we were fucking gods of the underworld. And meanwhile, I'm wishing that somebody could be the voice for *me*."

The other guys made no response to that, maybe because they heard echoes in it of their own unresolved conflicts. I drifted back to my notes while the light lasted, but I didn't feel so avid during the second round. I suppose my consciousness was just saturated enough with self-disclosure for the moment.

We got out in Akron during a downpour and sprinted into a sleek quick stop for provisions. Once stocked up, we stood beneath the roof eaves, facing the pumps, and watched the fat drops fall while Tommy and I smoked. Rainfall had a way of making the world feel small, and this could be a discomforting sensation for me when I was in a strange place that I had no reason to believe I'd ever see again. Apparently the road only truly exercises its therapeutic effect upon me while I was in motion.

"How far to Boston now?" I asked.

Carlos was the map reader, but Tommy had a better understanding of distances and mileage. They conferred for a minute. Then Tommy said: "If we're prepared to keep going straight on, and nothing delays us, then we could be there sometime tomorrow morning."

This snapped me back to the reality that we'd soon be playing again, before virgin audiences. While we were shooting the shit there, and finishing our smokes, we speculated about what our potential new manager might be like.

"Maybe this Maureen can put us up for a day so we can catch up on sleep and get showers," Carlos said.

"That reminds me," Tommy said. "One of us should call Chas here, pretty soon, and warn him that we'll be getting into the city earlier than we'd originally thought."

I watched as his face evinced signs of that memento being filed away in one of the file cabinets of his mind.

"I just hope that she's cool and that it works out," I said. "I really do. Then we can just concentrate on the music and let someone else make the deals. That's the way it should be anyway. Nobody asks their plumbers if they've produced any transcendental poetry lately, and yet somehow we artists are supposed to master this whole separate world of business on top of our art."

A few minutes later our luck turned and the rains abruptly ceased. I took advantage of the respite and went for a run, for probably twenty minutes, down the puddled sidewalks in the semi-dark. I ended up grateful for this activity, and for the fact that I'd gulped down some strong coffee beforehand, because I proceeded to hammer the pedal for a solid nine hours (minus bathroom breaks) after that. I saw us through Pennsylvania, a patch of New Jersey and then all the way to Milford, Connecticut.

We arrived there at a magical hour, as the sun was just beginning to stretch her fingers over the Atlantic Ocean, creating sparkles like the dance of a troupe of pixies over the waves. We rolled slow over a freshly-paved street that ran parallel to the beach and breathed in the sight. I'd seldom beheld sweeter azure than within that arc of sky that leaned protectively over the sea and her brood of white sailboats.

Aching for a stretch, we parked and got out. An old man apparently dressed for a day out on a golf course, brown leather cap on his head that somewhat resembled Tommy's, sat on a green bench by the stairs, looking out. He turned to gaze at us with open curiosity.

"Three days on the road!" I gushed. "We need to *move* these legs!"

He grinned and then turned back towards the wide ocean, pointing. "Tide's still going out," he mentioned. "Will be at its peak low in about an hour or so. Perfect timing. You can take the path all the way to that island there – Charles' Island – and have plenty of time to get back, if you leave now."

"You're kidding me!"

I conferred with the other guys; but we were, of course, of one mind on this matter. "Thanks for the tip!" I called out to the old guy, as we made our way down the stone steps 'til we reached the sand, pebbles, dry seaweed and salty air of the beach at low tide.

Many people will say that when you're out on the open road, nothing can catch up with you. I've made that assertion myself. But during this most recent stretch of driving – the most that I'd done the entire trip – I'd discovered that quite the opposite was true for me. The more miles I put between me and Sadenport, the more the souls of those whom I loved there – Rachel, Saul, June, Janie, even Robert Chane – seemed to tug at me, call me back.

But now that I was immersed in the low sloshing of waves rolling over fudge-colored sandbars, the peel of gulls overhead - seeing them scatter before us only to quickly find nearby beachheads where they could regroup - I was finally able to elude my personal phantoms. And once we were on the rocky path, momentarily unveiled by the ebbing waters - and wide enough for maybe six people to walk abreast - I seemed to leave the known world entirely. It was a journey with Biblical connotations, even for someone as religiously unidentified as myself. And the island itself beckoned like a half-recalled sanctuary sprung out of my childhood dreams.

We made some brief exclamations of our wonder and joy. But aside from that, we scarcely talked. We felt the tremendous marshalled power of nature – here in her mightiest bastion, the ocean – to both sides of us, and were utterly humbled.

When we attained the edges of Charles' Island we picked our way amongst the veritable reefs of washed-up shells, sponges and seaweed. Further inland, bushy trees waved in the warm breeze. I turned and surveyed the mainland that we'd left behind.

My reaction was compulsory, a commanding joy. With such eagerness that my hands fumbled at the laces, I undid my boots and removed them, took one in each hand.

"The sea, she demands a sacrifice!" I cried. And with that, I hurled each boot in turn so that it arced up and out, to be swallowed by the beatific and wild waters that cradled the shores of our newfound oasis.

17. Maureen

Afterwards, back on the mainland, we hung out by the stairs as Tommy made some phone calls. First he got Chas on the line, and repeated the directions to Maureen's house out loud so that I could take them down in my notebook. From what I could make of it, Chas' voice sounded thoroughly pragmatic, coming from a universe fundamentally removed from road fatigue, displacement and island epiphanies.

Carlos and I then took a walk while Tommy phoned Maureen, so I missed the minutes of that particular conversation. When we got back, though, he was smiling and shaking his head in semi-amazement.

"Well, I tell you what," he marveled. "She loves us. I almost felt like I was talking to a groupie rather than a potential manager."

My mind warmed and bounced to that revelation. But I stowed the reaction away in order to pursue a more practical point.

"Can we stay with her?"

"Well, she's got *space*," Tommy said, "and she's thrilled to have us. But we'll be sleeping on the floor - or, you know, fighting over the one couch."

"So, nothin' we're not used to," I summarized, while Carlos nodded his agreement.

"And Boston's not too far from here, right?" he said. "We can probably be there early evening? I'll drive the last leg."

I was feeling eager, now, for a place to land. And the fact that Maureen might prove to be an empathetic soul helped me to unwind. The drive was grueling due to our poor timing, hitting rush-hour traffic outside of Hartford at about four-thirty. In this way, we ended up paying for our excursion out to the island. But the trip was just a little over four hours for all that; nothing compared to my marathon of the night before. Carlos was, perhaps, not the ideal candidate to navigate Boston on account of his becoming newly-reacquainted with driving. The city's grid, if one could be content in calling it that, had obviously been made up as they went along. Either that or it was a deliberately diabolical labyrinth designed to torment visitors. And if you missed any crucial turn - like we did, twice – God knows when you'd find an opportunity to get back on course again.

"To hell with this!" I grated – my way of expressing some sympathy to Carlos. "If I lived here I'd just sell my car and take the transit everywhere."

My vehicle, incidentally, was at that moment sitting alongside Tommy's on Saul's lawn, kept company by rusted engine debris of yesteryear.

"I wonder if it might not come to that," Tommy mused from the back. "If we end up with a manager who lives here, and signed to a label that's based somewhere in the vicinity, then it may well be time for us to relocate."

And this brought us back around to the looming shadow of our uncertain future. I let the fear wash over me, refusing to either fight it or try to explain it away. No thoughts arose to offer comfort or resolution. Was "do or die" the only possible answer to the riddle of my existence, at every juncture? From whence did security come? Victory? Peace?

No matter. I had my Muse; and She would travel with me to any corner of this Earth.

"I'm itchin' to plug in so bad," I breathed. "It's been too long."

"Two days!" Tommy called back. "We're booked at The Hangman night after tomorrow."

I nodded in semi-satisfaction. While performing couldn't offer me any permanent answers, per se, it did enable me to depart to a mental and spiritual plane where the questions themselves no longer plagued me.

"It's a known venue for Metal, I guess," Carlos added, "so who knows, we may find an appreciative crowd there."

By this time we were passing through the dim and spectral yellow womb of one of Boston's tunnels. His eyes and brain operating swift as a hawk's, Carlos espied our exit and made for it. He had to cut perilously close to a car behind – inciting the driver's wrath and a heavy lean on the horn – to do it.

"Jesus!" he grunted. "You have to be *cutthroat* to even get around this place!"

"This is the most horn-happy town you're liable ever to visit, from what I've heard," Tommy consoled him. "Don't take it personally."

Maureen lived in an apartment in Jamaica Plain that faced, across four lanes of road, the resplendent beauty of Arnold Arboretum with its collection of trees from all far-flung climes.

When we got there, she was standing in her driveway, eagerness apparent in her very posture. I guessed that she was about forty, a brunette with the energy and freshness of a young lady just entering college. Maureen was dressed in faded jeans and a black sweater, and her thick curled hair was bound back in a green scarf, lending her a gypsy air.

She jogged alongside and began talking even as we were still rolling up to park. "You guys find me o.k.?"

Tommy leaned forward to speak out the front passenger window. "Oh, yeah. I figure Boston's gotta be befuddling to anyone who doesn't know it – maybe even for a lot of people who *do* – but your directions were great."'

"Well, I've got chicken kabobs on the grill!" she announced. I could see them smoking on the small red deck that extended from the side door of her building. Apparently this was a duplex. It had no upper floor.

"That sounds great!" Carlos enthused.

"Yeah, I figured you guys would be sick of road food by now."

And this was as far as we got by way of making formal introductions. Maureen just took it for granted that we knew who *she* was, and she got to know our names sporadically as we ate and talked. As versed as she was in our recording, this didn't take much doing. It was a simple matter of connecting new faces to names that she already knew.

I'd consumed very little in the way of vegetables for almost a week, so the grilled green peppers, onions and mushrooms, all cut thick, tasted scrumptious.

Afterwards, as twilight descended and the hiss of traffic formed a lulling backdrop to our conversation, Maureen fetched four glasses from inside and opened up a bottle of champagne. After toasting and taking her first sip, she finally got around to discussing the topic that obviously burned inside her: Our music.

"So, I've listened to your CD, like, a couple dozen times!" she gushed. "And I've been *dying* to hear the EP. Chas wouldn't send it to me; he said I had to be patient until you guys showed up. *Please* tell me you've brought copies!"

"We have," Tommy deadpanned.

"Let me go get it right now!" Carlos offered.

And then, suddenly, I felt alone with Maureen, as Tommy drifted to the other end of the deck and gazed at the shadowed gate of the Arboretum.

Maureen, carried on by her own inner rapture, continued as if there'd been no shift at all in the personal dynamics. "So, I've seen and heard a lot of bands that were reacting to *something*. You know, they rail against politics, or corporations, the rape of the Earth, whatever. And I definitely see the value in that, don't get me wrong. There's got to be people out there – preferably really *loudmouthed* people – who are a thorn in authority's side. But what you're doing... it isn't reactionary in that way. And yet it's not escapism either. These songs of yours... it's like you're not so much offering answers as that you're trying to get people to ask different *questions*."

I took a sip of champagne to purchase myself a moment in which to think. Her observation was both astute and thoroughly unexpected. "Huh. I never thought of it in that way. But yeah, I can see it now that you mention it. I guess I always felt like I was asking questions that no one else was. It's easy to find yourself frustrated with *what is*. Finding a new vision of how things *could* be, that takes more effort."

"That's real *art*," Maureen put in.

Her enthusiasm somewhat embarrassed me. "So yeah, thank you," I muttered.

She waved a hand. "Don't thank me – I'm not saying it out of charity. There's seriously maybe a *handful* of bands that have ever rocked my world like you guys have. 'What Casts the Shadow' blew my mind."

Carlos had returned by this point; and he and Tommy flanked me, facing Maureen, as if they sensed that she was reaching a crucial pitch.

And apparently she was. "I'd *really* like to manage you guys, if you'll have me. I won't make a bit of money off of it until you do. I just want to help expose your music to the widest audience possible."

I finished my glass. Here's the thing, man: I was a slow burner. Passionate, yes; but I liked to stir it up to a steady flame first. Maureen was forcing me to move at an unaccustomed speed.

"God... I knew it was coming, but I didn't expect you to pose the question so *quick*."

Maureen held her ground. "It's my way to be forthright. I hate to sound trite, but, life *is* short. Besides, I'd be kicking myself for a long time to come if somebody else snatched you guys up first."

"You've managed bands before?" Carlos asked, coming to my rescue with a practical question.

"Two," she said. "Well, one band and one solo performer. And not to toot my own horn here, but I was the one to score you guys the gig at Broomstick Belladonna's in New York. I've got as good an ear for the street buzz as any music fan out there. And then, if you ever attract label interest I can think like a lawyer on your behalf."

Tommy had been quiet this whole time, no doubt maneuvering through a stream of inner calculations that couldn't be verbalized until he hit pay dirt. Me, I resorted to the only thing that I knew how to do when faced with unknown variables: I followed my gut instinct.

"You *believe* in us," I said. "That means a hell of a lot to me."

Maureen smiled. "That's the main part of what I do. I won't take on a band that I don't *like*. And if I pass on one that goes on to sell a million records I still won't regret my decision. I'm in this for the music. And you guys *have* the music!"

Her grin widened. "I'll go open another bottle while you guys think about it." And with that, she pushed the screen door aside and disappeared.

We looked to one another at once. Tommy spoke first.

"Enthusiasm can be a double-edged sword. Sometimes a person in that position can have too much of a vested interest, have too many of his or her own ideas about the direction that a band should be heading in." Perhaps anticipating a possible protest from me, he rushed on. "I'm not saying that's the case with *her*. My instincts say she's trustworthy. But I'm just putting the idea out there."

I shook my head. We'd wandered into terrain where I felt like I had no secure footing. *Feeling* your way through reality is all very well, as a general strategy, but it becomes infinitely more complicated and uncertain when your whole emotional landscape is riddled with landmines of pain.

"I don't know *what* to make of this, really," I said. "I've been too scattered and just, like, mentally numb to grapple with the world of facts." I was rambling on about things they already knew; but reiterating it all steadied me somehow. "But then, that's kind of the point. It'd be a relief to let someone else do the thinking and planning so that we can just focus on the music."

"What about going into it on a trial basis?" Carlos offered. "We let her *act* as manager to the extent that she wants to – say, for the duration of our tour out here – and we just don't sign anything for the time being, no formal contract."

When Maureen returned we all took a moment to toast and drink. Then we presented our open-trial-period proposal to her.

She was almost laughing in her eagerness. "Look," she said, "that's all I'm asking for anyway. Just give me a chance. We don't have to sign *anything*. Just take some time and see what I can do for you before you consider somebody else, is all I ask."

"We don't actually know any other managers," Tommy acknowledged.

"If I have my way then that's the way it'll stay," Maureen said, with a merry twinkle in her eye. "You guys ought to know this business by now. It doesn't always attract the most upstanding types of people with the noblest of motives."

"No, it doesn't," I muttered.

For some reason my gaze wandered down to my feet then, and I saw the bits of sand from Charles' Island still clutching at the spaces between my bare toes. I thought about my old boots, past their prime of life anyway, sunk into a deep salt water drop-off where the shifting tides probably had them half submerged into the ocean floor by now.

Maureen, following the line of my sight, cracked a grin. "Perhaps my first order of business should be to find you some serviceable footwear?"

I won the coin toss for the couch, and I slept beneath the slow breath and peaceful emanations of two jade plants and one spider plant. I'd spent some time beforehand idly wondering why someone as attractive and vivacious as Maureen was without a man in her life; but I suppose she filled the void with floral companions. Each of the windows on the opposite end of the room were kept company by a trio of plants as well. I awoke with the vague sense that I had dreamed of being a chameleon that crawled in and out of the various pots in search of insects. "I" the lizard had ended up having to settle for some droplets of water.

Maureen continued to woo us with good food that morning: Giant egg, mushroom, peppers and cheese omelets with heaps of hash browns.

"Let's pretend to be undecided, so she keeps cooking for us!" Carlos chided, loud enough so she could hear from the kitchen. Maureen giggled.

About twenty minutes later, as we were finishing our plates, she said: "So you probably ought to set up in the living room and rehearse for a while today, don't you think? So you don't go out to the gig totally cold tomorrow?"

We were, of course, amenable, especially as she seemed confident that it wouldn't aggravate her neighbors so long as we did it in the afternoon. Maureen ended up watching almost the entire rehearsal; and she was laughing with delight and bouncing in response to every number.

"Oh!" She gushed at one point. "There is this truly great thing that rock'n'roll can be, but we so rarely get to experience it. This indescribable magic... oh, we must respect and honor it when it comes! And it's here! You guys *have it!*"

This was also the occasion upon which we discovered that our prospective manager *loved* to smoke grass. She confessed that she oftentimes would suck down a joint before she even got around to coffee or breakfast. I was tempted, at first, to attribute her lofty and oft-times elliptical praise to this very fact. But as you get to know Maureen you realize that her manner of speaking never changes much one way or the other, intoxicated or sober – although she *did* settle into a calmer and more free-floating state of mind when she was high.

And she, for her part, was astounded to learn that afternoon that none of us cared to indulge.

"Oh, God!" She actually blushed. "I just assumed, from the sound of your music – particularly some of the spacey moments – and the surrealistic kinds of lyrics you write…"

"That's a natural thing," I told her, striving to smile to put her at ease. "I get high *from* the music. Or, you know, I can slip into a different state of mind at other times, just naturally, too."

"There's all kinds of routes one can take," Tommy elaborated. "But basically people get involved in various different methods of trying to get at something that's already alive inside them. But that doesn't mean that we" – he swept his arm to indicate each of us, 'the band' – "harbor any kind of judgments about it. I mean, if smoking gets you there then that's all good with us."

Maureen smiled. She still looked slightly abashed. "O.k. Cool." She pointed to each of us in turn. "And just know that it will *not* affect my bookkeeping skills!"

She was so good-natured and forthright. Seeing her discomfort made me ill at ease. I glanced at my bandmates.

"Look," I said, "how 'bout we get past this thing right now, all right? We all know that we like Maureen and feel comfortable with everything that's happening here. I think it'd even be safe for me to say that our meeting wasn't an accident, that we can all sense that… let's just say that we're partners, all right? We're in this together now. Like, what other kind of sign are we waiting for?"

Carlos and Tommy just kinda pursed their lips and nodded, accepting this casually; and in the moment, I think we all realized that our minds had been made up, that this was all inevitable, but we'd just been trying to exercise some sort of 'professional' aloofness until this point.

"All right, Maureen," I said, turning to her, "you are now the manager of Edge of the Known, hands down the craziest band on Earth. How does it feel?"

She literally quivered with delight. "Like all my years in this nasty business have finally come to fruition!" She waved to us and simultaneously retreated backwards. "All right. You guys get back to playing. My head's swimming with so many ideas now, I gotta go write them down!"

We'd practically played our entire repertoire by this point. Before starting in again, we all shared a look, a communal exchange, that communicated our collective satisfaction with this turn of events. Tommy summed it up:

"Even if we found someone with twice the business sense... seeing as there's no way they'd possibly match that kind of enthusiasm, I'd *still* say let's stick with her."

***

Many of us go through a good portion of our lives feeling like our identity ends at our skin, the boundaries of the flesh. There's times when I'd be sitting in my room – particularly when in a bleak mood – and it'd seem like those walls comprised the uttermost limits of my personal world. Each of us are indeed unique, which implies a separate sense of consciousness.

And yet, there is a deeper part of our being that is *never* separate at all, not from one iota of Creation anywhere. Even if you wanted to be entirely pragmatic about this, you'd have to admit that our physical being is composed of the stuff of the Earth; that we share the same essential air and water again and again; that we all dip down into the same wellspring of Dream.

When I played music, that was when those artificial mental barriers were most likely to dissolve. That's how the miracle oftentimes unfolded at The Catacombs: First, I'd tune into this sort of cascading flow of mind and spirit that emanated from Tommy and Carlos. It swept me along to a certain juncture, an existential crossroads that was like a meeting place of souls. We don't often think about it consciously; but deeper down, we *know*. We came here to fulfill certain purposes, both individually and in the sense of a vast cooperative adventure. All of us who're alive in this time are passengers on the same cosmic ship.

And this is where Edge of the Known truly found its groove. Sometimes my awareness spread out to encompass everything around. I became sensitized to the memories of trees and the feeling sensations of shadows. I felt the warm inner intent of Saul's work; there was a light that emanated from his house, and I knew it was created, in part, by all those others who perceived it as an oasis, an abode of spiritual solace. The grassy yard supported this bastion, gave it a Place to Be. It knew and loved those who live upon it. The trees on the outer edges were more than sentinels: They were caretakers; guardians, even. Although they may follow their own unfolding thoughts over the sap-movement of decades, they still radiated compassion for those of us whose lives are more fitful and transient.

Under the influence of rhythm and beat and poetry, I could feel the vast undercurrent of love and cooperation that upholds the world. When we played The Hangman, I descended into this level of awareness, with Maureen standing in the wings and applauding every number like she was witnessing her child's graduation.

I remember that it was one of the most diverse crowds we ever played for. Peering into the dancing pit, I'd see a middle-aged man in a suit, a young woman in all black (right down to her lipstick and eye-shadow) and a fresh-faced kid in a college jersey and new jeans – a pint sloshing in his upraised hand – all weaving around one another. The onslaught of the music conveyed the essence of the journey we were proposing; and the audience, with their bodies and voices and minds, conveyed their eager assent to it.

Older songs assumed new significances for me that night. The image of The Hanged Man from the Tarot – upside down, mostly naked, his old and gnarled limbs demarcating the number 4 – ran along the dark wood ceiling in white. The lighting in the bar was subdued, perfect for our twilight shamanic tendencies. And I got the feeling that a good portion of the crowd was there to *hear music*.

I can scarcely describe how I'd ached, throughout all those restless hours on the road, for volume, electricity, release, clamor, the feeling of the stage beneath my feet. And those feet, by the way, were bare. Maureen had loaned me a pair of her sandals, but I left them off for the performance.

And this is how the three of us had learned to weather the storms of life with our own brand of sanity intact. Reality intensified to a keen edge, like the point of a welding iron, when I'd play and sing. That white-hot tip performed the act of alchemy. Pain was churned to ecstasy; fear to exaltedness; loss could spark the flames of victory. As I had often roamed amongst the trees alongside Saul's property, while rehearsing in The Catacombs, I now communed with every human being within The Hangman. Most of them stayed in the club and worked through to their own personal catharsis and recognition before the end. I've never discovered the proper word for what we did, for what Edge of the Known's art really was. I probably never will. But we applied it with a fine brush, that night in Boston.

Even our equipment seemed to appreciate the use, following a week of mostly dormancy and displacement. I kissed my amp goodnight before flicking her switch and extinguishing her hum. The exclamations and praise that was hurled our way created a din almost comparable to the musical ferocity – and how does one respond to that?

I packed up my guitar, left it on the stage for the moment, and stumbled off like a drunken man. People attempted to engage me. I nodded, smiled as best I could and kept walking. I'd never relished that aspect of being a performing musician. It's not that I longed to *get away*, necessarily. I'd just already expressed everything that was within me. What could I add to the conversation now?

For those of us who've experienced some degree of inner awakening, conversing with others can take on new levels of complexity and challenge. Although the words that are spoken may be the same as before, the nuances of meaning will have changed. And one's perspective may be from the other side of the fence.

To my right, a maze of tables cluttered the space between me and the Old West-style swinging doors that led to the restrooms. Every table was full; and easily half of those eyes were on me. To my left, and up ahead, was about three car-lengths of bar. All those seats, too, were occupied. Whatever the owners were planning on paying us, we'd no doubt earned it from them.

I squeezed into a spot, ignoring the glances to both sides of me, and ordered a scotch and water. About five minutes later I moved on to beer – and secured a seat that a young blonde smilingly offered me on her way out.

Maureen found me there a while later and began showering me with ebullient praise. The drink was working in me by then, mingling with the sweet simmer of post-performance adrenaline.

With my characteristic lack of tact, I skipped preliminary explanations and dove right into trying to describe the feelings that her presence evoked in me.

"I lost my mom when I was a teenager," I blurted. "My dad was hardly a father to me, and I ended up raising my little sister – at least for a few years there – like she was my own kid. I'm just saying… if you start acting motherly with me than there's a chance I'll get carried away in return. Just warnin' ya."

She'd frowned in sympathy while I was talking. But she grinned once I finished, and spoke with the most affected politesse. "I promise to always behave with the proper professional detachment, Brandon!"

Then she gave me a quick peck on the cheek and wiggled my ear. Withdrawing, she screwed her face into a mock-scandalized expression.

"Well, most of the time!" she amended.

18. To Have Chosen This Time and Place

So my spirits were lifted for a brief time, thanks to the audience's reception at The Hangman (where we sold about a dozen copies of each of our records, too, thereby making some road money) and Maureen's loyalty. Before long, though, the inherent conundrum of touring began to leer at me. No matter how well we went over with our audiences, in the end – once the dates were done – I would have to return to my old familiar nightmare. Was this creativity's sole efficacy, then – that it could simply stave off one's awareness of the Abyss for fleeting instants? Was I just sculpting sandcastles before an oncoming tide every time I wrote a song, or climbed onstage to sing?

I managed to stem this encroaching sense of futility by taking a hike, along with the others, through the Arboretum. Eventually we clambered up a hill, in the sweat-inducing sticky heat of the noon-day sun, where we could see the heart of downtown Boston beyond a green sea of deciduous trees. Maureen snapped some pictures, Tommy and I smoked, and Carlos paced back and forth while his eyes stroked the distant line of high-rise buildings.

"This is one of the oldest settled places in the whole country, isn't it?" he considered. "Just think of the history here! Man, we're in a place that has seen Puritans, witch trials..."

"Man, don't even bring that up!" I grunted.

I'd carried around the subconscious fear of persecution my whole life. "I can't explain, Carlos... but somehow, I just know the hysteria of being bound on that stake, or facing Inquisitor's hot tongs. It's not a pleasant thing to philosophize about."

Especially when I'd grown up believing that my very nature inevitably made me an enemy of the State.

Anxious to change the subject, I turned to Maureen. "Hey, are you gonna tag along for the rest of the tour now?"

"Of course baby!" she said at once. "I'm there for everything to do with band business from here on. I'm Edge of the Known's nanny. That big black beast of yours isn't going anywhere now without being stalked by my little yellow buggie!"

Then she pocketed her camera, retrieved a little blown-glass pipe of blue and green, packed it and lit it. After puffing for a few seconds she proffered it towards each of us in turn. We all shook our heads. I grinned. It was such an echo of how Tommy and I behaved with Carlos around cigarettes. I could tell already that she was probably going to do that every time she got high around us, despite the near-certainty that we'd never give in and partake.

Then Maureen apologized for having created a lot of extra driving for us on account of how the tour was arranged. What she was referring to was the fact that, having first fulfilled our rendezvous with her, we now had to backtrack to honor a date in New Haven, Connecticut and another in Hartford before returning to Massachusetts, rather than hitting the cities in their logical order. I assured her that I really didn't care. Bringing music to the people isn't a linear quest to begin with. No map can tell the real tale of it.

At any rate, we figured that we could get to New Haven in well under three hours.

"And a good thing, too," Maureen said, smiling, "because we're gonna have to get up at the crack of dawn tomorrow – at least by *your* standards!"

"What do you mean?" Tommy demanded, his eyes sharpening in the way that they often did when he was confronted with something that he didn't already know.

"Oh, surprise, surprise," Maureen said. She knocked her pipe on her palm, examined the debris and, finding nothing to salvage amidst the ash, blew it off. "This date that I lined up for you isn't in a club. It's actually an open air festival in the park. Two other bands are on the bill; and you'll play in the middle. This happens in the late afternoon – four-ish, I think. I'll have to check my book. But the event is pretty popular. This could end up being the biggest audience that you've played for so far."

A change of scenery felt welcome. We wondered how well our sound would carry outdoors, though. We'd only done something like this once before, at the Pumpkin Festival in Jennes where I'd first met Janie. Back then, our repertoire had still been dominated by loud, abrasive and primitive metal – with Tim Peralta, not Carlos, providing the propulsion. It was difficult to envision how the subtler musical dynamics that we'd developed since then would translate in an open-air environment. But there was nothing to do but blindly throw ourselves into the experience – which I suppose was our typical response to *any* challenge, anyhow.

"You do realize that we're more used to *staying up* 'til dawn than *waking* up then, right?" I challenged Maureen.

She cast us all an impish glance. "Sure you guys don't wanna puff? It'll help you sleep…"

***

The weather was gorgeous, both for the drive and for the festival itself. They'd set up stands with carnival-type viands along the broad mowed field and scents of fish, fried dough, onions and peppers mingled in the hot afternoon air. People of all ages and stripes were meandering: Tight-knit families to poor, lonely looking drifters. The stage had a tall black satin backdrop proclaiming the local promoter of the event. After creating our backline of equipment, we milled about, sampling the food (it's detrimental to stuff yourself before a performance) and talking.

I can't recall the name of the band that played before us, and I didn't care for them. They were too polished and professional: Total anathema to my ethic of putting honesty and passion before virtuosity. What does it matter if you hit and hold all the right notes if your sound is designed to be nothing more than crowd-pleasing and your moves are obviously scripted for video? Their front man, with his fashionably long hair and black leather lending him an air of harmless rebellion, even made a self-conscious spectacle of himself by hopping off the stage during one instrumental break and dancing with some of the little kids in front.

I almost felt sorry about having to obliterate this safe and tidy musical universe that they were trying to construct.

My impatience and irritation roughened the opening of our set – to its benefit. To test the mic I wretched from a dry hollow in the pit of my solar plexus, loud as I could. Then I punctuated this tortured sound by hammering on a raw, distorted E chord. Back and forth. Some in the audience began yelling in response. I offered them a feral grin as the feedback carried. Then Carlos began a ponderous roll, Tommy insinuated his deep pulse into the mayhem, and Edge of the Known unleashed itself upon New Haven.

Sometimes music carried me past the borders of civilization and into the perilous wilderness...

After about an hour of this sort of audible catharsis, though, my deeper world-weariness and sorrow rose up to claim me. I could literally *see* this mood ripening to fruition, much as a landscape is shadowed by thunderheads rolling in on a cold front. Although the volume soothed and relived, some deeper disturbance still lay unresolved.

I finished singing "Breath of the Deep", a number from our first record, and wavered. The audience was in black and white. My inner sea change had washed away all color. I pounded on a single power chord as fast and hard as I could and then stopped dead. I repeated this; and yet again. Machine-gun rapid-fire riffing finally released me from enough rage that I could actually speak.

"I could blame my mom for dying! I could blame my father for the beatings! I could blame my school for trying to shove me through the mental meat grinder! Or all those people who seem hell-bent on destroying this good earth and making sure that we're all stripped of every kind of hope and comfort before that end comes!"

The audience, easily a hundred strong, was predominantly quiet by now, milling and confused. And yet they were still waiting. I suddenly remembered that I was talking to real people, human beings with struggles and sufferings of their own. My voice dropped down into a more natural cadence.

"I *could* do that – and, you know, find a million reasons to back it up and feel justified for saying it. It's all *true*, right? And yet if I repeat that mantra, cling to it *as* my truth, it ain't gonna do anything but perpetuate this hell forever. Because I'm gonna keep *creating* the very thing that I'm trying to be rid of!"

I tried to let the murmurs, the scattered admonition here or there to "just sing another song, man!" all wash over me. Then... Screw it, I thought. "Hey, just because I'm being paid to play this gig doesn't make me a human fucking jukebox!" I told those couple of hecklers. That steadied me.

"There's only one thing for it," I went on. "One way out. One escape path. I have to just say it, admit it, that I *chose* this all. I *wanted* to be an outsider, see. I wanted to be denied all those tried-and-true roads that society loves, because then I'd be obliged to find my own answers. I wanted to ask the questions that no one else seemed to be asking so I could create the art that no one else was making.

"So no, I don't attribute my breakthroughs and victories to God, and I don't blame demons - or whatever other label you may want to use for dark forces - for my sufferings and misfortunes either. My life is my own creation in every respect."

I knew in that moment that I'd chosen my circumstances - not consciously, of course, but on some deeper level - because I wanted to use them as an impetus for my journey of soul-recovery. I might not have had the motivation to undertake that journey, otherwise. At some time - perhaps "before" time - all of us decided upon the paths that we would take in this life, for our own valid reasons. If we can look back over the course of our lives and say, "Yeah, I chose all those events as a backdrop against which I could hopefully grow and fulfill myself," then we can lay claim to what is really ours already: The power to create our own reality.

"And so then what *you* get out of it is *this*!" I told the audience.

And from there, my friends crashed in behind me and we delivered what was probably our most impassioned rendition of "Sea

Breakers" ever. This was my favorite number off of "What Casts the Shadow?" anyway, due to so many personal associations.

Because this was our last song, we milked its tail end with improvisation that included even a languid bass solo from Tommy that made my throat clench with the force of all my suppressed weeping. We wove soundscapes of feedback. Eventually this settled into a quiet, steady groove, initiated first by Carlos. It felt natural for me to begin scat-singing a bit of doggerel that I'd scribbled down on the dashboard of the van – whilst somewhere in Iowa, I believe.

> Guilt speaks in a voice from your past
> Says: "No plea-bargain for you
> I'll give you back your natural grace
> just as soon as your whole life's through"

There were a couple other verses like that, and I repeated them all several times. This quieted by increments. But my anger, at the same time, surged. I allowed it its life: I didn't judge it. And during a moment when I began to waver, I recalled an exchange that I'd had with Saul a couple months before: One of his lessons that had always stayed with me.

"Facing into any situation that provokes your anger is, in the end, just a matter of facing yourself," he'd said. "That's you you're encountering out there in the wide world! Anger - healthy anger - carries you out beyond your familiar boundaries. Saying that you're afraid of your anger, then, is essentially the same as saying, 'There's something inside *myself* that I'm scared to discover'.

"Every emotion serves as a kind of fuel that you can utilize to travel to deeper regions of yourself.

"Love is not always the passive and flowery sensation that popular sentiment portrays it as, anyhow. Self-love can be *fierce*; it may involve outrage. And the force of that outrage can be frightening if you've dammed it up for so long with shame and limiting beliefs. Anger in its healthy form – and by this I mean anger that's not been overly accumulating due to repression - it dissolves shame. It is the primal force within us that will not tolerate any lack of self-love. It won't allow you to pretend to excuse any kind of violation with rationalizations like, 'Oh, I probably deserved that' or 'I'm sure she, he, didn't really mean to do that'.

"Feelings carry motion - movement - and that motion can push you through the seeming barriers in your life if you allow it to. I'll be blunt here: This is a world where what's real is generally shunned and everything unreal is supported. Standing up for your right to own your feelings, to move through them and see how they're manifesting in your environment - as opposed to being *caused* by that environment - can be a constant battle. But it's the only worthwhile journey to make."

Dissolves shame... Yes, thank you Saul. Abetted by this revelation – and by this time I had scarcely any musical accompaniment - I finally screamed to the audience: "Guilt! Don't listen to that motherfucker! We were born to live free!"

And with that, the show was over.

Well, it was scarcely eloquent; but then again, it was one of the most *incendiary* performances we'd ever delivered. And I noted, with some satisfaction, that the applause was a lot louder for us than it'd been for the previous, video-prepped band.

On a personal level, I was satisfied – for the moment. Surrendering to the sweep of my own anguish had led me back to the only really potent response I'd ever found for any dilemma. I had to take personal responsibility for everything, both my triumphs and my tragedies.

This insight made me more sociable, overall, at the fairgrounds than I had been at The Hangman. I'd worked through my own emotional logjam, at least temporarily. I did notice that Maureen seemed a little furtive around me, though. I suppose even our records couldn't have fully prepared her for a spectacle like this afternoon. But she relaxed by degrees, and finally fessed up to being a bit startled.

"It really is all in the pursuit of real sanity," I said. "Sometimes the only safety lies in complete self-disclosure." This was actually the sincerest explanation I could think of.

If you'd really known what this journey meant then I doubt you could've taken the first steps, I told myself.

How could I possibly tell this woman, who I'd but recently befriended – and who I knew I'd already begun to burden with some of my most fragile hopes – that going for broke like I did onstage was actually my sole alternative to self-destruction, basically? For me as a teenager and twenty-something, life in this world as we know it was soul-dead: And life without the soul had always lent the idea of suicide a kind of obvious and simple logic. If there's no place here for what I feel, perceive, dream of and long for then I'm bound to have better luck elsewhere. And I'm sorry that I have to hurt you, precious body, to get there; it's necessary; I don't know any other way; I guess I'll never know what your promise was...

I was fighting a surge of tears, and at the same time trying to drive the memories away. But that was the irony of the release of performing, for me: It left me open to *all* the primal forces within me, not just those of creation and exultation.

And yet there was always that little voice among them in those moments, the voice that *can* not and *will* not give up on the promise of life: The beauty, the love, the hope that insists, *Just give me one more moment and maybe I can show you how it all can be different.*

In recent years, that voice had found an ally in Saul. And it came to teach me that there is no such thing as a hopeless life situation.

The headliners were setting up by this time. I was granted a little more space in which to breathe, now that people were drawn by the prospect of fresh entertainment.

I looked at Maureen, and at the same time my mind frantically groped for inspiration. Then it came, in the form of some more old words of Saul's.

When fear is with you, there is an opportunity for movement. Beyond it lies the unknown. Each step that you take towards it broadens the boundaries of your experience and forces you to redefine your identity.

It becomes a question of how much you really desire change.

"I wish I could explain myself better, Maureen," I said. "But please don't be afraid of me." I strove to dam up the welling water in the corners of my eyes. "I'm not dangerous."

"Aww!" She took a step forward, stopped for a moment to question the impulse, and then gave in to it, hugging me hard. She looked a little embarrassed when she withdrew.

"I guess I've just never gotten to see genius at work up close," she said, in a tone that sounded in no way patronizing. Now *I* was embarrassed. "It'll be a good learning for me!"

At Gladys Pub in Hartford we made the mistake of showing up early. The owner, a man in his mid-fifties named Elmer who looked and dressed like a cab driver and chewed a cigar, insisted that we go on right away. There were scarcely half a dozen people in the bar and the sun was still shining.

"What the hell for?" we collectively asked.

He wouldn't budge. So we did a sound-check, launched into a number and he immediately stalked over to the stage waving his beefy arms over his head. Too loud. Christ, we ended up turning down *twice* in order to please that turd. By the time the gig was properly underway, too much of my passion had been sapped by this unnecessary aggravation. I ended up hammered that night, sitting in the front seat of the van with my forehead against the dash, crying for June, Janie, Saul, Rachel – even Kayla from Alchemist Brews, who'd used me at least as much as I had her – while everyone in my entourage took turns trying to console me.

19. It Somehow Never Sticks

I nursed my hangover as we drove out for our second engagement in Boston, at a place called Grim Reaper Penthouse where virtually every punter was dressed in black from head to foot. Maureen had told the owner that we were the heaviest band on Earth and so he'd just booked us at once out of curiosity. None of us were feeling particularly high-spirited, but we managed to be professional and deliver the goods regardless. Besides, our collective unease and simmering frustration was probably more of an asset than a detriment when we were faced with an audience that was hungry for extremity.

Poor Carlos had to play both of our dates in Springfield with a fever. He refused to sit them out, but soldiered through with a clench to his jaw that suggested that his face might crack if he released it. Fat beads of sweat rolled into his eyes as he drummed, and he cast them off with furious shakes. *Hell with it*, I thought. *If he goes down we all go down – that's how this band works.* As it turned out, though, he was the only one in the group to get sick. We did opt to splurge on hotels, though, giving Carlos his own single-bed unit as a way of quarantining him. Although by this point we had some gig money to throw into the pot, this particular gesture left us in Maureen's debt.

By the time we arrived in Provincetown, Rhode Island, our drummer was rallying his strength. His voice gradually regained its lilt of eagerness and the keen light stirred again in his eyes. All of us combed the beach in the afternoon, passing by an abandoned car that was filled to the roof with sand. Then we got dinner at a café on the main strip. This was a city that I definitely wanted to return to when I had money to burn. It was a balmy day, and the very air felt lively. We were well caffeinated for our performance. I noticed that the poetry-heavy numbers from "Trust in the Unseen" drew particularly favorable responses.

This was a place where music could really insinuate its way down the hot streets and entice people to come and investigate its source. Thankfully, I didn't drink afterwards this time. Instead I stayed up late and wrote poetry. I was relatively settled and gratified inside, feeling like we'd played our best set (in a packed bar by the name of "Turkish Delights") since the festival in New Haven.

From there we shot over to Manchester, New Hampshire. You hear so many rock stars, of all genres, singing about life on the road – all too often, with that same tired refrain about the towns all looking the same. Maybe that's true if you're *jetting* from date to date and all you're seeing on any given day is the insides of hotels, limos and performance halls. But from my perspective - just a few feet above the pavement and rolling - Boston, Provincetown and Manchester sang distinctly different songs, each of inimitable beauty. All the locales of this Earth have *spiritual* climates as much as physical ones, to be sure.

We serenaded the long, gray hall of a V.F.W. bar and its small constituency that was largely twice our age. There hadn't been any advertising for the show, not even a flyer inside. This visibly upset Maureen, but we managed to talk her down before she jumped down the bartender's throat. In the end, we basically got onstage and played for whoever happened to be there. I was feeling restless with the repetition of our established songs, so I requested that we take a couple of our "open-ended" improvisational pieces and *really* stretch them – to the extent to which they constituted our entire set.

Really, I was just in the sort of free-floating state of consciousness where I could have explored the textures of a tree's bark and leaves, or the movements of a caterpillar, for hours. I wove in and out of Tommy's meandering bass and Carlos' jazz-like excursions. The free-form sections were pretty immaculate, I have to say, and they led to new musical territory that surprised all three of us.

Not everyone was thrilled by this experiment. During a particularly languid passage, I heard one guy complain to his lady friend that his pool game was sucking "because of this goddamn music!"

When you realize that you can't win over the audience, just treat it like a rehearsal. That was our attitude.

This spontaneous approach opened up so many enticing avenues, in fact, that we were inspired to try it again in Concord. At Taylor's Bar we were spurred on by a rowdy audience that was there to drink and dance on a Friday night. And we abetted *them* by holding to a chugging rhythm rife with attitude, occasionally working up to crescendos that would inevitably crash and collapse into dissonance and the wailing of amplifiers.

During one of these interludes I kind of echoed my "embracing your personal reality" speech from the New Haven festival, only this time it was a calmer, more measured narrative that wed well with the music. I also reprised my "guilt rap". Certain songs in our repertoire had evolved this way before: Favorite bits that emerged from one rehearsal were recalled and resurrected during the next. These would then slowly merge with newer pieces until, finally, a complete composition was formed.

Aside from this, there were certain songs that we would *never* declare finished. If the universe ever ceased to move and change then it would die. An element of unpredictability must always be preserved.

We'd been finding wooded and secluded areas where we could park the van and sleep through the late-night and morning hours while we were in New Hampshire. Following the performance at Taylor's, we shelled out a bit of money for a camping space so that Maureen could pitch her little orange tent and avoid having to pay for a hotel room again. Of course she was always welcome in the van; but given the odds, I could well understand why she was hesitant. I figured that within another month or so she'd realize how truly safe she was with us three guys, however rambunctious we might be onstage.

"So what are we doing after this, anyway?" Tommy asked, over the gentle cackle of the small fire that he and Carlos had just started. "I forgot. I know I've got the itinerary stashed in the van somewhere, but…"

"Two gigs in Portland, Maine," Maureen said, rubbing her hands a few feet above the flames. She looked even younger in the truculent yellow glow. "Then, Chas and I figured you guys could mellow out in the glorious Vermont summer before you go do your big showcase. The shows are small, but it's worth visiting the state, seriously. We lined up three appearances: Burlington, Montpelier and Stowe."

It was hard for me to believe that we'd already completed half of our dates, and in little over two weeks' time. Maybe it was my own inner turmoil that had made the days and performances and the onrush of new faces and landscapes all swirl and merge. And aside from this, I didn't want the tour to end. I didn't want to go back to my life of before.

I suppose that a spell was cast upon me by the fire, the baroque shadows, the quiet vigil of the ash trees and the clear stars above them. It's human culture that teaches us to hold our peace; and culture was far away at the moment.

It was too late for any of us to return to the state of the barbarian. Still, there were times when I carried this sense of anticipation and excitement; it would well up inside me whenever we were in the midst of some upheaval, like a natural disaster... I'd wonder if maybe, this time, society would be too disrupted to ever function in the same old way again.

It was just comforting sometimes to think that some cataclysm could raze this behemoth to the ground and then life could begin again in some purer and simpler way - just man and fellow man; sentient life, and the elements. I was well aware that this was a radical sentiment; and I was never someone who enjoyed seeing misfortune befall others. It's just that sometimes the only "solution" to our myriad dilemmas that presented itself to my imagination involved wiping the slate clean and starting over.

Yes, I knew that things were never so simple as my fantasy would paint them...

Culture, by and large, just had a lot of its priorities in the wrong places; so it seemed to me. Being immersed in nature provoked such thoughts. Society had a way of keeping our energies consumed in petty frustrations and toils so that we remained pretty oblivious to the larger entities and movements of life. That was the appeal of storms, for me. When we were faced with the unbridled fury of the elements, we had an opportunity to feel both our primal kinship with nature and our deeper bonds with each other.

That was something that the abstractions of the scientific and technological paradigm did not encourage; and perhaps natural disasters would continue for so long as we existed divorced from nature and estranged from our neighbors. Because those barriers fall away when it's life or death - man facing the primal spirit that birthed him and that can yet consume him. Such an encounter cuts through the pettiness, the slackness and complacency of civilized life...and oftentimes, it can draw out the best in people and lift ordinary men and women into the sphere of true heroism.

From there, I found myself thinking back to the few years in High School when I'd experimented with smoking pot. I suppose Maureen's presence evoked such memories. It'd been an altogether disorienting and unpleasant experience, which is why I thought that she had *very little* chance of seducing me with it now. There was a certain unsettling perception that I'd grown really familiar with, back then, with my sensitivity so stretched thin by the drug: When someone spoke, I could read from their demeanor and body language (as well as by *looking inside*, which I could do even then) that they really wanted to say something completely different.

And I saw the reflection of myself in this disturbing revelation. We were all following a kind of script; something subliminally understood that had its origins God knows where. We didn't trust the flow of our natural selves. It's fashionable to say, 'Oh, I lost myself there'. But I always *knew* what my real impulses were; I was just afraid, because I was convinced that the whole world was against my acting upon them.

And in that denial of what was real, I could feel a veritable heaviness descending: a stifling and suffocating presence. Back then I believed that this was a demonic force, with a will to keep humanity repressed and unconscious much like some alien slaver.

I'd since shed the belief in demons. But there was no denying that much misery was still bred in our world.

"I think that whenever we fail to act upon what is true for us," I announced, "from the place where our passion lives, then darkness gains the upper hand. That's why I go off onstage, when the mood hits me – why I can't hold that stuff in. Wasn't that our original idea, Tommy? Let the shadow *out*, so that then it could be dealt with?"

"A totalitarian regime is born out of a populace that fears its own inner reality," he responded. Tommy was quite used to me speaking up without preamble. "Control fills the void that is left behind. The enemies of fascism will always be an open mind, openness to feeling, risk and integrity. Truth.

"That's why I've always believed that it won't be revolution but rather expansion that will save us."

Maureen and Carlos *both* looked like they were itching to interject, at this point: But there was no stopping Tommy when he was on a roll.

"Freedom means you've got no one to thank or blame save for yourself – just like you said it onstage the other day, Brandon. See, it's become fashionable for people to criticize the repressive nature of the various world religions, for instance. But many, many people find comfort in rules and procedures. Then there's no need to feel and explore and examine the terrain within the untamed wilderness of ourselves. That's why rules oftentimes permeate even those spiritual practices that seem most liberal and modern, like the New Age movement."

And this summoned to my consciousness yet another memory of Saul and his words. I'd once asked him what he thought about humankind's "chances".

The darkness that humanity is experiencing at this juncture can at times seem insurmountable, I know. But it only appears so to the extent to which we deny ourselves. After all, it's our own creative power that has woven the tale of this age in the first place. The soul does not manifest where all is hopeless, and the inner self never sets us up to fail. These are myths spun from the mind, and supported by the same limiting and erroneous beliefs that keep so many of us from trusting and speaking our own truth.

"And yet there's something so overly-lofty about all of this, for me," I fumed. "Ultimately, I don't want to save the world so much as I just want a goddamn happy life."

I began to pace from one side of the fire to the other. "I'm not looking for any kind of response to that," I said, striking a hand down in response to a protest that hadn't actually even been uttered. I was just frustrated, and needing to move it through my body. I was caught in a war between my need and the part of me that *judged* that need as a sign of weakness. "I'm just sick of fucking riddles without answers!"

"I think your creativity rises up out of that very tension," Tommy said - in a tone that seemed to add, *Dude, you just gotta live with it.* "If you ever 'answered the riddle' then you'd stop asking those very questions that lead to your poems and songs."

"That makes a lot of sense," Maureen said. She looked and sounded unusually somber. "You probably don't want to go too far in either direction. If you totally make peace with the world and adapt to it then you'd lose that unique vision that you have and not have nearly so much to say. But then if you give yourself over *totally* to the vision – and this is what I think is the bigger temptation, for you – then you'll forget to share it with the rest of us. And what would be the point of even having it, then?"

That last point provoked her smile again.

I was grateful for my friends' input. I truly was. But I was wound up inside; and I kept pacing. Thoughts exploded, and their shrapnel fragments sped off in all directions at once. I tried to sift through the remnants of inane fears and the fossils of old, bankrupt beliefs.

"But all this pain and sacrifice for *what*?" I ranted. "I'm just this fucked-up guy in a world populated by billions. And everything else is so goddamn *big*. Governments, banks, corporations, religions..."

It always circled back to that, for me: The futility of individual action in the face of massive systems and institutions. They had claimed everything. They were ubiquitous and invincible. And not only was I insignificant, I was also too busy battling *myself* to be a threat to anything else in the world.

"Remember what you and me have been learning about, though," Carlos prodded me. "What you're saying seems true only if you're looking at the very surface of reality and not trying to go any deeper. Think about it. There's another source. Like, a government doesn't really *create* wars. It's the unresolved aggressions and pent-up frustrations within *us* that lead to wars. And it's our feeling – our belief that we're separate from nature that puts her in jeopardy. It's the fear of our own power that creates whatever kinds of oppression we might experience. The power structures in the world, these things you're talking about, they just mirror that internal battlefield."

I nodded, but answered noncommittally and in a tired monotone. "The answers are inside us. They're not out there in the world." Then I met his eyes. "I probably remind myself of that twenty times a day. Somehow it never *sticks*, man!"

He lifted his hands in a gesture of supplication, eyes looking sympathetic. "We're working against a whole lifetime of believing the exact opposite."

Maureen was now sitting on a short log that she'd dragged out of the woods. She lit and began puffing pensively on her glass pipe. "Well, I don't know about all that," she said through a long exhalation. "But I do know that the great artists really *do* change the world. Don't think for a moment that they don't."

"You just can't even *start* questioning the worth of yourself and what you're doing," Tommy put in. "It's challenging enough to make it in the world, on your own terms, when you *have* belief."

"And as far as making a difference goes," Maureen said, her voice a little high-pitched and disjointed from the smoke, "I think there's a lot to be said for seeing a guy wrestling his demons and working his issues out onstage. A lot more people struggle with these sorts of questions than you probably know. Your perspective isn't nearly as crazy as you think. And" – the fire was getting hot now, so she stood off her stump and retreated a few steps, "I *guarantee* you that there's still people in Boston talking about your performance."

Then for a while there was just the cracking of the fire, the light, the trees overhead and the breeze. Carlos took a long time mustering his resolve to address me, though I could see the words clear formed in his mind.

"But just the issue of belief doesn't solve it all, does it?" His voice was low, tentatively probing. "Because if you see life as your creation, then you gotta think that *you* somehow fractured a relationship you had with a woman you loved, right? And that your poverty, and the lack of recognition for your work, is somehow a reflection of your own feelings of worth. And even your family life... It hurts, having to see it that way, huh?"

"You think?" I said, in a voice so high it nearly cracked. It was one part wry humor and one part near-hysteria. I decided to move on, right then – force the pain down and enjoy the night as best I could. "Hey, let's toast those hot dogs!"

We'd picked up a package of them, along with some rolls and condiments, on the way over. Maureen, who was concerned for our health, had insisted in purchasing some fruit smoothies for us to wash them down with.

"There's nothing for it but to just keep plugging away," she summarized, as she handed me mine. "Convert the world to your vision of a better way, one entranced and ecstatic listener at a time."

20. Shattered Remnants

The night that we camped outside of Concord really cemented the feeling that we were a family unit now, us three guys and our new manager. I carried this comforting familial sense with me when we played in Portland, Maine. Thanks to road construction, and our own lazy attitudes beforehand, we barely made it there in time to honor our first engagement.

This was at an all-ages space, a converted warehouse that reminded me very much of the one adjacent to The Samurai in Sadenport where Edge of the Known had played their first-ever gig. I always relished the chance to play for younger people, many of whom I figured could relate better to the turbulent and confused emotions that I reflected in my songs.

I realize that I'm generalizing here, but it does typically happen that as people age they settle more into their "official identities", which often revolve around their careers, marriages, parental roles, all that. They may gain much that is satisfying to them in the process; but along the way, they may also lose many of the fruits of their earlier period of creative unrest. It's the hippies-who-grow-up-to-be-yuppies phenomenon; and I vowed to never fall prey to it.

We sold nearly fifty records at that show: A personal record for us. We insisted that Maureen accept a good chunk of the resulting money as but one token of our appreciation for all that she'd done for us. Though we didn't say so aloud, we all knew that she needed it, that her efforts on our behalf were slowly draining her slim resources. She, in turn, insisted that part of the money was going towards proper footwear for me. I wound up with some durable leather sandals, the kind that cover your entire foot but still allow your skin to breathe.

We spent the rest of the intervening day at the beach, witnessing the most frenzied waves that I'd seen since leaving the West Coast. The remainder of our recent earnings purchased us delicious food from a few outdoor vendors. I took Portland to heart right away. My guess is that artists had taken a hand in its design and philanthropists had comprised some of its earliest settlers. The vibe was one of open arms and acceptance, and I was able to breathe easy. After exhausting ourselves on her friendly streets, we returned to the beach that night to pass a whiskey bottle around until we finally sank down, one by one, to sleep.

The following night we lugged our gear into Creeping Vines of Wine, one of my favorite clubs of all those we ever visited. It was pretty nondescript by surface appearances, and dark. But the stage was high, carpeted and prominent. And it was here, no doubt, that all the offbeat, eccentric, radical minds of Portland had made tacit agreement to meet and celebrate their collective oddity with the kind of Dionysian revelry that befitted the venue's name.

You could *feel* intellectual fecundity in the air, the kind that questions, sifts and discards everything in its restless quest for a more expansive description of the world. It wafted over me as soon as I walked through the door.

Once upon a time, I'd wondered if I'd ever recover enough of myself to even function in the world at all. Life back then had been measured in heartbeats and breaths, not in hopes and dreams. Saul had taught me that miracles did indeed exist...

But therein, ironically, lay a trap for my twisted heart. Nihilism had once protected me from the sting of loss. I found reassurance in the shaman's wisdom, via Saul, because it told me that everything that existed possessed consciousness - and that all consciousness endures. But there is always still pain and loss in this life, because although consciousness will go on, it will never again be the same as it is in this moment. What we're attached to we will lose, and in that loss there is pain. The artistry of the shaman can transcend loss by showing us the eternal nature of the soul. But to be human we also have to come back down and find our personal sense of value and truth in a world in which all that we love will one day depart onto new adventures.

About midway through our set, I found myself airing my feelings about all of this. "Now, I know it's such a cliché thing to say," I began. "But you know, sometimes sentiments are cliché for a reason, because they really do bear repeating over and over. And it's like... there really is nothing in this world that guarantees that *any* of us are gonna wake up tomorrow. So if you've got some love that you're holding that you haven't expressed to someone, some words you've been meaning to say to someone special in your life... seriously, do it now while you have the chance.

"I mean, life will go on forever – that's really my belief. But it won't go on with ourselves as we *know* ourselves *right now* and with the opportunities that we have right now. So anyway, we're gonna do a song that I wrote one day in the park for my sister. She was sitting on my lap the whole time. And I wish she was here so I could tell her how much she means to me. I know she knows it anyway, but I never get tired of saying it."

This was the first, almost consciously recognized, warning sign that I was racing towards my breaking point. I could hear it in the way that my voice cracked a few times. I rolled into the gentle intro of "Sister/Satyr", Tommy and Carlos joining me just before I reached the first verse, and the cold, dark waves slowly rolled back. But that didn't last long. Thinking of that day in the park also brought Janie vividly to mind: Hand-in-hand with another man, ostensibly moving on from what we'd known and shared and hoped for. My voice came out raw as a dying soldier's. The audience whooped in response to every elongated high note. How often does it happen that one man's torment is a spectator's entertainment?

But aside from my personal trials, I was saddened to leave this particular branch of my tribe. And I wish I could describe in detail our performance in Burlington the following night. Unfortunately, though, I let myself get talked into swallowing a chunk of hash that looked like the bit-off tip of a brown crayon. This was down by the docks of Lake Champlain, at the bottom of Church Street. We'd set up early at Lester's; and then some hippies, who'd been slowly nursing pints at the bar, started chatting me up. Eventually they invited me to go for a walk.

I suppose I was seduced by the breezy atmosphere of Burlington where it feels like the darkness can't find you. Maybe I was fed up with my psychic civil war and longing for *any* kind of alteration of my mental state. For whatever reason, I got excited when the drug was proffered.

It hit me about a half-hour later, as we were making our way back up the hill. I began questioning things that I normally took for granted, even my posture and my walking rhythm. I couldn't converse at all, because I'd travel through four imaginative tangents that branched off from whatever had originally been said. Then I'd reply, and it would bear no relevance in any kind of context. I was completely in my own world, man. Those guys didn't care, but I was growing paranoid.

We learn that our own nature is suspect, you know. That's the major part of our education, whether it's science or media or religion that's delivering it to us. Many people can overlay that inner reservoir of self-doubt with a slick persona, a veneer of confidence. I never learned how to fake it. When I was high, there was no psychic buttress between myself and the mocking voices that I'd allowed into the dark recesses of my mind. I couldn't do or say a damn thing without judging myself for it the next moment.

Reddish light streamed over the lake from the cool, mellow sunset. Maureen caught up with us about two blocks from the club.

"Oh, o.k.," she said as she espied me. "You guys aren't expected on *quite* yet, but I was worried 'cause I couldn't find you."

Being a seasoned stoner, she of course immediately marked my reddened eyes, and the other telltale signs, and smirked.

I managed to introduce my friends. "Ernie. Jake. This is Maureen. She manages us. She's great."

They began making amiable greetings, which I cut into by announcing, "I can't sing tonight."

"What? Why?"

"I can't do it like this. I'm too high. Hell, I feel too exposed even *talking*. I got no armor, you know?"

"Shit – I'm sorry, man!" Jake said. He sounded genuinely remorseful.

"Nah, it's not your fault," I said. "I react differently from most people I know. I know my limits, and I should've just spoken up. But you gotta relax and let go in order to sing good, you know? And right now I'm just analyzing everything in the world at light speed and I don't know how to get loose."

The four of us walked back to the club together, the others trying to cheer me up as if I was battling depression rather than drowning in the mad sea waves of my frothing Unconscious. I always lived too close to those waters for comfort as it was. I didn't need to be chemically exploding the last few buoys that were left there to keep my sense of identity afloat.

When I found Tommy, I explained my predicament as best I could. Luckily, he knew me well enough to fill in the gaps. He was probably the *only* one there with the necessary experience.

"Well, we only have two choices, then," he declared. "Either we stick to my songs, and stretch them out as much as possible with instrumentation, or else I sing *yours,* too."

"*Could* you?"

"Sure, why not? I know the words by heart. And none of it's out of my range."

No doubt he knew that there was much more involved with it, though he didn't say so. My songs had all arisen from a very personal and vulnerable place: Hence my fear of the moment. Once again – for easily the thousandth time in the course of my life – I was profoundly touched by his loyalty.

"I think that way feels best," I decided.

The more things veered towards crisis, the more pragmatic Tommy became. "All right, then. We'll stick to the same set list and I'll just handle the vocals tonight. I'll go tell Carlos."

I wandered over to the bar and asked the tattooed lady dressed in black – Wanda was her name – for a cup of coffee. I didn't need the caffeine, but I figured that the familiarity, the associations of wakefulness and comfort, might be helpful.

Some old words of Saul's drifted up from the barren grottoes of my mind. *Fear is a reality. But at the same time, fear never tells us the truth. It's like that desert lizard that puffs itself and fans out its headdress in order to look twice as big and ferocious and scare off predators. Fear is just fighting for its own existence. And it's got an infinite arsenal at its disposal. Think of all the opportunities for tragedy that our world holds out. Think of all the ways that you could die. But the truth is that you and I will die when and how we choose to. And so what is the basis for our fear?*

I meandered towards the stage, mug's worth of warm coffee in my belly and in my mind. Some part of me felt like I was betraying my own songs. But no doubt they could forgive me a lot easier than I could forgive myself.

I was convinced that the gig was a disaster – until we got about ten minutes into actually playing it. Then the music told me a much different story, one that contradicted both guilt and fear. The vibe was powerful and righteously upbeat, for all the darkness that our riffs and words reflected. The crowd – there must've been forty or fifty bouncing around – were wildly appreciative. And above all, I was profoundly moved by the sincerity of Tommy's voice.

He sang *all* the songs like they were his own; and I doubt that anyone there could've guessed that these words had originated in two different minds. He did me a deep honor that night. His vocals opened up a window through which I could glimpse what these words and melodies had really *meant* to him throughout all those months – years, now – of rehearsing.

How could you really tell, with a guy like that? He'd always just sort of nod his head at the end of a run-through, indicating approval but not much else. Tommy was erudite and loquacious when dealing with *concepts* but reticent around open displays of feeling. And I never judged him for that, because I knew that those feelings were there. They just found their outlet through other channels, such as his music.

So Tommy was our band's frontman that night, and I enjoyed letting him have the spotlight. I poured my aching, longing too-full heart into my guitar, all the while thinking about the incomprehensible journey that had finally brought us to this stage in this time.

This was enough to help me rally myself for some backing vocals... and then, finally, I claimed my own mic for "Sensations of Spring Grass". This served, tonight, as our showstopper.

A dozen people pleaded for us to play more; but there was nothing more for us to play. I rolled up my guitar cord with a smile on my face. A gig that averted meltdown and snatched triumph from the jaws of catastrophe was even better than a gig that went full fury straight out of the gate. I realized that I loved every place that we'd played. Well, the pub in Hartford still stuck like a thorn. But, hell, the miseries make the joys sweeter; that's just the way of it. And the arms of Dionysus, which sweep us out of this world's woes and into that gold and silver-lined field that we've been convinced of, ever since childhood, embraces it all, unequivocally.

I was still acutely sensitive to swirling eddies in the atmosphere, unspoken words in the bar, shifts in the flow of probabilities. I hadn't come down yet. Maybe it was for this reason that I was aware of it, when us three members of the band all sat together at the bar afterwards. I'm sure it must be obvious by now that we spent a hell of lot of time together: In our shared house, at rehearsals, in the van... When duty relaxed her grip, we were all often eager to fly down the nearest open alley. We could hardly be blamed for that. But on this night we moved as a unit. It had something to do with our having weathered a potential crisis in our own inimitable style. It called for a shared drink or two.

"So am *I* gonna have to sing all the songs when we get to Montpelier, then?" I chided.

"Maybe *I* should start learning them all, so that we have a plan C!" Carlos suggested.

Then, finishing our second round of drinks, we piled into the van and followed Maureen to the capitol "city" of Vermont. In the aftermath of our previous epic excursion between the West Coast and here, this trip passed like a flickering intermission. I soon espied the gold-plated capitol building, with proud and unassailable Ceres atop it, all bathed in moonlight as we pulled off the highway.

Maureen had friends in town who'd agreed to put us up for the night. The couple, Edmund and Allison, were roughly her age and lived in a ranch house about three miles out of town, alongside Route 12. They rented half of it to a guy in his early twenties, himself a musician. He happened to be gone for the weekend so we didn't get to meet him. Edmund and Allison, though, were just the earthy and hospitable kind of souls that one hopes to meet beside strange roads and beneath unfamiliar stars. They had such a close, familial relationship with Maureen, though, that me, Tommy and Carlos were largely obliged to entertain ourselves. As it turned out, we were all keen to sleep anyway.

Our gig at Ulysses' Bar and Grill marked the final demise of my black spray-painted Telecaster, the guitar that had been with me from the beginning, since the days of my first awkward chords and feeble attempts at composition. I remember that, for a while afterwards, I felt as bereft as if from an amputation. Even though its splintered fragments lay in a damp green dumpster behind the club, I still seemed to carry it around with me at times like a phantom limb.

The destruction was difficult to comprehend, or even believe. It was ironic, too, that it should occur at the culmination of a great performance. We'd had a – by and large – rowdy audience that relished our heaviness and reckless delivery. Our set was *particularly* aggressive. But see, it was often those exultant moments that would then trigger feelings that were most difficult for me to cope with. As that last resounding chord was still ringing in my ears, and reverberating in the club... as Carlos' symbols hissed like snakes in a skillet and a whoop of affirmation hit us like a jubilant wind from the crowd... I realized that none of this changed a goddamn thing. The recognition of the fact, and my physical reaction, came almost simultaneously. I lifted my guitar high with both hands and then brought it down on the stage like the last chop of the ax that felled Rome.

But I destroyed nothing except something very dear to me; resolved nothing; I merely fulfilled my own self-uttered prophecy of alienation and failure. *Right on, you rock'n'roll cliché!* It was neither shamanic nor rebellious. There was nothing for it but to complete the desecration, beat that body and neck into fragments. Of course, if I'd been more lucid I would've realized that the original damage could have perhaps been mended. Now it was too late. It no doubt looked exactly like what it was: A lost young man's futile meltdown.

Of course, a lot of people clapped and hollered anyway, because a destructive spectacle – much like a man's agony – can serve as entertainment. Perhaps I could've immolated myself for an encore. The owner, Kristin, a slim middle-aged redhead who looked like she'd been settling barroom brawls since she was a teenager, was furious. Fortunately, she discovered that no real damage had been done to the (admittedly ramshackle, anyway) stage. My guitar had capitulated much more readily than the floorboards had.

"What the fuck?" she demanded anyway.

I was still trembling – and staring at the wreckage in incomprehension. "Do I look like I've got an answer? Christ, it's *my guitar*! I *slept* with the fucking thing!"

Then I glared at my bandmates, as if they'd confronted me too. "Have I *ever* claimed to be sane? Huh?"

Tears wet my face. My words were as fractured as my beloved instrument. I gathered the pieces and stalked off.

The steel bin was nearly empty. It clanged, hollowly, when the fragments hit, and then was silent again. I stared at the gnarled jungle of pain, guilt, confusion and resolve that had been my adolescence. I gripped the top of the dumpster with both hands and shook as I wept some more. I was sure that some part of me knew what I was grieving for, but I couldn't consciously name it.

21. Flight

No one bothered me out there. In fact, I began to hear music again: Tommy and Carlos were improvising a bass and drum groove. I managed to smile. I guessed that they were doing it to support me, to keep the people in there entertained so that I could have some privacy and peace. They meandered into a series of riffs that we'd experimented with in rehearsals but never managed to evolve into a proper song.

Just then my phone began vibrating in my pocket.

Not now!

I probably would not have answered it if it'd been anyone else in the world. But I checked the number and recognized it. Saul's.

I drew three slow breaths to settle myself. Him calling me here, now... it could not bode well. My thumb seemed to depress the green answer button of its own accord. Then I lifted the slim receiver to my ear and risked casting a word into the void. "Hello?"

"Hi there. It's me, Saul." His voice was so steady, with the underlying grit of sand, that it betrayed nothing, no hint of intent or of what was to come.

"Hi Saul," I stammered. Then I went for broke. "I just smashed my guitar, my dear sweet guitar, to bits. How are things?"

"I'm sorry to hear that." Somehow he did not sound surprised. Then, with a breath saturated with controlled emotion, he went on. "Listen, I'm taking a turn right now being the one who needs, the one who hasn't got the answers for everyone else. O.k.? So, since you asked how I am... well, I could really use a friend."

To this, my soul in response cast aside all my personal woes for the moment and insisted: *Nothing in the world matters now but this!*

"I'm here," I said.

Saul chuckled; more an expression of embarrassment than humor, it sounded. "I guess what I'm saying is that I'd really love to see you *here*, if that's at all possible."

"What? Like, immediately?"

It was here that my mental feet tread over empty space and slid into a chasm. The sense of dread lurking within me since he'd first rung was finally articulated. There could be only one explanation. Saul understood full well where I was, what I was doing, what was at stake. He knew the *significance* as well as my own bandmates did. Therefore, only a single circumstance could've possibly pushed him into such a state of desperation that he would actually make this request of me.

I swallowed hard. "I'm sorry, man. I'm here for you. I'll do what I can."

I glanced down at the remains of my guitar once more. It looked like the ruins of my whole life. But perhaps even that did not compare... Then, with a wrench of my insides, I realized that the wreckage of my instrument signified the end of the dream, at least for now. No New York. *Hell with that!* I berated myself. *What is that, alongside* his *loss?*

I lashed myself forward. "I gotta tell you though, Saul, that what I can do may not be *anything*. I'm on the other side of the goddamn country, broke..."

"I'll pay for it," he said at once. "If I get you the ticket, will you come?"

Still I wavered, much as I loved Saul. I couldn't stop thinking about the imagined culomination that my band and I had worked so hard towards; that we *deserved*, goddamn it!

"I've got the loft tidied up for you," he persisted. "I can pick you up at the airport and I can send you back out that way if that's what you want. It'd just mean a lot to me... if you could be here for a time."

God. *June*!

"Ah, hell; what's *that* matter, anyway?" I was trying to combat the void with a brusque outburst. "Didn't you hear me say that my guitar's in shambles anyway? The tour's over. We're done. At least for now.

"So yeah, just get the ticket. Burlington's the closest airport to me right now. Just tell me where to be, and when, and I'll do it."

"Thanks so much, Brandon. I fully realized what I would be asking of you when I called. Don't think I take this lightly, o.k.?"

I hung up with Saul just as Maureen, Tommy and Carlos were making their way across the parking lot to meet me. The street facing the club was noisier now with the bustle of drivers who'd been cast adrift by Last Call. Saul's bedtime in Oregon equaled a late night for us in the East.

I pocketed my phone. They came to a standstill a few paces from me, and I could hardly meet their eyes. "I have to go," I muttered.

Then I forced myself to look up at Maureen, the one person there who I feared might have a difficult time comprehending. Her eyes were wet. What a dear soul, I suddenly realized. We were so lucky; many bands would kill for a manager who actually cared like she did, who invested so much of herself.

"I so badly wish I could've given you something more substantial in return for your faith," I told her.

She shook her head, strove to deny the self-condemnation beneath my words. "I'm sorry," she said. "No judgment, just... so sorry." She swiped her eyes. "This is just a setback. There *are* going to be other opportunities."

This was also her way of saying that she would've purchased me another guitar on the spot if she'd had the means.

"Where are you going?" Tommy asked. There *was* an edge of bitterness in his voice.

"To see Saul. He's flying me back for a few days. He needs my support right now."

"Now?" Tommy demanded. He took a step forward, as if to grab me and give me a shake, and then – mastering himself visibly – retreated. "Don't you think this may be a good time for us to show solidarity as a band, maybe stick together and process what's happened and plan our next moves? This can't wait at least a couple days?"

"Jesus, Tommy!" I fumed. "The man saved my fucking *life*, all right? If he needs something from me then he's got it, no questions asked. He called before he even knew about the incident tonight. *Knowing* what we're here for and how important it is, he still made this request. Now what in the hell do you suppose that means?"

Tommy nodded slowly, casting his gaze to the dirt by his boots. "June," he acknowledged quietly.

Swept on by fierce and contradictory emotions, I bent my tirade around to strike at myself again. "*I* fucked this up! And it's done. This is what I do, man! Every joy that tries to spring up in the desert of my life, I strangle it before it can bloom."

"Oh, to hell with that, Brandon!" Tommy retorted. "This band wouldn't even *exist* if not for you. *I* couldn't have done it alone; and I doubt I could've ever done it with anyone else."

Hot tears raced down my cheeks. Goddamn it, I was sick of futility, of doubt. Sick of the darkness always *winning*. Grief bore me down until I was steadying myself on my bent knees. *June! Oh, Saul!*

Someone's arm was lain across my back. Carlos' forehead touched mine. I felt Tommy's hard shoulder. I'd trusted it, relied upon it, since way back in High School...

Gradually I realized that the four of us were caught in a football-style huddle, swaying; breathing as one.

"You're chasing after a ray of light that never left you, dude," quoth Tommy. That provoked in me a quick, sharp burst of laughter in spite of everything.

But I became aware that there was another thread within this convoluted emotional entanglement, one that had escaped my notice whilst I'd been consumed by my own private pain. I lifted my head and met Carlos' steady eyes. I needed clarity, and retreated from our communal huddle.

"Did you know about this?"

I sensed several different – and perhaps even contradictory - replies stirring in him. But for all of this internal tumult, Carlos didn't waver. "Saul and I have talked, yeah," he said.

Perplexed, I shook my head. "I don't get it, though. I mean, it's none of my business – and excuse me if I'm trespassing here – but you've been seeing him almost as long as I have; and more consistently, too. I know there's a lot of love between the two of you. How come he didn't ask *you* to go?"

Carlos was normally real transparent. Thoughts, words and facial expressions were so often perfectly aligned. I wasn't used to this from him, these long reflective pauses and measured responses.

"Look, bro... I think this is something that maybe *you* need as much as Saul does."

And with that I had to be content.

***

They all accompanied me to the airport: Tommy driving, Carlos riding shotgun and Maureen in the way back. She'd *insisted* that I take the seat, so now she was kneeling, steadying herself against the occasional bumps with one hand on Tommy's amplifier. She flashed me commiserating looks so often that I finally had to smile back at her.

"Well, there *were* some triumphant moments," I allowed. "New Haven, Creeping Vines, both Boston gigs…"

"It's all learning and growth," Maureen said. "Success and failure are just our own value judgments."

"Think beyond good and evil," Tommy concurred in his characteristic deadpan monotone.

The van rumbled on, perhaps reflecting on how the greater part of its duty was now accomplished.

Saul had booked me a flight on a Friday morning – 10 a.m. – which meant that we'd had to rouse ourselves at even a *normal* person's crack of dawn. You can't ask for a clearer declaration of loyalty and love from your friends than this. I'd opted to forgo coffee. Instead I sipped a beer on the ride, intending to drink another once I was in the air and then hopefully nap through the five-and-a-half hour main flight, the one from Boston to Sadenport.

Not a word was uttered about the showcase or my guitar. No one wanted to rub salt in the wounds.

My joy was fled along with my hope, for the most part, but I was not altogether unhappy. After all, I was flying from one oasis of love to another. I was aware of that. Disappointment made me see it more clearly, somehow. Despite the overall penury of what I'd thus far called my life, I'd always been fortunate with friends. In that sphere of endeavor, I was uncommonly wealthy. I'd not have gotten far, otherwise.

Maybe this would be enough, in time, to renew the dream – or to paint a new one.

"Goddamn it!" I grated. "I *hate* cancelling a gig. I'm sure they'll have no problem filling our slot at Broomstick Belladonna's. But I feel like I owe the town of Stowe a personal apology. Doesn't matter if not a single person there cares one way or the other."

Carlos immediately tried to soothe me. "We'll come back someday and make good, bro."

"And we'll *relax* next time," Tommy added, "like Maureen and Chas meant for us to do in the first place."

The airport was in view now, and Tommy made for the parking garage. He ended up finding a space on the third floor.

"Despite the ungodly hour," Maureen said, "at least you're flying out of one of the smallest and mellowest airports anywhere."

I nodded, too overcome with sudden emotion to speak. Then we all got out. I stood by the van.

"We might as well say good-bye for now, right here, guys," I said. "I'm pretty useless for conversation at the moment."

Tommy leaned in and clutched my shoulder, catching me completely off guard.

"So it makes the most sense if we wait for you in Boston? We're agreed on that?"

I nodded. "Saul already got the ticket. This is a quick trip. I'll be flying there tomorrow night." I tried to fathom the logic behind this, and shrugged. "Maybe he's worried that I'll be overwhelmed if I stay too long. Or maybe he figures he'll want space to himself by then. I don't know."

We'd all thrown our fates to the wind, trusting in the unknown – in the Unseen, like our EP so proudly proclaimed – and that leap had thus far landed us in a place where we couldn't even grope our way forward in the dark anymore.

It was surreal to the extreme, walking into an airport alone and preparing to board a plane that would take me *back west*. I lumbered through those broad halls, the great existential junctures of greetings and farewells, like a phantom. The last time I'd been in an airport I'd raced to sweep Janie up in my arms. The memory made my insides feel like a monstrous cavern of ice. I deliberately opted for stairs over escalators in an effort to exhaust myself. But I only had to pass two wings to reach my terminal. I tried to swallow my scowl as I was searched at the gate. I knew that those uniformed guys with their flashing and beeping wands weren't to blame for my world of woe.

I was grateful to be seated next to an old woman from a world fundamentally removed from my own. She made pleasant small talk for a few minutes and then resumed reading her Victorian drama. Sometime later I got my ridiculously overpriced beer and downed it fast. This drew her attention again.

"Does flying make you nervous?" she asked: Pretty intently, too. Her blue eyes were windows into a sharp intelligence that I had underestimated.

"No, it's not that." I broke eye contact, aimed my words at the seat in front of me. "There's just been a lot going on. Thought I'd sleep through my long flight to escape it. I won't bore you with details."

Her chuckle snatched my gaze back to her.

"I've probably got four good friends left in this world of an original twenty," she said, wrinkling her nose sassily. "But you apparently think I wouldn't understand someone having a rough day!"

I began to protest. Then I laughed, nervously. "I guess I'm just not used to people caring." I let out a long breath that was laden with tension and suppressed tears. "Ah, hell. I was here with my band. We had a gig coming up; it could've been our big break. And I smashed my guitar. I was just upset about a lot of things. Losing this girl who I love, most of all. And now I'm leaving everything behind because a friend needs me."

She laid a pale and wrinkled hand on mine. Her skin was cool but her presence was warm. "If you're going there for that reason," she said, "to be there for a friend who needs you, then you won't go wrong in the end. God takes note of things like that."

"Ah, man, don't even tell me about God," I groaned. "I'm tired of even hearing that *word*." I turned away once again.

She squeezed my hand. "Then don't use it. What's it matter? We've got all kinds of different words for the love of the universe. And then, of course, 'love' itself is a word." She leaned towards my ear to whisper. "Doesn't matter what you *call* it. What matters is that you *trust* it."

I stared off for a moment, reeling with a symphony of inner echoes. "Christ," I breathed at last, "you're an angel!"

When I turned to her, groping for more words to say, she just nodded in a way that told me, *don't knock yourself out trying to explain the unexplainable, kid.*

She reminded me of this exchange about twenty minutes later, as we touched down in the Boston airport and I stepped out into the aisle. "Find your own word for it!" she called.

"I think I already have," I returned with a smile. "The Unseen Source."

"Ah, poetic!"

I had another beer at a pub inside the terminal and then, thankfully, was able to catnap during my flight westwards. In fact, I awoke as the captain was announcing our final descent into Sadenport. That approach took fifteen minutes, just long enough for me to waken fully. The sun told me that it was early afternoon in Oregon.

I bought a sandwich and orange juice in the food court and sat down at a table for a while, watching the people pass back and forth and not thinking of much in particular. I wasn't feeling ready to see Saul. He'd once told me that we can only see as deeply into others as we've dared to peer into ourselves. What that meant to me, in that moment, was that my inability to grieve was a liability. *Saul* was grieving; and I didn't know how to meet him in that place.

I'd spent years – my adolescent years, prior to knowing him – damming up the channels of pain within me. I'd cried a few times over the course of a week when Mom died. Then I'd set upon a quest to drown my anguish with volume, aggression and screams. Hell, in a way I felt like my father had died back then, too. But I'd tried to disown that part of me, too – the part that mourned the loss of him. It was only since I'd begun working with Saul – going on two years by this time – that I'd begun to recapture, reawaken, my own capacity to feel pain.

He deserved my empathy.

Probably two hours passed, in that purgatorial terminal where it felt like the same people surged and receded like a shifting human tide, before I finally phoned him.

As before, Saul sounded like a man with a white-knuckled grip on the wheel of his soul-vessel.

"Do you want me to pick you up?" he asked at one point.

"You know, I don't think so," I admitted. "If that's all right, I mean. I could actually use the exercise. And I know I can make it to your house within an hour or two from here." I was still stalling. "Thanks, though."

Saul seemed eager to accommodate my wish. "We'll plan on about two hours, then?" – And in hindsight I can hear the peculiar emphasis he gave to the word *plan*. "I understand. I get the itch to move after sitting that long, particularly on cramped plane seats."

"Two hours it is, Saul." Finally I mustered the courage to expose some of the truth. "I need some time to get my head together."

I couldn't help but laugh, a bit sheepishly, at the absurdity of calling attention to my own personal struggle in the face of his tremendous loss.

But Saul just said, "I understand. I'll see you soon, then," and hung up.

My route from the airport to his place mainly involved cutting across the eastern outskirts of the city, which meant that I didn't pass by any familiar landmarks: No Alchemist Brews, Samurai, Pioneer or Robert Chane's house. I was grateful for this. I wanted to step lightly across Sadenport's verges, not get pulled into the emotional complexities of my life here. I'd only come for Saul, this time.

I began pondering whether he'd extended his invitation to anyone else. Surely I wasn't his one true friend, the only person he could turn to in his time of need. At the same time, he knew about my aversion to crowds, particularly large groups of strangers. He'd remember, right?

No doubt there'd be a gathering for the funeral. I suddenly realized that I'd forgotten to ask when that would be. Maybe I'd thought of it and had just been unable to utter the word.

I turned onto Glassbrook Road, a long two-lane strip with yellow heather flats stretching out from both sides of it. I saw maybe one car every five minutes. I smoked to pass the time. June had followed a healthy regimen and look where it'd gotten her. My momentary callousness made me tear up.

The road joined up with Townes Street; and I could see Saul's brown shanty – at least, the roof and chimney through the trees – as soon as I made that right. It wasn't far, now. As I drew closer, though, I was drawn into even deeper perplexity than before.

My father's dirty tan truck was parked in the driveway. And he was standing by it, hands driven in his pockets, waiting for me.

What in the hell?

My face must have framed the question, nearly screamed it, but he didn't answer until I was about ten feet away.

"Hey there. Saul told me you'd be coming. He scheduled a session with me this evening. Be 'bout ten minutes or so, we're gonna start."

I pushed down the throng of questions, my utter befuddlement, and forced myself to look at Robert. He was a bit leaner, his face more defined, as if privation – or confronting some bitter truths – had flensed the opulence from his cheeks. They had some color, too; color proper to sun and life. And he regarded me warily. I wasn't used to that. His brain had typically been too inebriated for that degree of self-consciousness, in the past. With an inward start, I realized his expression and body language, his whole *being*, expressed utter sobriety.

Spurred by unnamable regrets and longings, I began: "Look, about that last phone call..."

He waved away my guilt, dispelled it with the look in his eyes. "You've got every right to be angry, and to vent your anger the way you did. A man's got no business treating his son the way I've treated you these last few years. And I've beat myself up for it, too. But that don't get me off the hook. And it don't undo it, either."

For a minute or two, I was too strung out on adrenaline – the backlog of adolescent outrage and denied fury – to speak. "There's a part of me that would love to..." That's as far as I could get. But no doubt the way that I alternately clenched and opened both fists conveyed my essential intent.

"Yeah. I know." His voice was a curious admixture of petulance and stubborn resolve: His old and new selves, battling it out.

The newly emerging part won out momentarily. "Look, I can't wipe away what's done. I know that. All I can do is try harder, strive to be better, from here on."

I realized that my indignation wasn't going away because it was a *rightful* part of me. I allowed it to live and breathe. "Well, if you still want contact with me then I guess I have to say that I won't settle for less than that. I've been fighting hard to build a new life for myself, and there's nothing that says you necessarily have to be a part of it."

He just acknowledged this with a nod. I tried to soften my glower. Then Robert Chane glanced at his watch – a new acquisition, I noticed. He'd had it cupped in his hand, as the cuffs of his shirt were pulled up high – presumably to hide his scars.

"Welp... it's about that time."

By quiet consent, we made for the front door side by side. Both the air and the light had cooled. The yard was quiet and the crickets were distant. Saul's house looked peaceful and beatific, as if it was oblivious to loss. I stomped up the three steps, opened the screen and rapped on the wooden door behind.

When it was pulled back, some ten seconds later, I saw June standing there.

I remember that I gulped when I witnessed the vitality, the raw health and *presence*, manifested in her. Then Saul's head appeared over her right shoulder. That sonofabitch, he couldn't even conceal the mischievous gleam in his eye! Probably he didn't try. But he adopted a mask of professional solicitude.

"Robert," he said, "you wanna come in?"

My father slowly moved past me.

"Have a good session, Dad."

Why *shouldn't* I say that? What the hell was real anyway? I glanced up again. There was no buttress now between my eyes and the impossible, effervescent fact of June.

She moved down a step and let the door close behind her. The two steps that remained put her only a bit higher than me, as I'd retreated back to the ground.

"It looks like they'll be busy for the next hour or so," she observed, in a voice like the soft essence of spring. "Shall we take a walk?"

22. June

We began making the same circle around the property that Saul and I had traversed previously. It occurred to me that I'd first heard about June's illness during one of my walks with Saul. Neither she nor I said a word for the first ten minutes or so. June was dressed as if to work out in the garden: worn blue jeans and a sturdy brown flannel shirt rolled up to her elbows. Her light flaxen – nearly white - hair was tied in a ponytail. Try as I might, I couldn't in any way account for her presence there beside me.

I finally gathered enough stray strands of consciousness together to voice the obvious. "I thought I was coming here to your funeral." This, in turn, opened the floodgates to an irrational surge of anger. "All right: I don't know what the hell is going on! If Saul lied to me, if this was all a goddamn game from the beginning..!"

"Oh dear," she interjected, "you mean about my sickness? No, no. Oh, Brandon, we would never do such a thing; not to you or anyone else."

Then she bit off a laugh. Her eyes sparkled like a pixie's in a flight of wild fancy. "My husband *does* have a bit of the trickster in him, as I'm sure you've noticed. But no... the pain, the danger, all of that was very real. Often I'd wished that it would just *kill* me. There was a fire in my tissues that made my corner of the universe feel like hell on earth."

She glanced at me then in a way that allowed me to *see* the agony that she referred to. "I tried to escape it in sleep," she went on, "and would wake up to pools of sweat that had collected right where my back met the sheets. It got to the point where Saul would constantly have to clean it up, because I had no energy anymore. No,

Brandon, nothing that he told you was any exaggeration at all. I was truly on death's door."

The ground was damp, almost spongy. Sadenport must have been doused while I'd been away. We stopped a short distance from the Mason's pond, where Saul had once revealed to me *the true source of power and knowledge*: Myself.

"Obviously this has been profound for the both of us," June said. "My recovery, I mean. It was a path of learning that was outright harrowing at times. But as much as I feel the urge to apologize in the face of your shock, I have to say that I agreed with my husband about this. He felt that there could be a powerful lesson for you here, and that it might have its greatest impact if you were not told before you came."

Then she spread her arms wide and smiled, in case I'd failed to notice the way that her very being offered an ebullient cry of "Yes!" to all of Creation. I shook my head, as if in an attempt to awaken from a dream that I couldn't rationalize.

"You healed yourself!" I stammered.

June nodded. "I risked everything, these last several months. I let go of all of my supports and went inward, searching for the true source of that illness. Assuming that the cancer – I didn't even want to label it, see? – But assuming that it was my creation, then what convictions and imaginings and fears of mine had given birth to it? That was my question.

"My body ailed because my spirit did not reassure it. I did not tell it, 'This is your place to be,' and so it found no reprieve. *I no longer chose life*. And my body was going to continue to suffer – eventually giving up the fight entirely - until I committed to either being here or there, so to speak."

Her somber moment of reflection granted me another glimpse of the grim struggle that she was describing. "But I won't beat myself up for all of that anymore," she said. "I think the pain was probably necessary. The mind must at times be shaken free of what it expects, so that there's room for the unforeseen solutions to emerge; and also so that they're not discarded."

No words were adequate to convey my amazement. "Without chemo, drugs, surgery..."

In silent acquiescence, we resumed our walk.

Although June was a head shorter than me, I felt daunted by her new stature. She exuded a kind of quiet surety and strength that surpassed any of my previous conceptions of personal power.

"I have been very afraid, Brandon," she confessed, as if contradicting my assessment. "The truth is that I was so scared to be here... that some part of me preferred the slow capitulation of terminal illness to all other possible fates.

"So that was the work that needed to be done, the place that needed to be confronted. But I didn't only have to uncover the reasons for my fear, see. I had to make a decision, to commit to physical life in the first place. I had to find it within myself to affirm the beauty and *value* of it."

She glanced over at me; and I saw that, although the spritely sparkles were still there, they were mingled now with fleeting reflections of rue. "There were many moments when it seemed easier to just surrender to the beckoning of death," she admitted.

I nodded. "I *do* understand that part. There's been times when I felt like it was only my love for Rachel, or maybe Tommy and Carlos, that kept me here."

"You've suffered a lot, and have had little support in your life," June acknowledged. "I know a bit about that, just from what my husband has shared with me. I think he sees himself in your struggles, at times.

"And in my case... what I was really fantasizing about, of course, was a world that I could go to where my fear couldn't follow. But what if my unfinished work pulled me back here to face it all over again?" She laughed. "Oh, *that* thought was a motivation at times!"

I swallowed hard. I wasn't ready to explore the implications of this idea, and I knew it.

"I get what you're saying," I told her, after some hesitation. "And I don't mean to in any way minimize what you've gone through and overcome. But... *cancer*. God. I mean, it's cell growth run rampant. It takes over the other cells and literally, like, *devours* your body."

It took my mother away! I know what it does!

I stopped moving then. I literally couldn't nurture my perplexity and navigate my course at the same time.

I pushed both hands through my hair, rubbed my war-torn head. "I just don't see how you can *combat* something like that with your thoughts, or by confronting your fear, or embracing life, or..."

Grinning like an impish child, June leaned over and pinched my left arm. "Don't you believe Saul when he tells you that what we are in this world is our own *idea* of ourselves?"

"Well, he's never used those *particular* words, but..."

She pinched me *again*, harder this time. I gasped, and flinched, before I could even catch myself.

"Even many physicists are learning that this 'matter' here is not nearly so solid as it appears," she said. "Someday they will have to acknowledge that it follows the dictates of thought and belief, that consciousness comes first in all things. Now, if this applies to our 'o, too solid flesh' then surely is applies to germs, viruses and cancers?

"It was not so much that I *combatted* the disease, Brandon, as that I learned to stop creating it in the first place. Now, do you feel the difference?

"I had to change paths. That old way, the way of fear, was already dead for me – had been for a long time."

I tried to breathe it all in, to let it settle within me. Something was digging its way beneath the very roots of my world. I felt my intimate foundations tilting, shifting.

"Wow. I guess, well, I never really took what Saul said so literally."

Then I forced myself to look at June, to focus on her and accept the physical proof, there before me, of everything that she was telling me. "So you're no longer afraid?"

She pursed her lips as she considered her reply. "I know that my life is *mine*. It is not given me by the world, or society, or fate."

We began walking again; and as we did so, I could literally see her sink down into a deeper level of personal truth. "It may be that there will always be some fear in me, so long as I remain in this physical world – with all the thorns of life!" – She giggled. "But another part of me also knows now, without question, that fear does not reflect reality. I exist in a safe universe."

I realized, in that moment, how nearly everything I'd ever heard since early childhood had, in one way or another, essentially argued for the opposite view.

"My illness had accomplished precisely that," June went on. "A precious gift had lain wrapped within all those layers of pain. And once the prize had been snatched, the accompanying pain was no longer necessary."

By this time we'd reached the front steps once again. Telepathic exchanges still deciding our joint course, we sat side by side on the second step.

There, the full emotional realization of what had occurred here finally swept over me. I turned and impulsively offered an embrace that Saul's wife accepted and eagerly returned. I clutched her.

"Oh, June! You did it! It's a miracle!"

One of her hands worked at the knots of tension in my back. "It really is," she whispered. "*We* are a miracle."

A few minutes later, the door swung open and Saul and my father emerged. The sun was beginning to dip below the level of the trees and the light was a mournful kind of cool. I stood up and met the eyes of my mentor, the man who'd taught me to steer my life away from the Abyss.

"I hope you've enjoyed all this!"

"Enjoyed?" Saul grinned. "Why speakest thou in the past tense? The evening is yet young!"

June moved up the steps to embrace her husband sidewise, as Robert came down. Saul took a moment to acknowledge his wife – a brief glance that nonetheless seemed to encompass all that they'd suffered and transcended during the course of this, their most trying year together. Then he looked back at me.

"You probably ought to get going," he said. "I have a feeling that June isn't the only one who wants to talk to you today."

I felt my eyes narrow with suspicion. "What, you aren't done with surprises and secrets *yet*?"

Saul adopted a look of mock surprise. "Me? Oh, I assure you that I had only the most peripheral involvement in this one."

I couldn't sustain my questions, though. My aching heart was too prominent; logical concerns stood no chance. I felt my eyes itch and moisten. Then the wet warmth began sliding down my cheeks. All of this was overwhelming.

June! Somehow she'd claimed final authority over her own life and death. And goddamn it, I was crying while my old man was watching me. But who the hell cared?

My throat was so clenched with emotion that my words took twice as long to emerge as they normally would have. "I have a feeling that, somehow, this changes the whole world for me."

Saul lifted an open hand as if in salute. "And you've got the rest of your life to figure out exactly how." Then he gestured towards his barn. "You're all set up in there with bedding and some food in the cooler, by the way. Make yourself at home, like you did way back when." Then he ended with an echo of his previous ambiguity. "That is, assuming you end up still wanting to sleep there."

Then he and June said good-night to my father and me and disappeared inside.

I walked with Robert Chane back to his car. He looked *raw* in the way that I'd often felt, coming out of a session with Saul. This kind of work could dredge up poltergeists or nuggets of gold, depending on where one was along the path.

He stopped, with one hand on the door handle, and finally met my eyes. "Damn," he said. "That guy has a way of making you see your whole life in a different light."

"Yeah," I muttered. "So does his wife."

As if on cue, my phone started vibrating in my pocket as soon as I got inside Saul's newly-refurbished barn. Come to find out that there were electric lights in there now; but as I was clueless about it at the time, I didn't search for switches. The glow of the phone would have to suffice. I fished it out, opened it and then trembled when I saw the number.

Janie.

Christ! How rubbed raw was I going to be before this day was done? I gave myself no time to think, lashed my will into motion and answered.

She plunged right in as soon as she heard my voice.

"O.k., you were right! *I got scared.* I made choices out of fear. You don't have to rub it in my face anymore because I'll just admit it to you! You told me a *really heavy thing*, all right?"

I veered. My dizzied mind required that my body find a place to land. She wasn't just sobbing; she sounded nearly on the edge of hysteria. I couldn't find a chair anywhere, and so settled for propping myself against the iron wood stove.

"Whoa... take a breath, Janie. Easy. What's going on?"

"*What's going on*? I turned my back on something beautiful in my life, first man I probably ever really loved, because of fucking fear! And I hurt you! God, I know..."

"Shhhh..."

This was the second conversation of the day that I somehow couldn't believe was even happening. "Don't beat yourself up, all right? If there's one thing that I've learned over this past year it's that guilt is a useless emotion. You don't spare *anyone* pain by punishing yourself. And besides, like you said, I *did* tell you something pretty disturbing. And you had no way of knowing that I'm not really that kind of person."

"But I *do* know; that's just the thing." Her very words were wet. "I believed in you. I believe in you now. But I didn't follow it, act on it. I let the things I was scared of turn me away."

In a strange way, her emotional extremity enabled me to forget all about my own bereavement. I set aside my wounded ego. I only wanted to be there for her.

"Well, I forgive you, if that's what you're asking. I'm able to do that because I can forgive *myself*. Seriously - my whole life shouldn't be judged by one of my worst acts, during a very unclear and fucked-up moment. When you think about it, that kind of self-condemnation ends up doing even more damage than the original offense.

"But anyway, enough about me and what's in the past. I never stopped caring for you, you know."

"I never stopped caring for *you*. I never stopped *loving* you."

That brought me up short. What little there remained of my 'ordered universe' was now obliterated.

"I love *you*," I stammered. Then, suddenly, I felt compelled to come clean with her, to continue this conversation with total transparency.

"I tried to have something with someone else – you know, a sexual relationship. It didn't work out at all."

"Yeah, and I slept with David, the guy you saw me with that day," she said, hurriedly.

This was like the clean slash of a finely sharpened blade, one of those cuts that you look at and think *this is gonna hurt like hell later*; but for the moment, it's as if your nerves haven't figured out what's

210

happened yet. I quickly stowed my reactions away. *Bleed over it some other time, man!*

Janie seemed equally intent on moving forward. "So what do you think?" she ventured, in a small voice.

Ah, another question without answer. Whoever believed that the gods lacked a sense of humor had obviously never witnessed the bizarre twists and turns of *my* life.

"I think I've got until tomorrow afternoon before I fly back east."

"What? You're *here*?"

This time I chuckled aloud. God, I'd missed her fire. "I came because Saul asked me to. I thought it was because June had died. Turns out she's very much alive... more so than most people are, probably."

"Yeah," Janie said, almost in a whisper. "Seeing her, watching her transformation... that's what set me to reconsidering everything, weighing what's really important in life. How I don't want to let fear decide my courses anymore."

If working with Saul helped you to come to those realizations, I thought, *then I owe him my life twice over, for real.*

"So then what do *you* think, Janie McCabe?"

In her sigh, I heard the full weight of all the disappointments, regrets and wounds that she'd nurtured throughout that 'lost time' during which we hadn't communicated much – the time during which I could only guess at the turmoil that might have been churning about within the heart and soul of the woman I loved.

"I think," she enunciated, "that I am not going to make the same idiot mistake with you twice in this life, Brandon Chane. You get your ass over here, o.k.?"

23. Paint a New Picture

Those of you who've experienced it won't need me to describe the keen joys of makeup sex. When heart and desire get chugging at full throttle together, all while you're moving in harmony with one another, it's a sensation that can whisk you clear off the face of whatever world you'd previously been rooted to.

Janie wasted no time at all. Her mouth found mine before I'd even made it through the doorway. I guess we both figured there'd be time enough to talk and play catchup later. Her eyes were full of promises and apologies. I imagine mine were too. But we both knew that we were forgiven anyway, come what may.

Her responses to me were urgent. There was a point when I thought about that man – David – and she panicked when I went cold. I saw no way out of the dilemma but to confess what had happened. That set off a flurry of reassurances. Ah, hell... what did I *care*, really? She wasn't the only woman *I'd* ever made love to, either. But she was the only woman I loved. I grappled with my jealousy, false sense of inadequacy and fear – it was much like taking a bull by the horns – and finally thrust it all aside. This was *our* time; and nothing else in the world was permitted entry.

Love scares us all because of its ferocious power. Maybe Janie had run in response to *both* of our fears, me just being silently complicit and therefore appearing like the victim of the whole thing. Saul always insisted that it takes two. If there are no accidents then this means that, in the wider scheme of things, there really are no victims.

We didn't talk for a long time afterwards, though our eyes said much. Janie was still in the same apartment that the hippy couple had painted in sunburst colors and vibrant slogans. Her bed was low, scarcely raised above the ground, 'cause that's how she liked it. Close to the Earth, this woman, in all ways.

"Does it just *feel* like we travel someplace else when we're together like this," she whispered, into the pristine silence of pre-dawn, "or do we really *go*?"

I smiled. It was a pure lover's moment, you know? Only she would ever have asked me a question like that; and only I could have ever known what she *meant*.

"Paint a new picture on the inside," quoth I, "and you step right out of one world and into another. That's what Saul says."

She hugged me hard. "I'm so grateful that he helped me to see, to know, that I was listening to the wrong voice."

"Me too," I breathed, giving her ear a little nibble for emphasis.

I got to experience my blissful epiphany twice, as it turned out. Somehow, during my brief period of sleep, I forgot where I was, and about trials overcome and barriers dissolved. I hadn't *intended* to sleep in the first place, honestly. I didn't want to miss one moment of Janie's breathing, of her warmth, her hair, her scent, her skin. But contentment wields a powerful pull over a weary body and soul. And so it was that I awoke not knowing where I was; not recalling, at first, that my heart's long grief had been annealed.

Then I heard Janie's voice coming from the kitchen.

"*Pleeease*, Krystal! I just patched things up with Brandon after a really painful time apart and he leaves again *tonight*! What? No, of course it's not your *fault*; I'm just sayin'... Oh, *thank you*! Thank you! Anything you want covered, morning or afternoon shift... I will make this up to you!"

She came back into the room dressed only in a long white t-shirt with some kind of pretty "tree of life" design emblazoned across the chest. She looked relieved.

"Called in to work?" I asked with a grin.

"I found somebody to cover for me, yeah. Otherwise I would've had to leave, like, now."

"You didn't have to do that, you know."

"Yes, I *did*." She walked over and knelt on the edge of the bed. She swiped my forehead gently with the back of her hand like a nurse from olden times checking my temperature.

"We need this day," she declared, in a voice that almost dared me to contradict her. "Now, tell me about your tour. I want to hear *everything*." She wagged a finger at me. "No leaving things out because of your false modesty. I want to know about all the awesomeness."

I knew that her interest was sincere, but also that this served as a means of steering away from the subject of *her* and how she'd filled her life in the time that we'd been apart. I didn't want that specter casting a shadow over us. I decided to confront it.

"Tell me this first: Do you have to break things off with David, now?"

Janie, true to her new commitment not to shrink in the face of fear, answered at once. "It ended about a month ago, actually. He knew that I had feelings for you, that all my talk of moving forward was just a brave charade. I have to give him credit for that."

"Pretty chivalrous, really, to be so understanding," I marveled.

"O.k.," Janie said briskly, as she rose. "Now that that's over with, I'll go make coffee. Then, in return, you give me the whole odyssey."

The wafting scent of the strong brew somehow reminded me that this was all real. Wake up and smell the coffee, indeed. For once, I *was* awake in a sweet dream rather than asleep in one. Gratefully, I accepted her mug – white, with a picture of an orange cat and a funny caption – and smiled.

Even though the story came to such a lackluster conclusion, I discovered that I was filled with such plentitude that I didn't mind relating it. I delivered the details, beginning with Chas and all his plans for us. I described our two interviews and our race across America.

Like many periods of trial and travail in my life, it all seemed more heroic – and less arduous – in the telling. Hindsight has a way of highlighting the secret luminosity behind events, the unnamable quality that lends nostalgia its keen ache.

I even tried recalling everything that I'd said onstage at the gigs, because I knew Janie enjoyed hearing that kind of stuff. I got on such a roll that by the time I finished my narrative I realized that I'd hardly touched my coffee. When I tasted it it was lukewarm.

"Well," Janie concluded, "we're obviously gonna have to get you a new guitar."

I pulled her down beside me, wrestled her into a bear hug while she pretended to struggle and then surrender.

"What do you mean, hon? I'm completely broke. And you should see Maureen. She looks after us like a mother hen to her chicks. If there was even the *remote* possibility that she could've afforded it she would've offered right away. And Chas already parted with all the petty cash *he* had on hand to send us cross-country."

"I have it," Janie said softly. "I've been saving practically the whole time I've been at the jewelry shop. Nearly three years now. And if it's used, or a decent copy, I can swing it no problem."

My smile dissolved. "Oh, I can't let you do that!"

She wiggled around to face me, and I was treated to the tigress smile of hers that I'd so sorely missed. "Excuse me? You are my lover, Mister Chane. You are *not* my master."

"It's a lot of money… you should use it for something really important, for yourself."

"And maybe helping the man I love to pursue his dream," she argued, "and not only that, but to fulfill the thing that this world *needs* for him to do, too, is the most important thing that I can think of at the moment.

"Besides," she added, "I seem to recall you shelling a few hundred out on a plane ticket for me, once."

I finally found what I thought was a potent protest. "I *owed* you that, as far as I'm concerned."

Janie's eyes had flecks of sorrow dancing amidst the resolve, now. "I think I owe *you* one, this time."

I discovered a Les Paul copy at a local pawnshop. Janie tried to talk me into shopping around before settling upon anything, but I fell in love with this guitar as soon as I pulled it down from its peg and started playing. It had a real solid, dependable feel against my hip, easy action; I even liked its curves and blood-orange-colored swirl. A more jagged flying-V may perhaps have better served the original incarnation of Edge of the Known… But much had changed since then.

"I *am* paying you back for this," I told Janie as we approached the counter.

She didn't answer, but instead just insisted that we get a case for it as well. This all comes along with one getting involved with a spirited lass. Recognizing this fact, I swallowed my protests.

"So you think she'll do you justice for the big showcase?" Janie asked, as we stepped out onto the afternoon's sunlit sidewalk.

I just stared back at her, momentarily shoved out of the seat of logic and words.

Janie made a ludicrous face when she realized how caught off guard I really was. "You *did* realize that this was half the reason we were making the trip out here today, right?"

"Ah, hell… I told you, we had to cancel that along with the other gig, the one in Vermont."

"But it hasn't *passed* yet, right?" Janie argued. "You said it was early next week. Maybe Maureen can still get you guys on the bill."

I smiled, trying to convey my appreciation for all her support, but I imagine that it probably came out all askew. "It's not just the gig itself," I explained. "She and Chas had also convinced artist and repertoire people from two different record labels to come see it – specifically, to see *us*. That's why we've been calling it 'The Showcase'.

"God, Janie… it really doesn't matter. I told you once already, how I realized that if I could just feed myself and pay rent off of this band then I'd be happy. I don't need to be on a big label."

"I understand that you're probably not motivated by the money you could make," she acknowledged. "But think of all the *people* you could reach."

I hesitated. Perhaps I'd never explored my own feelings, in that area, to the extent to which I could take a stance one way or the other.

"Call her!" Janie insisted, glancing down at my pocket where my phone was sheltered. "There might still be time."

I couldn't repress my grin. I shook my head. "So is this 'have your way day'?"

Janie matched me sass for sass. "You do this one little thing for me and then we go back to the apartment and you can have *your* way!"

"Imp, imp, imp!"

"Who knows," she persisted. "It could end up being a repeat of last night."

"All right, I'm calling!" And I made a dramatic display of fishing that phone out as frantically as I could.

I caught Maureen just as she was sitting down for coffee, in her home in Boston, with Tommy and Carlos. She probed me delicately at first. "How are you?"

"Oh, I'm good."

"Really?"

I suddenly realized that we inhabited fundamentally different worlds of perception and understanding; and I wasn't sure how to bridge that gulf – leastways, not in brief.

"Umm… yeah, I'll have to explain it all to you later. But June is alive and very well, and I'm standing here with Janie and with a new guitar in my hand."

"O…K.…" For a moment, Maureen sounded like she was questioning my sanity. But, being an empathetic soul with a business head, she was capable of navigating the most unexpected waters. "I can't wait to hear it. Sounds like one hell of a story. So, you're booked to come back late tonight, right?"

"Yeah. But listen –" Now that the moment had come, I wasn't sure how to broach things. *Just stumble through and don't think about it.* "Uh… is there any possible way we could still do the gig in New York? That we could get the same people to come out to it?"

"You know…" Maureen laughed in a way that told me she was embarrassed. "O.k., I actually never told anybody that you guys *weren't* coming. Oh, God, you're gonna think I'm such a flake! I get these little nudges inside, and I've learned to trust them. Crazy as this sounds, Brandon, I just had the feeling that, despite everything that's gone wrong, somehow you'd still end up playing there." She laughed again, but it sounded much lighter – less laden with self-doubt – this time. "I've actually been waiting for a call from you with, like, baited breath."

"God, Maureen, you're a genius!" From the way that Janie had started grinning beside me, I assumed that she'd grasped the essence of this exchange. "I could hug you. That little voice knows more than the brain could ever compute in a hundred years. You're wise to trust it."

"Oh, all right!" Maureen sounded relieved. "I thought maybe you'd call me crazy! Yay, we're doing the gig! Unless, of course… I've got you on speaker phone, Brandon, if you want to put it to a vote with your band," she finished, teasingly.

"Speaker phone, eh? Hey, Carlos!"

A moment later I heard him. "Right here, bro."

"You're busted! You *knew* about it. You knew what I was flying back to discover." I hoped that my essential good humor would carry over the line.

His reply set me at ease. "You were losing your belief. You had been for a while. When Saul asked me what I thought about it, I just said that the best thing for you would be to see June with your own eyes."

"You're like a brother to me!" I called over. "You too, Tommy! I'll see you guys tonight!"

Under other circumstances, parting with Janie like this – even while the sweet scent of our reconciliation still lingered – would have strained my heart to the bursting point. But I had walked with June and witnessed her resurrection. A love-borne state of quiet ecstasy was stealthily awakening in me. There were 'rules' that had once banished the realm of the miraculous, of the magical, from my mental and spiritual domain. Now those rules had been crucially undermined. Oh, yes, the possibilities were truly unfathomable. We're fools to ever think otherwise. My brain lacked the fingers to grasp it all, but my heart had resolved its last lingering doubts.

Life was sacred. No longer was this conjecture, or poetic fancy or empirical deduction. I *felt* it with the kind of certainty that held me aloft with such buoyancy. It was as if my body sought its soul-marriage in the kingdom of high winds. Every glance and kiss and breeze and bereavement was sacred. The *other place* existed as verily as this one; perhaps it was 'more real'; and that fact sustained me.

In the midst of all these buffeting winds, Janie and I decided that we would be together. If it was my destiny not to return then she would rejoin me in the East. Our love was not going to conform to the dictates of the world. Rather, those other circumstances would have to adapt to our shared journey.

She saw me off at the gate that night, dressed all in earthy browns. Janie had light amber complexion, so the color suited her. Her loose-fitting leggings were made from a kind of material that I couldn't identify. But it looked so silky-furry that I imagined it'd be much like petting a deer, running my hands across it. I regretted that this was neither the time nor the place to try the experiment. A strip of yellow twine served as a belt. Over her skirt she wore a shawl of light-colored leather with fringe that splayed over her breasts and shoulders. My indigenous princess. My heart throbbed like a stubbed toe. Sensing my tangled emotions, Janie leaned in to meet my kiss.

"I'm sorry I can't be there for the big gig," she said. Then, acting on sudden impulse, she began undoing her makeshift belt. "These stay up just fine without it," she remarked. Once she had the twine loose she began wrapping it around my right arm, over the bicep. Finally, she fastened it tight.

"There. Now you can be like one of those knights of old who'd ride into a joust or battle in full armor, bearing a lady's brooch."

Her smile, and the unabashed affection in her eyes, nearly made me weep.

"I love you with everything in me, Janie. You *will* be there."

It was scarcely a whisper. And she didn't answer, probably because the lack of any need to respond was the truest testament to what lay between us. I had to go. The East was calling me back, for one more round – the final campaign in this war. And there was nothing more to say. I hugged her quick and hard.

Every life seems to have its definitive beginning and ending points. That's how we learn to frame it all in our minds. Most children are a lot looser in this regard, though. You can hear some of them talk about the world that they came from, not so long ago. They'll play at being orphans in order to grapple with a deeper sense of inarticulate loss. And when they pretend to be parents, or elderly, it isn't mere imitation. Perhaps their knowledge is culled as much from the *future* as it is from the past? For they understand, and take for granted, the elasticity of time.

June had, in many ways, reminded me of this child's view. My life suddenly appeared open-ended again; no longer was it a fixed narrative with 'birth' and 'death' as its bookends.

The trick is to be awake for the moment, Saul had once told me. *When you do that, you step into an ocean that touches upon every shore on every world.*

When I met Carlos, Tommy and Maureen during the surreally-late-night hour at the Boston airport, beneath the garish and artificial white glow, I tried to somehow convey this state of 'silent knowing' that I'd stumbled upon. Fortunately for me, the two guys were already accustomed to my occasional blazes of right-brained madness. And Maureen was learning fast. They took turns filtering my elliptical epiphanies and translating them into their own personal brand of philosophy or metaphysics. It just made me acutely aware of my deep love for each one of them. Realizations of this sort are highly personal: They should never be proclaimed as The Truth, with a capital T, for all.

"Wow. She beat cancer," Maureen marveled. Then she looked at Carlos. "And you knew about this?"

"Saul called me right before we played in Montpelier, the night Brandon destroyed his other guitar," he said.

I just drifted along, my mind in a free-floating space. My thoughts could not attach themselves to facts, certainties or expectations. I learned to just appreciate my questions without demanding that they produce answers. And I came to discover that the deeper region of *knowing* carries its own form of certainty. It just isn't arrived at through deduction.

I suppose you could compare it to the phenomenon that sportsmen remark about sometimes: Just knowing that you're going to sink a basket, or bowl a strike, before the ball even leaves your hand. It's as if the essential thing, the miracle, has already manifested. It just needs to play itself out in the field of time.

That's how it was when we played Broomstick Belladonna's a couple days later.

A month or so earlier, I'd been nervous about this gig. So much hung upon it. But my brief interaction with Saul's wife, the woman who had reversed her own self-created death sentence, had granted me a glimpse of what lies on the other side of this life. And from that place...

There was nothing to fear.

There is never *anything* to fear.

And I saw how fear had always lain beneath my anger, my perceived need to prove myself, my outbursts of violence. Releasing fear – at least for the moment – I simultaneously relinquished the thoughts and emotions that had always revered it, supported it.

For the first time in my life, I climbed onstage and played for nothing other than my sheer love of it.

24. The World is Your Mirror

"New York!" Tommy intoned. "Let us now create a space wherein our souls may breathe!"

And so it began: An extreme band like ours, with a frontman with a penchant for openers like that. I suppose playing in Edge of the Known was similar to being a professional comedian in that regard. There were times when I thought half of Tommy's job involved just being able to keep a straight face.

When we finished rousing the club with the sheer bombast of his "Stone Soul Etchings", we segued into a newer thing of mine. I had, in fact, just written it since returning to the East, in the wake of what some people may refer to as a spiritual awakening. This night marked the third time that we'd ever played it together as a band.

I'd just been trying to arrive at the *essence*, the thing that I somehow knew I hadn't understood before, the inner recognition and awakening that made life lighter and yet infinitely more precious, both at once.

I called the piece "The Jaws of Time".

Life's infancy, and the echo

through our weary days remains

But you were well worth a

lifetime's quest to reclaim

My guitar parts in this song never resolved themselves into any recognizable riffs or progressions. I'd shown Tommy a baseline: Probably not the most exciting thing in the world for him to play, as it was simple, repetitive and hypnotic. But sometimes the simple part is the right part. I wanted the song to rolllllll... like a waterfall, endlessly. Over the languid groove that Tommy and Carlos laid, I painted with aural color: A shimmering minor chord here, some ghostly arpeggios there; sometimes, just a single haunted note bent and sustained to the point of fraying.

Like hounds, we hunt only

after a sniff of your meat

Or else, blind fools, we race

up and down illusory streets

Relishing what rapture we can

snatch from the jaws of time

All is born from our minds: Both the cliff and

the thrill of the climb

It was almost jazzy in its unexpected deployment, its lack of identifiable structure... something dredged up from the deep swamps where the reptiles croak melodies as old as the Earth itself and the birds overhead respond with calls that are the promises of Eternity.

Like hounds, we hunt only

after a sniff of your meat

Or else, blind fools, we race

    up and down illusory streets

    Womb of the soul that

    can't be taught to kneel

    Remind us of what the child knew:

    The faith that makes illusion real

That was the crucial paradox. The world was, in some sense, illusion; and yet it was utterly real and dear to me. June had brought herself back from the brink of death and yet June could never really die. And I looked out, once the last chords of the song faded into evanescent reverberations. I beheld this gathering of souls, at our agreed-upon meeting place of illusion and truth: Broomstick Belladonna's.

It had a high stage, one that was level with my chest when I stood on the stone floor. That floor was bulging now with bodies and perspiration and collective need. What little breathing room there'd been had been consumed halfway through our first song. The darkness was apt for the journey we were embarking upon. And our high vantage lent us the kind of remote mystique that we'd once sought – misguidedly, perhaps – behind our liquid light show.

I'd actually enjoyed the previous band and had made a mental note to meet the guys after the performance. Perhaps they were somewhere out there in that milling mass. Supposedly an A & R guy from Phantom Hordes was there, as well as another from Widowed Soul Records. I could scarcely see the bar, off on the left-hand side. The overhead televisions in that anteroom area had been turned off, as no one was paying attention to them.

It's almost as if I thought that I owed the audience an explanation for the song, even though music should never *be* explained. But I figured that the story of June Mason was something that the world should know, because it was essentially *everyone's* story.

My voice ventured out into that dense and expectant darkness.

"I used to have these fears, man, that someday someone would find out about the things that were living inside my head and then that'd be it: A cell somewhere, maybe a padded one, to the end of my days."

There were some cheers in response to this. Maybe they thought it was a planned part of the 'evening's entertainment'. But hell, even *I* didn't know where I was going with this. I'd just passed through experiences that had shaken my existential certainty to its foundations.

"Thing is, I'd made my own life a kind of prison – and so what did it matter whether or not there were actual physical bars there in front of me? I'd adapted to the cell already. It was home. I thought it was the full tale of the world."

Then, just as I was faltering, Carlos produced some heavy punctuation behind me as if to say *Keep going, bro! Let it out!* I grinned, then masked it and soldiered on.

"I just flew out here for this gig a couple of days ago," I explained. "There wasn't nothin' to do on the six-hour flight but read the paper. That's not something I normally do; and while some people will say, 'Dude, you gotta stay aware of what's happening in the world', I always figured that if you spend too much time *making* yourself aware of horrible things, things you feel you have no power over, then you're bound to drive yourself fucking insane sooner or later.

"So basically, I'm kind of a dim bulb when it comes to world events. And for that reason, I probably can't give you a lot of accurate details about what I read. Maybe it's all old news to *you* anyway. But I think I can summarize it pretty well. Many thousands of people were gunned down or otherwise killed. And many times that many starved, or died from illnesses that could've been prevented.

"It's always the same with me, man. I read stuff like that and I immediately wonder what the significance of my own life is. I'm one out of several billion, you know? What do my thoughts, feelings and choices *matter*, one way or the other?"

More musical encouragement arose, this time from Tommy: An echo of the hypnotic thrum of "Jaws of Time". I silently thanked and blessed my bandmates.

I started following the cadences of this impromptu music. "See, but I'd just gotten back from visiting a woman who we were all sure wasn't gonna make it," I went on. "She had an illness that, supposedly, you don't recover from. But she *did* recover. And it wasn't because of any drug or miracle of modern science, either. It was because she understood that her life was hers, that it's her creation. The *power* was hers, hers to choose: Illness or health, life or death.

"And if not for her, I wouldn't be standing here telling you all this. It's all connected, see: *We're* all connected. And there really isn't a world that exists outside yourself to begin with. Think about that the next time you question your own worthiness for life. You were born into the time and place where your voice would be needed, as my friend Saul says. Everything you experience is your mirror. The whole goddamn world depends on who you are!"

Carlos started pounding out a beat then, responding to something that the three of us up on that stage all knew: It was now time to rock *hard*. We did so without apology or restraint.

The finale, which came maybe a half-hour later, took the form of several minutes of frenzied inspiration. I couldn't help but grin as I heard the manic propulsion coming from behind me. Carlos had no doubt weathered his own death and rebirth over these last few months, a process that I, sadly, had been too embroiled in my own personal struggles to fully notice or respond to.

I tried to make it up to him in the groove. He was like a wide receiver who, having caught the long pass and sailed past the goal line, proceeds to run up the bleachers, hurl himself from the top of the stadium walls and then land in a somersault to sprint off into the sunset. At this point, his cymbals sizzled, faded away, and we were left with no doubts that he'd said the absolute last word on the matter.

Afterwards I relinquished myself to one of my favorite places on any stage: The shadow of Tommy's tall amplifier. I'd first met Janie in a comparable position. The gods could ask no more of me, or anyone. I was exhausted and sated in equal measure. I grazed my hand across

Janie's strip of twine and mused, "What did you think of that, sweetheart?"

As if by way of delivering the Universe's reply, Maureen stopped a few feet in front of me. I recognized her shoes. I looked up to meet the beaming – and tear-wet – face of a proud mother.

"Tommy and Carlos are now caught having to *schmooze*," she said. "I tried my best to draw the attention. You probably made a wise choice, hiding out here."

Then her eyes grew more intent. "Look, I have no real control over what happens from this point forward, as you know," she said. "But I *will* make you this promise: If that performance you just gave didn't earn you guys a contract, I will *quit* this goddamn business!"

I regarded this woman, who had done everything she could to succor and encourage me through one of the most trying months of my life, for a moment longer. Then I realized that I'd absolutely had enough intensity for one day. This thing had to be diffused.

"Maureen… you're stoned!"

Sometime later, after Mike Makand Nobody's Business began tearing up the club with their brand of heavy blues, I was able to pull away from the social circle of 'industry insiders', musicians and patrons who continually offered us drinks and lofty praise. I stood on the sidewalk outside as the daunting skyscrapers hovered overhead, reminding me of my mortality. And yet my world was as vast – and some parts of it seemed still as remote – as the one that surrounded me. I fought the sweeping sense of insignificance by reminding myself of my own earlier 'sermon' onstage.

On impulse, I retrieved my cellphone and dialed the Friedman's number.

I was hoping the change in time zones would save me. It wasn't quite nine p.m., where Rachel was…

Gail answered at once, catching me off guard. I said hello in stumbling fashion and, as humbly as I could manage without sounding phony, asked if I could talk to my little sis.

"It *is* her bath time," Gail said, "but I guess it's o.k."

There was that undercurrent of affection in her voice, of respect, that had but newly grown up in the spaces between us. I felt so grateful for old animosities dissolved, for this newly-emerging human warmth, that I tilted my head up towards the light-obscured sky and mouthed a prayer of thanks. Not that I believed in 'somebody up there', per se, but... I guess some mental habits are tenacious.

"Hello?"

Rachel was always informed of who was calling and yet she consistently answered as if she had no idea.

"Hey kiddo!"

"Brandon! Where are you?"

"We just played our last show of this tour," I explained. "I'm in New York City. It's way huger even than Sadenport. Anyway, it went really well. Afterwards we met some guys from two different record labels. They wanna wine and dine us. You know, take us out to dinner and talk business."

I could hear her tasting the foreign word. "What's a label?"

I laughed for the sheer joy of connecting with her. "Oh, that's a word for a record company. I guess 'cause their label goes on every CD that they print up. Kinda like it is with cereal boxes."

Rachel's mind leapt from there straight to the gold. "So does that mean that you and Tommy and Carlos are going to be famous?"

My smile was a little bittersweet this time. Perhaps I caught a glimpse then of what lay ahead, the twists and turns that were to dwarf all of my previous conceptions of *craziness*. And as naïve as Rachel may have sounded, I had to admit that my own thinking had not been so far removed from that, not so long ago.

"It may not mean much at all," I said. "But what ideally happens is that a record company gets your music out to all the people out there who really want to hear it. It helps the music to reach them. Doesn't always work out that way, but that's what you hope for. We'll have to do our part and put in a lot of work, too."

Following a period of silence, I risked a piece of myself in the space. "I'm actually a little nervous," I admitted.

"How come?"

"Well... geez, how do I even describe it? If you make it big then there's that risk that a lot of people will think that they love you, and for a lot of the wrong reasons."

I was still growing accustomed to her new tendency towards thoughtfulness; towards taking a moment, before speaking, for reflection.

"But you don't have to change how you are for *them*," she said. "If people think of us a certain way it doesn't mean we owe it to them to *be* the way they think. And besides, there's people who love you for real."

That nearly brought forth tears. "I know." I gulped hard. "I've been really lucky with that. And I love *you*." Then: "Hey, why don't you ask Gail and Ernie if I can tell you a good-night story, like we used to do?"

"O.k.!" Her answer was brisk; and by the sound of things, she must've run right off to do what I suggested. She returned mere minutes later.

"It's all right. I didn't play outside today because it was raining, so they said I could skip my bath."

"All right, then," I said, over the hiss of traffic and the plod of pedestrians and the distant sirens. "I'll tell you about the girl who woke up one day to realize that she'd woven the whole world out of her dreams..."

This was the story that I was always struggling to believe. There's times when I still do, I'll admit. Maybe I will - at least to some extent - to the end of my days. It may be that we really "graduate" from this schoolroom that we call life the moment we fully realize, without any lingering voices of doubt, that we were the authors of this dream all along.

In the meantime, it seems that – ironically – both our joys and our bereavements stem directly from our *forgetfulness,* our ignorance of this crucial fact. And the tension between them, the longing for the one and the fear of the other, creates the adventures that we call our lives. Certainly that first kiss with Janie was a lot sweeter, after months of believing that I'd lost her forever, than it would have been without that sense of bereavement. And no doubt I wouldn't have felt such a fierce, piercing joy in beholding June if I hadn't mourned her beforehand.

It's the thing that I tried to express in song. It's the Divine Bait. We humans are like hounds of the hunt, in that respect.

We'd never run if we weren't first offered that quick sniff of the celestial meat before it was all, seemingly, taken away.

Made in the USA
Charleston, SC
12 August 2014